I want him. I want a man so desperately. Grant has spoiled me and I won't deny myself this unexpected opportunity. I pull him close and rub against him. His hands release my head. They skim my shoulders, tickle my ribs. My breasts ache for his touch, but he teases me. Sides, waist, belly. I arch into him. He pulls back slightly. I moan with frustration. His tongue traces a path along my collarbone. I raise my breasts for his mouth. He ignores them. Neck, shoulder, chin, jaw, eyes, and then back to my mouth. I groan and seek his hardness. My hands are taken and held behind me. Gently he pulls me backward till his hands hold mine on the ground. I'm stretched before him on my knees, legs wide, breasts thrust out. I'm pleading with him with my eyes. He ignores me. My breath is ragged, my chest heaving.

Also by LYN DAVENPORT:
The Guardian

TESSA'S HOLIDAYS

LYN DAVENPORT

MASQUERADE BOOKS, INC.
801 SECOND AVENUE
NEW YORK, N.Y. 10017

Tessa's Holidays
Copyright © 1996 by Lyn Davenport
All Rights Reserved

No part of this book may be reproduced, stored in a retrieval system, or transmitted in any form, by any means, including mechanical, electronic, photocopying, recording or otherwise, without prior written permission of the publishers.

First Masquerade Edition 1996
First Printing March 1996
ISBN 1-56333-377-5

First Top Shelf Edition 1996
ISBN 1-56333-885-8

Cover Photograph © 1996 by Robert Chouraqui

Cover Design by Dayna Navaro

Manufactured in the United States of America
Published by Masquerade Books, Inc.
801 Second Avenue
New York, N.Y. 10017

I keep the determined smile on my face the first couple of days of school. Having to listen to everyone's commiseration about not receiving the position of principal is worse than not getting the job. Especially since half of them are silently gloating inside and do little to try and hide it. On top of that it always makes me realize how narrow their world is and how terribly dull and boring my life has become.

My quaint little town in the heart of Iowa has lost its charm. One incredible, hardly believable, secret summer has ruined my old comfortable world for me. I'm no longer the person I was. I'm no longer content with what I have. I view it all through wide-opened eyes now. What had been a satisfying, cozy life now drags along at a snail's pace as I wait impatiently for next summer to arrive.

How will Grant arrange for us to be together to travel and explore new worlds? I can't even begin to imagine, but I don't doubt for one moment he will contrive it. He's a wealthy, determined man. A manipulative man. A man who has turned my life completely upside down within a short seven-week period. A man who wants to do it all over again next July.

And I want it too. Desperately. More so as each long day passes with a sameness that smothers me. I have been whisked from one continent to another and tasted forbidden fruit that before that time I'd hardly dared to fantasize about, never mind ever expected to experience, to come to love, to crave, to need. Now I slowly stagnate and smolder as the yearnings build hotter each day, yet remain unfulfilled.

The sharp memories both entice and haunt. I find myself daydreaming, reliving, desperately trying to recapture parts of last summer at the oddest times. One Sunday in church I found myself tuning my brother-in-law's sermon out, and once again I was high above the Mediterranean, Grant's hands working their magic on my naked body as I stared out over the watery expanse. My happy sigh caused a few heads to turn my way, and I shamefully tried to cover it with a hasty yawn. Is it a sin to sit in church and recall such decadent behavior? My mother looks at me curiously a lot lately. Maybe I should think of getting my own place.

Would Grant come to me if I did? No. I know he won't. He'd been adamant about us not knowing each other in public. Not that we ever meet, even by accident. His age, reputation, and position would stand the titillating scandal that would sweep though my small community. I would be doomed and, knowing his thoughts about the subject, so would our relationship.

I miss Grant constantly but the nights are the worst and seem to be getting more so. My hand has once again become my lover and a very poor substitute it is indeed, especially since I now know what another's is capable of doing to me.

The summer days hadn't been all total pleasure, but even so, no matter what had occurred each time, they had ended in my being consumed by the raging fires of Grant's passion. The good parts, the yearning for more, have made many of the other memories fade and become insignificant. I'd gladly endure all the bad moments again for one blazing night in Grant's arms. Even his rage and retribution would be preferable to this nothingness I now live through, each long day slowly, tortuously passing to bring me one day closer to seeing him. But that is not to be for another nine months. How will I ever endure it?

The school bell rings and almost at once the students begin to pour into the classroom. Noisy. Boisterous. Sullen. Expectant. They're just at the age where they are desperate to appear more worldly. More macho. More sophisticated.

I notice some of the boys seem to scrutinize me closely. Assessing me. Weighing the odds of who knows what in their minds. Do they tune me out and daydream about their fantasies with me? Do they wonder what it would be like to love an older woman? Do they stare more this year or is it that I'm more aware of the strong, steady, sexual undertone that seems to hum and vibrate from their young, vibrant bodies?

Am I different? Do my experiences proclaim themselves in my expression? My demeanor? Does my yearning show? Can some of the more mature boys tell I'd be an easy target? Would any of them dare? Do I wish they would? Are they just fantasizing about their own forbidden dreams as they struggle through the end of puberty or do they wish I was a part of it? Do they have any idea how many different ways there are to make love? Would someone so young, so eager, so open to new ideas make a good lover?

I stand quickly and force myself to concentrate on the lesson that the state demands I teach. Thoughts like that will lead to nowhere but trouble.

I swear each minute becomes an hour as the day progresses. The teenagers have as little interest in learning as I do in teaching. They're still reliving their summer vacations and aren't ready to buckle down and concentrate on the day-to-day routine. Neither am I. Will I ever be again?

I rush down the steps of the porch knowing I've hurt my mother's feelings, but I'll start screaming if I listen to her tell me about Mrs. Carroll's stroke one more time. How have I stood it for so many years? Has my life been so meaningless that someone's misfortune was the topic of conversation for weeks at a time? Mom's hurt eyes haunt me and guilt invades my soul, but now it's not enough to stop me leaving. I've learned to be a little selfish when it comes to my needs and desires. I've learned, too well, that I have needs and desires.

The seats in my car are hot. The backs of my thighs tingle and burn. I feel the stinging high up. Immediately it reminds me of the hot passionate days on board the yacht. Sun, heat, the burning of my buttocks and thighs, the burning of my insides always before the sweet relief of rapture.

A drop of perspiration drips off my chin. The air is stifling. Summer is lingering this year. I flip the switch for the AC as soon as the car starts and back out of the gravel drive without glancing at my mother on the porch. I have to get away. Everything is closing in around me.

The street is straight and wide open to the sun. Not a shadow appears. Not a spot of shade to protect the smallest of creatures, never mind man. The air shimmers with heat, distorting the horizon I'm heading for. I imagine standing naked on the hot pavement and feeling the heat shimmering, humming along my body like a thousand infinitesimal invisible hot vibrators. Prickles of sweat break out on my brow even as the cool air hits my face. I step on the accelerator and drive aimlessly.

The roads are empty. I steer automatically with no thought of direction as my mind wanders back and forth between today and last summer. Everything is dry and dusty. It makes me feel old, used up. The farmers will begin to harvest their crops soon, and the cooling fall breezes may then flow over the land.

A long while later a patch of blue beyond some trees catches my eye and I slow down. A small lake glistens in the distance. I pull over to the side and stare at it. It's so cool looking, inviting. An obscure dirt track leads from the road to it. White-tipped prairie grass waves gently to and fro in the hot breeze as if beckoning me, defying me to trespass, to do what I never would have done a few months ago. Daring me. Challenging me with its inviting color and promise of coolness to bury my guilt and make myself happy.

Opening the door, I ignore the blast of heat that hits me. Standing, I see nothing but fields of crops stretching far into the distance, the spot of blue with a few trees around it looking more remote than before, more tempting. There is no sign of the farm that I know is probably just over the rise. There is no sign of life in any direction.

To be in the midst of someone's vast property but so totally alone is both thrilling and intimidating. My heart beats faster. The fields of crops and grass go on forever, the gently waving tops seeming to offer caresses if one should choose to walk amongst them.

What would it feel like to walk naked through the undulating fields? Would the tips caress with feathery touches, reminding me of long, languid caresses? Or would they be sharp and stinging, reminding me of harsher, keener moments with Grant? My nipples harden with need and I look out over the neverending fields with both trepidation and yearning.

The magnitude is staggering. I feel like a tiny speck in the universe. The only friendly thing in sight is the inviting blue of the lake. I heed its call. I'll stay with Mrs. Carroll a few nights to relieve my mother of the burden and me of my guilt.

I stop the car under the largest tree and shut off the engine. Immediately, the car becomes hot, and I quickly open both windows, the thin, hot breeze slightly cooler in the shade of the tree. The water ripples softly, the almost nonexistent waves lap the shore and I envision myself once again on Grant's island.

I can almost feel the sand beneath me, cool in the summer night. My nakedness is caressed by the silent, balmy breeze. My legs are open and the gentle waves lick and lap at my source. It was such a gentle climax. A necessary one that calmed and soothed so I was finally able to let Grant love me as he wished to.

I jerk from my reverie when my arm touches the burning-hot metal of the car. Rubbing my arm softly, I stare at my dress. Light blue. Thin. One that Grant bought me. Then, I was forbidden to wear undergarments. Here, I don't dare not to. It took me a long time to get used to the confines of bra and panties again. And I'm still not used to it completely.

I throw the keys in my purse and open the door. My eyes scan the horizon in all directions. I'm so alone. So deliciously alone with all that cool water in front of me. It's impossible to resist its allure, and I don't even try.

The dress falls onto the soft grass, the bra and panties following. The cushioning grass is soft beneath my feet. The air whispers around me, slightly cooling my sweat-soaked body. Insects hum. Time seems to slow down. A bird lands on a high branch and sings me a song as I step into the silky liquid.

This is heaven. I toss my short tresses and stretch my arms high above me. The breeze kisses me with featherlight breath. I wade deeper and then plunge. Cool, heavenly water laves my body, and I stay below in its delightful embrace as long as my lungs allow.

This is bliss. Grant would like this. It's not as exotic as the oasis on his island, but he'd appreciate its beauty. I float on my back, hands languidly propelling me along. The oasis had been a place of pain and pleasure. Of storm and calm. Of raw sex and fiery passion. I wish I were there. Will we return next summer?

I hear a buzz that grows louder than the insects that whirr and buzz as they pester me occasionally. Shading my eyes I see a small plane high up in the sky. A sly, devilish smile curls my lips. Is it the owner of the lake? Can he see me? Do I want him to? What would he think to find a naked woman in his lake, breasts bobbing merrily above the water, my once-again-thick thatch peeking up at him?

Will he land and come storming over here? To what? Throw me out? Throw me down and ravish me? I can't help laughing at myself. The plane is so high I'm sure he can't see me. Wishful thinking has lately been unfulfilled and this time will be no different.

I dive, relishing the silkiness of the liquid on my skin. The water is so still, so silent. Nothing at all like the pounding of the ocean on Long Island's east end. I clasp my legs tightly together and relive the first time I swam in the ocean. Grant had made it a memorable occasion. But all my times with Grant have been memorable.

I open my eyes and my world is now a silent, cool, shimmering green. Grass grows on the bottom, its swaying dreamy movements hypnotic. Erotic. I rise, gulp in a breath of air and dive down, swimming low and letting the blades tickle and tease my breasts and belly as I skim them lightly. Silky, slick edges of green make me yearn anew for the strong, steely fingers that used to caress me. I'm gasping for breath by the time I give in to my body's demands and surface.

A cloud has covered the sun and my mood of decadent naughtiness fades. The magic dissipates and the too-familiar gloom intrudes. How sad to have something so wonderful and no one to share it with.

I drag myself from the water and shake my head like a shaggy dog. My hands roam over my body, flicking the water beads from it. They linger on my breasts but I stop myself. That is less than satisfying lately.

The shade of the tree is cool, and I shiver slightly before stopping dead in my tracks. Wide blue eyes twinkle with amusement as they watch my progress. He's sitting cross-legged where my clothes and purse had been. Youngish, early twenties perhaps, almost platinum hair and the most roguish smile I've ever seen.

Instinctively I cover my breasts, then my mound, then try to do both at the same time. I feel my belly churn with want even as the blood suffuses my cheeks. His smile is beguiling. I'm torn between warring emotions. His chuckle breaks my silence. He's too superior.

"How dare you spy on me!" What an inane, spinsterish thing to say. His roving eyes make my body tingle.

"I believe you're trespassing, ma'am."

"That has nothing to do with your despicable behavior. Would you please leave and I'll be off your land as soon as I can get dressed." My attempt at outraged haughtiness is having little effect on him. He grins wider and rises slowly to his feet in one fluid movement. I hate myself for being so weak. He has such as nice body.

"Not my land. You can stay as long as you like as far as I care. I kinda like the view myself."

Too many emotions rage within me. I feel no fear of him. It's myself I worry about. His total maleness is so obvious. I have to leave quickly or I won't want to leave at all. My eyes flick around but I can't spot my clothes anywhere.

"Did you move my clothing?"

"Hid them." He grins at my startled expression, and my mouth goes dry as he begins slowly to remove his shirt. He's tan and muscular. His hands are large and rough from whatever work he does. His eyes continually slide up and down my body. And my body is responding. My breathing is ragged and irregular. My nipples are harder than stone.

I don't know what to do. I should run. I want to stay. It's exciting and adventurous. Risky and scary. And by the look in his eye I'll have very little to say about it.

That's what makes me finally turn and try for the car. I don't want to be under anyone's control again. I'm surprised he doesn't try to stop me till I reach for the door handle. It's jammed. I can't lock myself in. I just stare at it stupidly till I sense him behind me and turn. I'm a little frightened but still don't think he'll hurt me. His grin is so confident, so wonderfully wicked.

"I think we'll be more comfortable on the grass. Your car is on the small side, ma'am."

I can't take my eyes from his. They probe and seem to read my thoughts. His grin widens and he raises his hand for me to take. It all has such an unreal quality about it. Like a dream one once had and can just scarcely remember. Like a dream I've had too many times since Grant and I parted. He takes my hand when I don't take his.

His touch is light but firm and his skin is rough. He leads me to a soft grassy knoll and kneels, taking me with him. I haven't uttered a sound or made any attempt to get away from him. Is this really happening? His eyes are so blue, so knowing.

Rugged hands frame my face and then firm lips slant to mine. The touch of his probing tongue breaks my trance and I give a jerk of resistance but he holds me. My hands push against an unyielding granite chest. He doesn't seem to notice. His tongue is making my head spin. It seeks and investigates the recesses of my mouth. It searches and soothes. My tongue is sucked into his mouth, and his teeth nibble it gently. My hands are holding onto his shoulders. I'm drawn close. His coarse chest hair tickles and teases my heaving breasts. I rub them against it in delight. I feel my hardened peaks skim over his tiny, equally hard nipples. His penis is thick and solid. It slaps against my belly.

And I want him. I want a man so desperately. Grant has spoiled me and I won't deny myself this unexpected opportunity. I pull him close and rub against him. His hands release my head. They skim my shoulders, tickle my ribs. My breasts ache for his touch, but he teases me. Sides, waist, belly. I arch into him. I want to feel the tube against my mound. He pulls back slightly. I moan with frustration. His tongue traces a path along my collarbone. I raise my breasts for his mouth. He ignores them. Neck, shoulder, chin, jaw, eyes, and then back to my mouth. I groan and seek his hardness. My hands are taken and held behind me. Gently he pulls me backward till his hands hold mine on the ground. I'm stretched before him on my knees, legs wide, breasts thrust out. I'm pleading with him with my eyes. He ignores me. My breath is ragged, my chest heaving.

"Please." I hate myself for begging.

His eyes watch me silently for a long moment. "When I'm ready."

And then I know. He won't harm me. He'll get his kicks out of tormenting me. I want him desperately and he's going to use it. My body is screaming with frustration, and I'll do anything to find my release. And he knows that, too.

My hands are released, and he leans back from me

and watches me. It takes everything I have not to reach for myself. He knows it, too. I can see it in his eyes. I hate him and he grins wider. He knows that as well, and he's enjoying it.

I raise up till I'm kneeling in front of him. His sandpaper hands reach for my breasts. He takes the nipples and squeezes them gently. I can't stop my gasp of pleasure. The pressure increases and I lean toward him, seeking his mouth. His hands push me back by my breasts. I'm to be touched, to be toyed with, but not allowed to touch. I would give anything to have the strength of character to leave, but I need him too much.

His hands knead and stroke, over and over. My mouth is slack, my breathing tortured. I would clamp my legs tight but his knees are between them. My hands reach for him, but he gently smacks them down. My clit is throbbing, pulsing with need. My hands seek it. They're taken and raised. His eyes bore into mine.

"Put your hands behind your head."

I hesitate.

"Now, or I leave." No raised voice. Just the effective, quiet threat. I do as he says. My breasts thrust out more. He flicks the turgid peaks with his tongue. I almost swoon. My legs grip his knees hard. I hear his chuckle. Feel his tongue glide from one tip to another. My body is trembling with need.

A finger touches my lips. "Suck."

I do.

"More."

I do.

A rhythmic pinching on my left nipple. I bite my lip with yearning. If he would just keep doing that I know I could come. I want him to touch me between my legs.

Tessa's Holidays

The finger leaves my mouth. He leans toward me, teeth grab and worry my right nipple, his finger jams into my ass. I grunt and fall forward against him. My hands grab his shoulders. His mouth leaves my breast. His finger slides in and out steadily. His other hand kneads and molds my ass in time with his probing finger.

I'm a mass of sensation. I'm almost there. My belly heats up and then he stops and stands up. I collapse in a sobbing heap. My hands cup my mound.

"Do it and I leave." His words stop me cold. I lie panting, staring up at him. He's broad and tanned; the dark green leaves above silhouette him perfectly.

"Why are you doing this?" My voice is strangled as I fight the need to help myself.

He stares at me for a moment and then grins wickedly. "Because I've never in my life seen a woman more desperate for a man."

I wish I could stand and defy him. I wish he couldn't read me so well.

"Get on all fours."

I do. Slowly. Reluctantly. He kneels in front of me.

"Suck it."

I do. He's thick and short. It stretches my mouth but doesn't make me gag. I can sense him watching my lips close around his shaft. Why do men like to watch? I never want to see a man make love to me. I want to feel the man make love to me. He stays perfectly still. I move up and down steadily. I feel it swell.

"Turn around."

I do.

"Back into me."

I do. I slowly crawl backward till I feel his hard knob nudge my sphincter.

"If you want it do it."

And much to my shame, I do. I push against him till I feel the muscle give and slide onto his cock. He stretches me but doesn't fill me. It's another tease and I know I won't be able to climax this way. How could he possibly know it too?

He works me back and forth with his hands on my hips. If he'd only touch my clit. Just once. Just for one minute. I'm so far gone it wouldn't take much. Why can't he fondle my breasts? Why do men love to torture women this way?

I'm pushed forward and he pulls out. He hasn't come. I still have a chance.

"Stand up. Hands behind your head."

I do. I thrust my chest out proudly. I suck in my belly slightly and part my legs. Grant has taught me to be proud of my body. Grant loves my small, perky breasts and boyish hips.

The man reaches out and draws me close to him. I can feel his breath on my mound. He blows on the hair and parts it delicately. My legs tremble. My clit is engorged. It peeks boldly out of the swollen lips. I know he can see it. Please touch it. Please. I feel myself sway. His hands tighten around my thighs and then, with no warning, his mouth devours me and I'm screaming in ecstasy, my fingers digging into his hair, holding him to me as spasm after rapturous spasm shakes me to the core.

But he doesn't stop. His tongue licks and teases. His teeth nibble lightly. His finger seeks and invades my tighter tunnel. Heat, incredible heat, seems to engulf me, and I rock and grind myself into his feeding mouth. Only his strong arms around my thighs keep me upright as he continues his assault. I'm spent, done, but still he continues and the sensations become hotter and hotter. I'm trembling like a leaf in a storm. My head whirls, my body shakes, my senses no sooner recuperate from one orgasm and he's bringing me relentlessly toward another.

"No." The word is so weak the gentle breeze carries it away. His tongue refuses to stop its invasion of my body. It's intense, not quite painful, but mind shattering in its ferocity when it takes me. I sag, a finger pushes harder into my anus and still the tongue probes my inside depths. It's too tender but he won't listen and continues on as if obsessed.

My body is limp. I'm almost draped over his head. He lays me down and pins my hands to my sides and still he ravages me with his mouth. Sucking, licking, nibbling. I'm moaning with yearning. This is the worst kind of torture. Tender, aching deliciousness.

My clit is sucked in and chewed lightly. Bolts of painful pleasure travel up my body. My hands are released. My nipples grabbed, pinched, pulled, and twisted, but so gently it does nothing but make me want him to continue his onslaught. And he does until I finally scream in aching bliss.

I have less than a moment to try to regain my senses. He drops on me and enters me fast and furiously. His pounding is harder on my hips than my cunt as he grinds away, but he's finished in a scant minute and rolls from me. He's gone when I wake.

My clothes are exactly where I left them. The door handle is back in place. If not for the soreness of my pelvis and the dried semen on my thighs I'd have wondered if I'd dreamt it. My body is stiff as if I've been pummeled, and I only walk normally after a long, cool swim in the lake. I feel calmer than I have for a long time but it's still not Grant. He's the one I ache for.

The days go by with the same dull routine. It's Sunday and I'm going to stay with Mrs. Carroll to give her nurse some time to go out. I've assuaged my guilt by taking one of my mother's nights. I sigh ruefully. How exciting my life is. A four-day weekend because of Columbus Day and here I am going to sit with a woman who is just waiting to die. Does she know it?

The nurse can't quite hide her eagerness to be away from the elderly woman and promises to be back by eleven as she hurries out the door. Mrs. Carroll sits in her wheelchair in front of the TV. She doesn't know the nurse has left. She doesn't know that I'm here. I sit on the couch and watch the pictures flash on and off the screen without actually seeing them. I wish I were back in Paris. I wish I were anywhere but here.

I can't sit still, so I wander around the house. Pictures on the wall depict the life of the woman in the other room. A young girl in a white dress and high-button shoes holds the hands of a stiff-backed father and a frail mother with pompadour hairdo. The adults all looked so solemn then. Was everything a chore? A duty? Or did they change into ravenous sexual beings after blowing out the candle. Did they ever make love in the daytime? On a boat? Anywhere but bed?

Another picture shows the same girl, older, shyly standing next to a dashing man with derby and full mustache. Was he gentle when he showed her what love meant? Did her heart pound with excitement or dread, or, worse yet, indifference, as bedtime neared each night? Did she cry out in ecstasy or wasn't that considered correct female behavior? Hard to believe this pretty young thing was the catatonic hulk in the living room.

Another picture shows the same couple proudly surrounded by four strapping children. Where are they now? Where did they fly to? Why am I wandering around in her house and they don't care?

I check on Mrs. Carroll. Same position. Same blank stare. Realizing I might one day share her fate, I suddenly can't bear to be near her. Rubbing the gooseflesh from my arms I make my way down the small hall and let myself out the back door onto her porch.

The night has closed in and surrounds me like a warm blanket. Won't the cooler nights ever start? Night creatures buzz and call to each other. Cicadas drone and whirr. I slap at the mosquito that hums and pesters me. An owl hoots in the trees far behind the house. None answers his mournful cry. Is he lonely?

The trees' dark silhouettes show against the sky. Soon they'll lose their leaves. Stars twinkle brightly and wink at me. It is so familiar, so comforting for all its boringness.

I listen to the droning of the insects. I can hear the inane noises of the television in the house behind me. I lean back against the railing and sigh deeply.

A hand covers my mouth and thick tape stops my yelp of surprise. I'm pulled over the railing. Rock-hard arms pin my own to my body, and I'm lifted and carried toward the trees. I instinctively twist and fight, my screams no more than muffled tones, my shoulders meeting nothing but hard body behind them. My foot makes contact with a shin and I hear a quiet grunt. Arms tighten till I swear my ribs will break. My heart is hammering away as I'm carried deep into the trees. We don't have rapists in our town, I think in blind panic.

The moonless night is dark, almost black beneath the trees. I hear my assailant's light panting. A large tree that has fallen during the last storm appears before us suddenly. My hair is grabbed and I'm bent over the tree. My wrists are grabbed and pinned to the small of my back. The rough bark scrapes my belly where my blouse has pulled loose. My toes barely touch the earth. I feel my underpants ripped from me and then nothing but pain.

My ass contracts against the first swipe of the crop, my screams muted by the tape. Over and over it bites into my soft flesh. I can feel my buttocks bouncing and clenching with each blow. No mercy. No letting up. My screams seem to spur him on but I'm helpless to stop. I feel the welts rising on the tops of my thighs and ass. My body burns. Each reactive kick of my legs rubs them against the rough bark of the tree. Only when I subside into ragged moans does he stop.

My arms are released and hang uselessly along my sides. My breathing is tortured through my tear-clogged nose. I flinch at the sound of a sharp crack and wait to be violated or killed.

Nothing.

Not a sound. Not a movement behind me. I start to tremble uncontrollably but am terrified to move. My body is on fire, my ass and legs like molten lead, heavy and heated. I move tentatively and nothing assails me. My arms tremble with the effort of raising them to my mouth. The tape peels off easily and I gasp in lungfuls of air before the sobs take over. My ass throbs with each movement as I gingerly lower myself to the ground on my hands and knees. A riding crop broken in two lies at my feet. So do two pictures.

My hands shake but I force myself to pick them up. I can't make them out in the dark. I bite my lips to stop the groans of pain as I stand. I barely stay on my feet. I can't locate my underpants. I half stagger, half limp back to the porch, my self-pitying sobs subsiding into shaky sniffs and gulps by the time I reach the dimly lit platform.

The single bulb seems harsh after the dark of the trees. I can't stop shaking. I don't dare try to sit so I lean heavily against the railing and try to get some control over myself.

The first picture is me on my hands and knees sucking the blond man by the lake. The second is me standing wantonly beneath the tree, hands behind my head, his mouth at my source. I wave away the mosquito buzzing about my head. The sound brings back another buzzing I had heard that day. High up in the sky. I start to shake.

I've been warned.

Thank God for the holiday. I needed the two days just to be able to walk without appearing stiff. I know the nurse stared at me curiously when she arrived, but I made some hurried excuse and departed guiltily. Maybe she thought I'd almost been caught with a boy, as if I were some teenager who was baby-sitting for her.

I feigned the flu and aching joints to explain why I groaned and moaned as I stayed in bed away from my mother's knowing eyes. I dreaded going to school on Wednesday and sitting at a desk all day.

Grant's warning was clear. I wasn't to pick my partners. He liked watching me with others but apparently it would be his decision when and with whom. Rodney had been merciless with the lesson but then Rodney has always taken great pleasure in teaching me a lesson. It wouldn't be wise to give him another reason.

I hate the thought of being forced to wait till next July for sex. I hadn't realized when I'd promised to travel with Grant again next year that this was part of the deal.

The days pass, one like another. The kids settle into the routine of study and homework, as do I. My bruises fade. I accept few dates and keep the few I do confined to dinner and a chaste good-night kiss at the door. I have no intention of inviting another meeting with Rodney.

It's a funny feeling knowing there is probably someone watching you at all times. It both frightens and reassures. At first, I constantly watched and looked but never saw anyone or anything suspicious. I would look up quickly, trying to catch someone in the act of avoiding my eyes but to no avail. It made most of my dates very uncomfortable. One man asked me if I was in therapy.

Maybe Grant thought the lesson sufficient and there is no one keeping tabs on me. Maybe part of the punishment is making me wonder.

The talk at school every day is all about the upcoming Halloween party. Eager to keep the kids off the streets as much as possible, the town has decided to throw a whopping big masquerade bash for the entire community. The teachers are just as excited as the children and will act as chaperons for those whose parents are unable to attend.

My mother and I have been making my costume for

the past week. Relishing my secret summer, I can't help but choose an angel costume. The irony will be lost on everyone else, but I'll know and it will make it that much more exciting to wear. Angel indeed! If people ever guessed.

The night is finally here. The children were more than useless in class today. Everyone is thinking about the coming night, even the boys who try so hard to seem above such things. I must admit it does promise to be something special.

The huge gym in the high school has been transformed into a spooky mansion. The art and tech teachers have truly outdone themselves. The area is divided up into sections made to look like various rooms of a haunted mansion.

When I see the dungeon, the mock manacles hanging from the wall, I am immediately transported back to the yacht. I can feel myself moistening at the memory.

The living room is done in dark, Gothic style. I roared when Kevin Daly sat on a chair to rest and it promptly tilted back and deposited him onto a mat on the other side of the breakaway wall. After that, every time he wished to sit we'd see him pushing and prodding to make sure the chair was a chair before sitting.

The bedroom features a huge canopied bed with hangings that slowly lower to suffocate the unwary visitor. Hidden staircases abound. Groans and shrieks will be heard throughout the night. The kitchen is dutifully full of turn-of-the-century appliances as well as bloody cleavers and frozen corpses. The effect is amazing.

Dancing will be in the cafeteria. The DJ hired for the affair arrives in proper mummy attire. His assistant has a hatchet buried deep in his skull, blood realistically dripping down his face. The room is papered in black crepe. Dim orange bulbs replace the usual bright fluorescent lighting. Skeletons will join the dancing, suspended from the ceiling.

I arrive early, the first excited children following shortly after. Costumes of all kinds mingle and mix. The older kids try hard to scare the wits out of the younger ones and too many succeed too often so I'm kept busy wiping tears and uttering reassurances. One little girl, refusing for the longest time to be soothed, finally looks up and her eyes open wide at the sight of wings sprouting from my back. Rounded baby blues travel the length of my diamanté gown and her small mouth forms an awed O.

"Are you really an angel?" she asks breathlessly.

"Yes, she is," a familiar voice answers behind me. My heart skips a beat and then begins pounding. My mouth is dry. I see the small eyes widen still further as they look beyond me. Reassuring words flee from my tongue. Strong fingers cup my elbow and raise me to my feet. I can barely breath. Please don't be an illusion. Ice blue eyes meet my green ones and I have to lick my lips. My nipples harden under his penetrating stare. I see the skin around his eyes crinkle. He knows. And he's pleased.

Satan stands before me. Magnificent in his wickedness, he fits the costume well. Only his eyes behind the full mask tell me I'm not dreaming. He leans toward me and I to him. I wish I could see those wonderful sensuous lips. I want to feel them all over my body. I moisten.

His voice is husky. "You look beautiful. Ready to be ravaged and taken to new heights but so angelic it makes one hold back. One mustn't corrupt the seraphim."

I hear his intake of breath. I see the blue eyes narrow slightly. "Unless they want to be tarnished. Are you willing to be corrupted, Tessa?" I almost sag with desire. The long-missed caress of my name on his tongue weakens me as effectively as his hands can. I want him so desperately.

My world is all lightness. It once more has meaning. He heard of the party and dared to come because of the costume's anonymity. I would happily suffocate slowly under the descending canopy if only we could use the bed for a scant half hour.

A tug at my gown and I tear my eyes from his and bend to hear the whispered words from Little Bo Peep about needing the toilet. He's gone when I straighten. I blink the tears back quickly and take the tiny hand that lifts trustingly to me. I'm almost shaking with frustration.

Has he come just to tease? Is this punishment for the blond man? The party is no longer fun or special. It's keeping me from Grant. Is he here? Has he left? I fight tears and paste a smile on my face. My eyes constantly search, each glimpse of red making my heart begin a new dance within my chest before I once more deflate with disappointment.

"Hey, you look like you need a break. How about a dance?" Kevin Daly is smiling at me, his easygoing manner enhanced by his Robin Hood costume. He's beginning to get a beer belly, I think, as I unconsciously compare him to Grant. I think I do that with all men now. Very few seem to measure up to him and he's twice their age.

I nod and take his offered hand.

"Great party, don't you think?"

"Yes. Everyone says it's a great success." We enter

the cafeteria and melt into the group on the dance floor. Kevin holds me lightly and keeps up a steady chatter of school things that don't require an answer. I can't stop looking around, my heart beating fast every time I spy a devil's costume. I don't see any that could be Grant.

"May I?"

My skin tingles, suddenly alive with electricity. I don't wait for Kevin's agreement but turn and step quickly into Grant's arms. His hand is firm and cool beneath my own. His other pulls me close to him. I'm sorry now for the voluminous angel's gown. I want to feel his body on mine. I want to drown in his kiss. I want him filling every pore of my being. I want him.

His blue eyes are studying me when I look up. I can't keep the happy smile off my face. I sense his own tender smile in answer. I resent the red and black plastic that hides so much of him from me.

"We appear to represent both sides of the eternal question."

His voice is so rich. I wish he'd continue talking. He's waiting for my reply. I try to think clearly. We spent hours sharing our thoughts and feelings. I know he respects my intelligence, my banter. I want to flirt and entice him to stay. I need him to stay.

"Good and Evil? Pure and Sullied? Prim and Wanton? Naughty and Nice?" I bat my lids flirtatiously and hear his chuckle.

His hand tightens on mine. "And which are you? Outwardly, you represent one side of the question. But do you wish it were the other?"

I bat my eyes furiously and allow a coy smile to spread my lips. "Why, sir, I would think you'd be the best judge of that."

I see the crinkles appear around his fabulous eyes. His head cocks to one side. "I think everyone has a little evil inside of them."

I swallow quickly and lick my lips. "I wish I had some evil inside of me right now. And not just a little bit."

Laughter booms out of his chest. Only a few of the closest people bother looking at us. Everything is loud—the voices, the colors, the music.

I'm pulled closer to his body as we move among the other dancers. His gaze is so penetrating. "You never answered my question, Tessa."

"What question?" I can't think. I'm mesmerized by his eyes. I've missed him more than I knew. Will this brief interlude make it harder or easier to part and wait till summer?

"Are you willing to be corrupted?"

My clit throbs with expectation. My nipples become hardened pebbles. They pulse with need. "Only by you," I whisper.

"And who I choose."

"And who you choose," I agree. I try to move closer but Grant maintains a dignified distance. Our steps are without thought, a perfect blending of motion. The song ends too soon, and then, with a low bow, he turns and leaves. I'm devastated when I follow and see him exit the building. He's actually gone.

My legs clench together. My heart is a leaden weight in my breast. The party seems to last forever. My mouth hurts from the forced smile I maintain all night.

The gym is finally empty. A few teachers linger and help me check the various rooms of the haunted house to make sure no one has been left or overlooked. A once-magnificent masterpiece is now a ruined, wilting shadow of its former self. The custodians begin the cleanup, and we all leave by the side door.

The air is brisk, the hint of the coming winter easy to feel. A large full moon hangs low in the sky, its reflected light bathing the parking lot with properly eerie moonshine for this night of the year. One by one, each car is entered and, with a shout and wave, a quick toot of a horn, the parking lot empties out and I find myself alone.

The ending of things, most things, is usually a relief yet always seems sad. I don't think I've ever felt so alone in my life as I do right this minute.

The streets are deserted. The moon slowly climbs higher into the sky. The night is still and peaceful, no hint of the mischief that surely occurred on this infamous night of tricks and pranks.

The buildings thin out as I head toward home. Houses become fewer as the land opens up and the smaller farms begin. I like where we live, still in the town, an almost separate community, but on the fringes of the vast farms that stretch across the state. We have the best of both worlds. The moonlight disappears as I enter the stretch of woods before the houses will start once again.

And he's there waiting for me.

My headlights show him clearly. Satan; tall, fiery red, devilishly commanding as he stands in the middle of the road, arms crossed over his chest. Magnificent. I feel myself moisten with expectation.

I stop the car. He approaches. A swish of his cape, the door is open and I'm lifted in his arms. His eyes are dark slits. Unfathomable. I want his lips but they remain hidden behind the hideous red-and-black mask. I shiver despite the fact that I know it is Grant.

"I…"

"Quiet." The command is whispered, almost growled. I'm being carried into the woods. The sound of my car starting and moving away reaches me. Memories of the woods behind Mrs. Carroll's house make me tremble slightly. I've done nothing wrong.

He shifts me and I feel his hand on my bare thigh. Nerves pulse madly where skin now touches skin. I tighten my hold on his neck. My gown trails down, starkly white and glittering against the red of his costume. My wings are in the back seat of my car. My heart is picking up its pace with each step that takes me deeper into the woods. I'm ready for him. I crave him. I will do anything for him.

We enter a cleared circle ringed with stones. Two trees about six feet apart fill the center. There is a small fire burning within a circle of rocks both in front and behind the trees. I'm deposited in the center in front of one tree. I stand and watch Satan move back from me. The fire outlines his form, darkening his features. The cape is tossed back over his shoulders. I see his chest expand, his hands resting on his hips. I feel as if he'll devour me as his low voice washes over me. I want him to. Completely.

"You've chosen the wrong night to travel, innocent one. This is my night. This is the night when all who know me come to worship me. This is the night that goodness and purity are sacrificed to me, Satan." He leans forward slightly, and I see his hand point to me, long, curved nails threatening silently. "You are mine."

I try to look demure, virginal, not rampant with lust. My heart is hammering with excitement and a touch of fear. This is all so easy to believe. The firelight flickers, throwing grotesque shadows that seem to twist and weave like claws trying to grab at me. They move obscenely over the pristine white of my gown. The silence is so total as evil glares at me. I'm hypnotized by his presence.

My hands are gripped and pulled wide. Two black-robed figures have me stretched and helpless, the long black cowls hiding their features as they grip me by wrist and arm to keep me still.

Satan moves closer. I'm panting and start to struggle, suddenly unsure if this is really Grant. I open my mouth to scream but steel bands take hold of my chin and my voice is stilled. "You will make no sound no matter how frightened you may become." The command is snarled and harsh, but the strength of his fingers reassures me it is really him. I see firelight dance in his eyes as they peer at me through the mask slits. He leans closer. "Your fate is sealed." I nod my assent, my eyes shyly lowered.

I will play the part of the doomed maiden, the sacrificial virgin. I will play any part he wishes as long as he makes love to me.

His taloned fingers skim my jawline. I shiver. The figures who hold me are silent and still, their grip tight enough to be convincing. My breath is rasping in my throat. The finger moves to my neck, my ear, under my chin. I raise my eyes. The evil visage makes my throat constrict.

"Kneel and pay homage to your master. Kneel on this holy All Hallows' Eve and vow to bind yourself to me with body and soul."

My shoulders are pushed down and I fall to my knees. The diamanté on my gown picks up the firelight and shimmers. His penis is large and waiting. I see the veins stand out in the firelight. I lick my lips as my head is pushed forward. I resist as if indeed I were still virginal. Cruel fingers clasp my neck. My tongue snakes out tentatively. I lick the ivory-smooth knob and flick the vent. It pulses beneath the warmth of my tongue.

"Open your mouth." I obey with a whimper. I hear his groan of pleasure as I take as much as I am able. He rocks back and forth slightly and then he is gone, my mouth empty. I'm lifted and dragged backwards. Leather binds my wrists to the trees so I am stretched between them. I'm on tiptoe. My breathing is becoming harsher. I feel his breath on the back of my neck.

"Do you know my name, sweet seraph?" His whispered taunting raises gooseflesh along my spine. "I am called Lucifer, Mammon, Beelzebub, Belphegor. I have many names and guises but from this moment forward they all mean master to you."

A finger runs up my spine, so light, so menacing in its gentleness, its intent. I feel the zipper lowering slowly and try to twist in my bonds. I'm held motionless, stretched, vulnerable. Shivers of excitement make me tremble. His breath is warm on my neck. I flinch under the swipe of his tongue up the side of my neck. He breathes into my ear. His tongue licks the lobe. I wish I could see him but he stays behind me. The unknown is always more terrifying, more exciting.

The two figures in robes stand in front of me, one to each side. They are motionless, sinister, threatening in their silence. My dress loosens as the zipper reaches my lower spine. Long nails tickle my ribs, then reach around and grasp my nipples. I sag with need as bolts of pleasure course through me. My breathing is tortured, my body alive as it hasn't been for too many weeks.

The silent specters move forward and unbind me. My dress slips down my arms and falls to my waist. My bra is unhooked and whisked off, and then I am once more bound to the trees. I feel the coolness of the air. The heat of the fires doesn't reach this far. Hands from behind ease the fabric over my hips. The nails scratch lightly along my belly, snake a trail up the length of my crack. My underpants are ripped from me and tossed into the fire. I get a whiff of burning fabric. My feet are lifted out of the gossamer fabric and it is placed outside the circle.

Satan stands before me, the mask removed, his face reddened. Grant looks like evil incarnate with the makeup on his face. High-arched black eyebrows. Goatee wickedly pointed. The leering smirk of superiority. The three figures stand before me and gaze at my nakedness. The firelight throws flickering shadows over my white skin. A breeze sweeps over me and I shiver. Shadows seem to caress my body and play with me. None of them move. Every pore of my being awaits his touch.

A taunting chuckle rumbles from his chest. "Here she is. The pure seraph waiting to be ravaged by her demon lover. Does she quiver with fear? Or with anticipation?" His tone is mocking. Too quiet. I'm suddenly uneasy.

"Grant…"

"Quiet!" The sharp command hisses through the air. I'm panting, my throat is dry. The specters move and I lose sight of them. Leather on my ankles, legs pulled wide. I'm gulping in air. My heart will surely burst from my chest.

"It's been too long since I've had someone at my disposal. I've missed being able to do what I wish, when I wish." His fingers curl into my hair and he forces my head up and back. His evil face is in shadow. It's too real and I'm once more afraid. He smirks when he feels me tremble.

A finger softly traces patterns on my belly. I try to clench my legs but can't. My breathing is irregular, frantic, the finger relentless. Light. Sensuous. Tortuous as it ever so slowly lowers.

Glittering eyes watch my face, note my every expression. I bite my lips. The lightest of touches on the silky hairs. I rasp in a breath. Lips are parted as the finger seeks my slit. I'm penetrated, rocked gently on the slow movement of his finger. The knuckle rubs and teases the engorged bud. I moan and burst, shaking in my bonds.

A tongue licks my neck, nibbles my earlobe, and still the finger works inside of me. "Please," I beg.

"Please what?" His jeering words make me pull at my bonds. His thumb begins to massage my sphincter. "Please ravage me? Please do it again? Please let me serve you? Please what, my angel?" His finger sinks in to the first knuckle. "What is it you really wish, sweet one?"

Teeth clamp onto my right breast and I suck in air. Heat invades my belly. My toes curl in delicious agony. He straightens. He circles me. A finger flicks first one, then the other, tumescent peak. Electric sparks rush from tip to tip. Clawlike fingers brush and tickle my cheeks. My anus is probed so gently. The tight muscle circled and massaged.

Two hooded mouths attach themselves to my breasts. They suck in unison. Steadily pulling and licking. I tremble with need. A tongue licks a wet path along the back of my neck. So many mouths making me mindless to all but the sensations that wash over me.

"Will you accept Satan as your master?" The hushed sibilance of his words laves my body. I try to lean into the mouths that are lapping at my turgid peaks. My clit is throbbing with need. I'm helpless in every sense of the word.

"Yes."

Another wet path up the side of my neck. I feel his hot breath in my ear. The mouths never pause. "Will you lick and suck when commanded?"

"Yes." Anything.

"Will you obey all my wishes?"

"Yes." Teeth chew lightly. I moan with pleasure.

"Will you let my minions enjoy your body?"

"Yes." I will do anything to feel him inside of me. I moan with need. I hear his pleased, victorious chuckle.

His voice is quiet, husky, persuasive. "Shall I come to you as an incubus? Shall I assume the likeness of a goat? Would you like to feel my sharp cloven hooves roam your tender soft flesh?"

I shake my head. Another moan of pleasure escapes as tongues begin to lap harder. I barely remember to play my part. "No, Master. It is you I wish. It is you I want to show me how to be wicked."

"And I shall, child. And I shall." His whispered words waft over me. The mouths leave and he stands before me. The fire has died to embers. The red glow just enhances his maleficence. I tremble in both fear and anticipation. I want to be ravaged. I want to be filled as never before. I want to scream and rage as he stands in front of me and makes me wait for it.

I feel his huge tool slap against my leg. He rubs it slowly back and forth along my netherlips. He beats it gently against my mound. Fingers part my thick outer lips. My slit is sought. The knob spreads them wider. And then delicious sensation floods my body as he slowly, endlessly, fills me. I strain to embrace him but remain stretched wide. Open. Vulnerable. Accepting. Moaning softly with desire.

Hands on my shoulders pull me down slightly. Leather tightens on my wrists. My arms strain. I give a sob of frustration. "I want to hold you," I plead quietly.

"I want it this way." I hear the determination. I can imagine the glint in his eyes. He takes long, slow strokes, the length of his penis dragging and pulling along my soft inner walls. Heat centers and pulses. Nerves scream commands from brain to clitoris. And my clit obeys and I gush, sagging as much as my bonds allow, Grant's penis still rock hard within me.

He holds me close, still moving slowly within me as I whimper in happy exhaustion. My breath finally evens out and I rest my head against his shoulder.

I sense another body behind me and then my mouth is covered by a warm hand, my head pulled back onto a hard shoulder. Grant's eyes glow red in the reflected light.

"All fallen angels suffer pain, Tessa." I see the fascination as he watches my reaction. I try to struggle. The body moves closer, pinning me to Grant. His hands reach around and part my buttocks. I feel the hard knob, seeking, searching. My screams sound like a muted foghorn. And then pain streaks up my body as the specter fills my bowels with one hard thrust.

The hand eases off my mouth. I'm gasping, panting in agony at the double impalement. Grant, the perfectionist, has thought of a way to bring the fires of hell along with him. My body shudders between the two strong ones that sandwich me. They stay still, allowing me time to adjust and accept the fullness of both of them. I am stuffed, filled beyond capacity. My anus throbs. I feel the penis answer with its own pulsings.

"Lay your head back on Bill's shoulder. I want to watch your face."

Bill. Why aren't I surprised? He's going to hurt me more. Bill loves to hurt women. I whimper but obey. I have little choice. Why would Grant do this to me?

"Grant..." I choke on tears. A finger flicks my cheek in gentle warning.

"You were told to be quiet." I sniff and obey. I don't want him angry. Light fingers stroke my cheek. "Bill will not set the pace. Rodney will."

My eyes widen. I don't understand. I feel Bill shift position. His legs widen and he pulls out of me slightly. I bite my lip to muffle the groan. My eyes are glued to Grant's. His expression reminds me to remain silent. I feel Bill tense, hear his low grunt and then feel his penis leap up into me and expand as his excitement builds and Rodney fills him.

Rodney sets a slow and steady pace, his movements within Bill forcing his penis to glide back and forth within me which in turn makes me ride helplessly on Grant's engorged prick.

I see Grant's eyes glitter in the dull glow. They go from me to beyond me. Do Bill and Grant's eyes meet in excitement as they feel themselves rubbing against each other's penis, a thin membrane all that separates them? Grant is an ass man, I wonder why he let Bill have me there?

Grant takes my mouth and kisses me long and deeply, absorbing my muted whimpers. The pain diminishes slowly. He nibbles my lips, my chin. His voice is slightly strained, almost harsh. "When Rodney says to, you will come."

His fingers seek my clit, the practiced thumb making me forget about my discomfort. I feel my breath quickening. The bud heats up, grows, throbs. I'm squeezed tighter between the muscled bodies as they grasp one anothers' arms to keep their balance. The pace increases. I'm panting. Waiting. I want to. I mustn't. I hear Grant's strained breathing. I hear Bill's low moans of pleasurable agony and then finally Rodney's panting voice demanding we all come. And we do.

I'm filled with pulsing cock, and my liquor spills as they both give satisfied grunts and spew into me. I'm crushed, kissed, humped. Heartbeats throb on my chest, my back. My skin absorbs each pulse of them as my own slowly quiets down.

I'm left, untied, lowered gently to a blanket. I'm bathed, soothed, dressed and carried to my car, which is back on the road. I haven't lifted a finger to help myself. I haven't uttered a word. Gentle lips on mine, a whispered "I miss you," and then I'm alone. Only the quiet idling of the engine breaks the silence. I barely make it home, I'm so weak. So sated. So completed satisfied.

The Halloween party was the hit of the decade, and everyone agrees it should be repeated next year. So do I but for entirely different reasons.

I fight the urge to return to the woods all morning

but finally gave in. I want to relive my experiences. I want to sit in the circle and conjure up all the wonderful feelings. I'm completely thrown when I find no evidence it has ever happened. My tender insides assure me it has, but the undisturbed woods say no. No ringed circle, no rock-rimmed burnt fires. Nothing. Everything seems to shift and move. I feel as if I've entered another dimension. The *Twilight Zone* in Iowa?

I return to the road and scan the stretch of woods over and over, reentering the trees at different points, retracing the steps I thought we'd made, but the only thing I find that looks familiar are two trees about six feet apart. Leaves and twigs lay scattered on the ground all around them as if they'd lain that way for all time. I get down on my hands and knees and search the underbrush for specks of burnt wood or some of the many rocks that had bordered the circle. I find absolutely nothing.

Grant would make an excellent criminal. He knows how to cover all angles and tracks. If it had been done to anyone but me and they'd reported it, the police would have sworn they was nuts and ignored it.

I return home but can't relax. I rue the loss of something tangible to help me relive my adventure. I need time to think, to sit on the porch to contemplate how he arranged everything. It's beyond me, or maybe it's I just don't care. As long as he had arranged it is all that matters.

The air is cool and dry, and I breathe deeply. I can't quite shake the feeling of restlessness. Tilting the chair, I rock slowly on the back legs.

Last night was the first time Grant had asked me to play a part. He had lived some of his fantasies with me this past summer, but we'd never done role-playing. I can't quite decide if I like it or not. It was different, but it had been hard for me to stay within the role he wanted because I wanted him so desperately. Had it been a whim because of the costume? If so, it'd been a very well thought-out one. But then Grant is a master at planning things so they go as he wants.

The breeze is sharp. My hair tickles my face, and I drag the light blanket off the back of the chair. The sky is a brilliant blue, the air crisp. Leaves twirl their way from limb to earth with each puff of wind. They remind me of pinwheels gone berserk.

The yard is awash in color. Reds, browns, yellows, burnt orange. As usual, they have mostly blown against the east fence. Images of Polly and me romping in the piles of leaves intrude. I see my dad pretending to be mad when we disturbed all his hard work. I even hear his delighted chuckles when he'd shoo us away and threaten a never-to-be spanking. A sigh escapes me. So many things over and done that can never be again. A wispy smile, a muffled giggle, a scream of pure delight given and gone for all eternity. Can they ever be recaptured?

Polly is probably watching her own children play the same games we did at this very moment. A touch of loneliness, a small yearning deep in my belly spoils the memory. Will I ever have my own family? Will I ever watch my own offspring leap and shriek with delight as they hurtle through the air to land softly in a big colorful pile of leaves? With a determined shake of my head I force myself to become practical. We'll have to finish raking within the next week or so.

My mind keeps wandering back to last night. It's

been almost ten weeks since I've been with Grant, and memory hasn't exaggerated his effect on me. Why is it something special with Grant? Even as a stranger, his first kiss had excited me immensely. It has to be more than just the prodigious size of his penis or the lack of good sex before him. Is it because we also share a love of travel and can talk for hours, each genuinely interested in the other's thoughts and feelings?

Is it because I know he really cares for me? His tenderness at times is enormous, and he'd always drawn back when I couldn't take any more. Thoughts of Jack and the yacht drift through my mind. Realizing I had reached my limit, that I'd lost any interest, Grant had stopped Jack from pursuing anything further and we had docked. The last few days spent together had been the most tender, the most wondrous. I wish we could relive them again.

A car passes and honks its horn. I wave without thought, not caring who it is. I'm restless but lethargic at the same time. I want to lie down and have Grant's mouth roam my body. I want to smell his smell. I want to taste him. I want to touch his skin. I want to be loved, caressed, licked. I miss those lazy nights at the beach. I miss him.

The porch door slams and I jerk guiltily. Mom shakes her head as she looks at the pile of leaves. "I don't know whether to try to keep up with them or just wait till they're all down." I smile but don't answer. Speculative eyes turn back to me. "Where were you this morning?"

I shrug but soften it with a smile. "I felt like being outside, so I drove for a while and then took a walk in the woods."

"Pretty time of the year to be in the woods." I hear her sigh as she settles into a chair opposite me. Mom seems to do it more and more lately. She's lost interest in too many things. She doesn't even yell about me tilting the chair back. I couldn't even get her to go to the Halloween party. Guiltily, I'm now glad she didn't come.

"This was your father's favorite time of year. Not yet cold but the heat is past." I nod but make no reply. I hear the same observation every year. I know she misses him terribly. So do I sometimes.

The days pass by, one like the other. It's hard to concentrate sometimes, and I find myself staring out the window till the kids' nervous coughing and shuffling draw me back to the present. Some must wonder if I'm not entering my dotage. Every time I see a young couple kissing or holding hands I think of Grant and my insides clench with need.

I've driven past his bank so many times but never dare to stop. I've never even dared to park and hope for a glimpse of him leaving. If I see him, the wanting will be too strong and I might do or say something that would destroy his wanting me. And I couldn't bear it.

He's so strong, so determined and in control I don't think he'd accept my reasons for inappropriate behavior no matter how flattering to him they were. He says he admires my sophistication, my intelligence. He expects better from me. His reaction to simple foolishness in New York City had been devastating.

Wonderfully devastating.

The house smells of baking when I come in after work. Glorious rich, spicy aromas that remind me Thanksgiving is only a few days distant. Mom is muttering to herself when I walk into the kitchen. She slaps my hand from the slices of peeled apple I try to filch.

"Your Aunt Helen just called. Seems Dan took a spill down the stairs and had to be hospitalized. I guess we'll be spending Thanksgiving at home." She rolls out dough with a vengeance, her movements quick and angry. "Never saw it fail yet. Trust something to happen whenever the holidays approach."

Time freezes. Her voice fades to nothing. The slap and thud of the rolling pin is mere background noise. Is Halloween considered a holiday? My heart starts to beat quickly. I mutter an unintelligible excuse and hurry out to the porch, wrapping my arms around myself against the sudden cold.

Columbus Day. Halloween. Both holidays. Both times something had happened. Will Grant attempt to get in touch with me over the Thanksgiving holiday? My mouth goes dry. I swallow and work some saliva into it. Do I dare to hope?

Three days. No, that's wrong, I quickly chide myself. He couldn't try to contact me on Thanksgiving itself. The day after? Or Saturday?

I rub my arms with excitement. I'll have to make an excuse not to go shopping with my mother as we always do the day after Thanksgiving. Maybe Polly would go with her and I could watch the kids? No. That wouldn't be any better than being with my mother. Worse. Kids see and repeat everything.

My breathing is rapid. I'm almost perspiring. A blast of wind hits me and robs me of breath. I hurry inside and run to my room. I have to be alone. My heart is racing. I can't stop thinking about the possibility.

The bed is soft beneath me as I lie stretched out, my body tense as my mind works frantically. It makes sense. Grant misses me. He told me so. Why wouldn't he seek any opportunity to be with me? Ripples of excitement wash over my body and I hug myself with joy. I can hardly suppress the cry of sheer elation that threatens to emerge. I'm going to burst with happiness.

High on excitement, I ramble on and on about the Thanksgiving holiday at dinner till my mother firmly but politely asks me to please shut up for one moment so she can get a word in edgewise. I do, but nothing can wipe the smile from my face.

And the days drag by. I daydream more and more. The kids take advantage of it and goof off. I don't care.

Where will he meet me? Where will we go? Will it just be us or Bill and Rodney too? Will he warn me ahead of time or will I just see him? How can he plan things when he doesn't know my plans? Or does he?

He's always known as much about me as I do. He knew about my needs and wants before I did. He knew and used my feelings to his own ends. And I love him for it. How will I ever get through the day?

The company starts arriving after services. Mom has decided to invite the widows and widowers from church. I don't care how much extra work it causes as long as the day doesn't drag endlessly. It's probably a good thing because I'll be so busy I won't be able to think about tomorrow too much.

It's all I think about.

I smile and murmur agreement to the many conversations that buzz meaninglessly around me. Mr. Kirby's loud comment that he's never seen me so happy makes me realize I have to control the excited smile that constantly settles on my lips. I'm more than happy to clear and do the dishes. I need to be away from the senseless chatter, the moans and groans of fullness. I need to plan.

But for what? Do I stay inside? Will he telephone? Do I go to the woods? Do I take a walk? Watch TV? Lie naked on my bed? Go into town?

I feel a frustrated desperation trying to take hold and I force myself to calm down. Grant will get to me somehow. I have to act normally. I cannot take a chance of drawing attention to myself. That is the last thing Grant would tolerate and the first thing that would turn him from me. He loves his anonymity.

"I'll lend you a hand, Tessa." Mom's words pull me back to the here and now.

"No, you go on and entertain your guests, Mom. I don't mind cleaning up. Really," I insist when I see her hesitate. "You worked so hard with the cooking, go on inside and lap up all the praise. You deserve it." I feel less guilty seeing her happy smile.

I toss and turn all night. Vivid, wonderful dreams keep me too aware of what might be. I won't satisfy myself. I want to wait for Grant. What does he have planned? Where will we go?

A few of Mom's friends expressed interest in her shopping trip last night so she isn't insistent at all when I beg off. The relief is overwhelming. The silence when she leaves is thick with expectation.

I shower and wash my hair, always wondering in the back of my mind if the curtain will suddenly open but, unlike *Psycho*, my man would love me to death with his penis instead of killing me with a butcher knife. My skin glows as I rub it hard.

The room is steamy when I step out of the bath. I breath in the sultry air and shiver with anticipation. I check myself in the floor-length mirror for any sign of imperfection. Am I putting on weight? A dab of perfume behind each ear. A lightweight wool dress, loose and comfortable. No undergarments. And I wait.

Time crawls. I pace back and forth. I pick up a magazine but see nothing. My ears prick up at the slightest sound. I flip on the TV. I switch it off. I sit near the phone. I look out windows. I pace. I go outside but don't linger for fear I'll not hear the phone. I push my lunch around my plate. I drive to the stretch of woods and sit in my idling car for an hour.

Every move of the second hands of the many clocks in my house seems to mock me. Their ticks grow louder as time passes. The gong of the grandfather clock jeers at my stupidity regularly each hour till I think I'll scream with frustration. My body is tight with tension as the time moves relentlessly ahead, the gongs now tolling their news of doom. Of aloneness. Of abject misery.

Elation has slowly turned to doubt as afternoon arrives. Now as it ends, crushing disappointment takes its place. He isn't coming. It's a bitter blow to both body and soul. My throat is tight.

I sniff back the tears and finally admit it to myself. What a fool I am. I talked myself into believing I knew how Grant's mind worked. I have never been a good reader of other people's minds. If I had been, I never would have married Greg.

I can't shake the overpowering feeling of discontentment that wraps around me like a shroud. It is so heavy, almost unbearable. I'd been so sure. I'd been so positive he would take any and every opportunity to be with me.

An odd sensation settles deep in my belly. Does he

see other women? Does he have casual sex with them? Does he want me only because I'm willing to go along with his more outlandish requests?

I feel my anger rising steadily. How dare he be with others if he won't let me be! How dare he pander to his own needs and deny me the same. I won't stand still for it. He can't always be aware of my every move. And if he is that's just too bad. It's time it was brought out into the open. It's time it was spoken of and the air cleared. He'd been the one to tune me onto my body. If he couldn't keep it satisfied, then others would.

I slam around the kitchen, whether angrier with myself or Grant I can't say with any certainty. Pots rattle and contents spill as I slop leftovers into them haphazardly. And just as quickly the anger dissolves into hurt. I'm jealous of what might not even be, but I'm helpless to fight the feelings.

And I resent feeling this way. I don't want a lifelong commitment. I have no interest in marriage right now, and I know full well that marriage to Grant is impossible. I don't think I'm jealous of Grant's possible relationship with others, I think I'm jealous that he can probably get it when he wants with no worry for the repercussions.

If I carried on with a man in this town my reputation would be shot. I could even lose my job. I don't know anyone but family outside of my own town. Could I go to a distant town and sit in a bar and get picked up? Would I want to? Am I that desperate or am I trying to hurt Grant? Would he even be hurt?

The questions spin wildly inside of my brain. What happened to the fiercely independent woman I'd been before last summer's trip? Why can't I lose myself in academia anymore? Why is the quest for knowledge not enough any longer? Why did I ever let this man into my life to turn it completely upside down?

Polly and I take Mom out to dinner for her birthday. The restaurant is about a half-hour drive from Polly's, so we agree to meet there since Mom and I wish to shop in the larger town before dining. We don't have a mall in our small town. This one is large, two-tiered. Before long Mom and I agree to separate and meet in two hours.

The mall is crowded with Christmas shoppers. People surge in and out of doorways singly and in groups. Santa is on his decorated platform at the end of one aisle, the children both eager and frightened to speak with him. I gaze at the dressed windows with interest as I roam idly along, hoping some wonderful brainstorm will happen and I'll instantly know what to buy for everyone. Should I buy a gift for Grant? I'd like to wrap myself up and send me to him. But I don't even know where he lives. I refuse to allow myself to wallow in self-pity, and I move on, determined to finish some of the shopping.

I pause too long in front of a doorway, and the next moment I'm flat on the ground.

"Gosh, I'm frightfully sorry." The deep voice is somewhere above me. Hands grab my arms and urge me upwards. I can't seem to put my thoughts in order. I feel my purse pushed into my hand and wince as my wrist turns backward.

"You're hurt."

The true dismay in the voice penetrates, and I clear my muddled brain. A young man, very dapper in a three-piece suit, is watching me with worried eyes.

"No. No, it's nothing," I protest halfheartedly. My wrist is throbbing. I try to get a better grip on my handbag, but it slips when the pain snakes up my arm.

He deftly retrieves it, and I suddenly notice people lingering and staring. My face heats up. A security guard approaches looking both annoyed and officious.

"What's the problem?"

"It's nothing, Officer...."

"It bloody well is." A determined chin juts out. I see him square his shoulders slightly. "It's my fault, Officer. Wasn't watching where I was at and opened the door too quickly, knocking this young lady down. She's hurt her wrist, so if you show me the way to a chemist's shop I'll buy the proper bandages to put her good as new in a jiffy."

"What the hell is a chemist's shop?" The guard's eyes narrow suspiciously and I hastily cut in.

"I believe he's referring to a drugstore. It's really all right. I don't require any assistance." I try to take my purse from Godfrey's resolute fingers, but he won't release it.

"I can tell you've been harmed, miss. Totally my fault and I really must insist that you let me tend to it. Did a stint in the reserve and know my bandages. Won't take more than a moment."

He's my height. Slender. Dark hair and short-clipped beard. And his steady dark eyes declare he's absolutely determined to get his way. I nod my acceptance rather than remain the object of curiosity. "I believe there is a drugstore in the middle of the mall."

"Keep your arm against your body between your breasts. This way it's high and no one will jar it before we can tend it." My other elbow is cupped and I'm led away without any further fuss. He doesn't speak any more but weaves me between oncoming people. His stride is brisk, his posture upright and stiff. I can almost imagine him having been a queen's guard once.

He steers me into the shop and unerringly finds the Ace bandages. My utterances of not fussing, not necessary, etc., are completely ignored as if not spoken. He selects one, pays the price, and takes my elbow again.

"We'll have a cup of tea and I'll tend your wrist."

"It's really not necessary," I protest again. I wonder if he's deaf or hard of hearing. He doesn't even acknowledge my words. When I try to slow down, he just tightens his hold on my elbow and tugs me along after him.

We enter a dimly lit small restaurant. Without waiting to be seated, he guides me to a booth at the back. A waitress hurries after us.

"Sir, I'm sorry but this section is closed."

"My friend has had an accident and needs her wrist bandaged. You understand, love. She hates to attract any attention to herself. Shy, you know. Be a love and fetch us a pot of tea and some biscuits."

"Biscuits?"

He waves her away with impatience. "Cake or anything you Yanks eat with tea will do."

I watch the girl waver for a second and then, with a resigned shrug, go off to do his bidding. His eyes twinkle mischievously at me when I turn back to him.

"Now, isn't this cozy?"

I lower my eyes demurely. "Surely too cozy for someone as shy as I."

I hear his chuckle and join him. "Can't fault a bloke for trying to be alone with a comely wench such as yourself."

"Flattery will get you everywhere, sir," I joke but see the spark of interest in his eyes. My heart picks up speed and I hastily try to change the subject.

"Do you really know your bandages?" His closeness is making me slightly edgy. He moves even closer.

"Very well. I could bind any part of your body and make you comfortable, if not ecstatic."

His voice has lowered suggestively. Am I so transparent? Have I no secrets? I have to swallow and concentrate. "I'm sure my wrist will feel better after it's supported."

"Yes. Everything feels better when it is bound tightly but cocooned in softness."

His whispered words make my skin tingle. Am I reading something into them or is he asking me? I can't quite seem to meet his eyes. I'm afraid of what he'll be able to read in mine. My hand is taken gently. His fingers are slim and long and very light in their touch. A shiver of pleasure runs up my spine. I feel his lips on my palm. A slow swipe of his tongue. My breathing quickens.

"I would never hurt any part of your body unless you wanted me to." His thumb rubs small circles on the pulse at my wrist. I can't tear my eyes from the hypnotic movement of his finger. "Do you want me to bind you? To caress you? To bring you to a fever pitch and then take you higher still?" He's so close, the warmth of his whispered breath kisses my ear.

I nod, helplessly caught up in the eroticism of the moment. His small, satisfied chuckle breaks the spell.

I blush and try to take back my hand, but he holds it securely and deftly begins to wrap it expertly.

"To help the swelling it should be held like this," he says, eyes watching my expression as he raises my arm and slants it diagonally between my breasts. A thumb scrapes my nipple, which erects instantly. I see the spark of interest flicker in his eyes. I try not to squirm when his finger again caresses the peak. His fingers hold the bandaged limb tightly to my chest. I know his sensitive fingers feel the thudding of my heart. His other hand lands lightly on my lap. My legs tense. I feel a thumb circle too close to my throbbing bud, and I shift slightly. This can't be happening in this restaurant. My mouth is bone dry.

The waitress approaches and he immediately sits erect.

"Does it feel better?"

"Yes. Yes, it does," I murmur, unable to meet the girl's eyes.

He fusses with the pot of tea, making comments on how Americans don't know what good tea really is. "Have a piece of cake," he offers, and then gets up and takes the other bench so he's facing me.

"My name is Godfrey York."

"I'm Tessa Duncan."

"So tell me, Tessa, you Americans are supposed to be outspoken and brash about things. Would you like to be bound?"

I choke on my tea. My blood is racing. "What?" It comes out more a squeak than an outraged denial.

"No need to get fussed. I like it. Like a strapping now and again, too. Thought you seemed the same sort."

"You mean you let women tie you and hit you?"

"It's a jolly good turn-on sometimes."

I'm dazed. I can't believe I'm sitting here in a public restaurant talking to a stranger about bondage and discipline. And he likes it.

"Haven't you ever been spanked?"

New York City pops unbidden into my mind. He sees the answer in my expression and doesn't wait for my reply. "Be honest. Wasn't it a turn-on?" Again he doesn't wait for an answer. "And tied. Have you ever been tied and at another's mercy?"

Iceland. The yacht. The woods. I nod without thinking. I can't take my eyes off my teacup.

I sense him leaning closer to me. "And would you like it to happen again?"

"I don't like being hurt." I'm surprised he hears me, my voice is so low.

"But there are all kinds of pain, Tessa. It doesn't have to be the agony type." My hand is taken. His fingers curl softly between mine. "Would you like to see if you like giving it instead of receiving it?"

I'm completely at sea. A man is offering me the chance to tie and spank him. Do I want to? I'm so confused. So at odds with my feelings. To be in control. To call the shots. To do to instead of being done to.

Suppose Grant found out?

He must see the confusion in my eyes because he slowly smiles and presses my hand lightly. "You don't have to decide now, Tessa. Here. Let me give you my card and you take all the time you want. If you ever decide you'd like to give me a try, either way, you call me and we'll make plans to get together. Fair enough?"

I nod. Speechless. Do things like this happen to everyone else? Is there something about me that draws this kind of person?

He slips a business card into my hand and kisses my cheek. I give him a weak smile and then watch him walk away from me. He pauses to slip money into the waitress's pocket and then pays the bill. He never looks back as he walks out the door.

I look down at the piece of white paper. His name, his business address, and telephone number. And then the nature of his business. Leather goods.

"What happened to you?"

"I was knocked down by a door opening and sprained my wrist. It's nothing serious, Mom. Did you get any shopping done?"

"Only a few things. The lines were too long."

I see her looking worriedly at my wrist and quickly suggest we leave to meet Polly. The ride is short and before we know it we're inside the restaurant. Polly joins us a moment later.

"Good timing," she exclaims with her usual vigor, her smile bright and sincere. "I'm so glad we could spend this time together. It's rare we get to be just the three of us."

We chat comfortably. Our relationship has always been easy and congenial. Mom is supportive without being too interfering, and it makes it easy to relax around her. Polly and I have always been close even though we are completely different people.

We're given menus by the hostess and peruse them enthusiastically. "Everything sounds so good!"

"Are you ladies ready to order yet?"

The low English accent makes me freeze. I feel my face paling. I strive to keep my hands steady. Lifting my eyes a bare inch, I see the buttoned coat, the vest rising above it. Godfrey.

Please. Please don't seem to know me, I plead silently as I lift nervous eyes. His meet mine unflinchingly. Steadily. I pray I'm the only one who notices the wicked twinkle in them. I swallow and relax slightly when I see my sister and mother studying their menus.

"Would you like more time?" The question is directed to me. I see his eyes sparkle with suppressed merriment when I finally understand the double meaning. I swallow quickly and nod silently, returning my attention to the menu. I can barely keep my breathing steady.

"Is something wrong, Tessa?"

"My wrist throbs slightly. That's all, Mom."

"Would Miss like a cold compress?"

"No. No thank you." Why can't he go away and let us decide without him hovering? He's too solicitous making suggestions to Polly and Mom. It's almost as if he enjoys making me uncomfortable.

But of course he does. Why wouldn't he when he thinks nothing of admitting to me, a stranger, that he would enjoy tying me up and strapping me or having me do the same to him. I wonder what it would feel like to have such control over another's destiny?

"What are you going to have, Tessa?"

I force myself to concentrate on the menu. "I think I'll have a Greek salad. I'm really not too hungry today."

"Well, I am. I don't get a chance to have a fancy dinner without cooking it too often." Polly proceeds to order soup, salad, appetizer, and entree without hesitation. Mom orders the same. Godfrey leaves and my breathing resumes a normal rhythm.

We chat amicably, but I'm too aware of Godfrey watching me from the kitchen windows. I see his tongue peek out now and again, a wicked grin spreading his lips a moment later. I complain about the heat in the restaurant to explain my flushed face. Tiny tingles skim over my breasts. The peaks harden and pull slightly. I'm never going to be able to eat without choking.

The soup is served and a moment later their salads arrive. I excuse myself and leave them to munch merrily as I make my way to the ladies' room. I need time to get myself in control. Godfrey doesn't give it to me.

He's leaning against the wall in back of the door. The room is tiny, maybe five feet by four feet. He slides over and leans against the door the minute I close it. I barely swallow a scream of fright when I first see him. My heart is pounding. His grin is so wicked.

"I thought you were a salesman for leather goods." My stalling for time fools neither one of us. I'm breathless. Nervous but excited. I can't stop rubbing my hands together. He just leans there and grins at me. I back up and hit the wall. The frosted glass is cold against my neck. I move away from it. He moves toward me.

"I sell leather goods for my own and others' pleasure. It's just a sideline." He's so close but doesn't touch me. I feel his breath on my face. "Would you like to come over and I'll give you a demonstration on how to use them? Some are very simple and self-explanatory. Some are ingenious and complicated." He moves a hair's breadth closer. I can't seem to inhale enough air.

Godfrey stretches his neck and moves his jaw closer. I feel the minute stubble graze my chin. He hasn't touched me otherwise. He hasn't lifted a hand. His eyes never leave my own. I can't seem to swallow. I feel his lips on my cheek, his light breath making the warm spots turn cold. The roughness of his suit rubs against my nipples. They harden and pull, the ache making me moan softly.

"You want me, Tessa." A quiet statement. Not a question. Why doesn't my name sound like a caress when he says it?

Grant. The thought is like a douse of cold water. Worse is the thought of Rodney. I pull back violently, cracking my head against the window.

"No."

"You don't mean that." Godfrey leans closer, but I suddenly realize the position I've allowed myself to get into and all my emotions freeze, fear being the only one I feel now.

"Yes, I do." He allows me to push him back, a puzzled frown on his face.

"I don't understand." He moves further back and to the side, eyes narrowed, head tilted as he watches me speculatively.

My voice trembles. "I just can't do this right now. I'm sorry, I can't explain." I feel so jittery. Is it already too late? Is it possible that Grant is still having me watched? "Would you please leave?"

I see his shrug, watch him readjust himself and then the wicked smile returns. "You'll call me if you ever change your mind?"

"I promise." And I mean it, too. I am curious. And he is nice. I had half expected to have to fight him off, but he accepted my answer and took it graciously. I smile, a tinge of regret burning deep within me.

I see his head tilt once more. His eyes seem to glitter with amusement. "I wish I knew what stopped you. I know it isn't me."

I shrug and smile harder. "Maybe someday I'll be able to tell you."

"I'll have to be patient till then," he says and with

another wicked grin in my direction, opens the door and slips out.

The shaking takes me the moment he's gone. What is the matter with me? A year and a half ago I wouldn't let a man who had wooed me for four months touch me. Now I've turned into some sort of sexual being. A word. A touch. A certain look and I'm ready and more than willing to engage in a frenzied sex match.

Was this the reason for Rodney's visit two months ago? Was Grant aware of what I've become, no, what he's made me into? Had he taken the steps he thought necessary to stop me from going from one to another? Grant had claimed he knew immediately that I had an untapped smoldering sexuality, and he'd been right. And he'd tapped it. Oh, so well had he tapped it. Released it. But I'm the one left to try and control it.

Oh, God. Does he know? Am I being watched? Will he think something happened? Will I meet Rodney one dark night soon? I vow I won't go out by myself. I feel the anxiety building, taking over, and I splash my face with ice-cold water again and again. I can't stop shaking. How can I let him know nothing happened?

The knock on the door startles me. "Tessa, are you all right?"

I take a big breath and let it out slowly. "I'm fine, Mom. I was just rewrapping the Ace bandage."

I paste a smile on my face and open the door. Worried eyes go from my face to my wrist. "Maybe we should have it looked at by a doctor?"

"No, it's fine, Mom. I think it was just a little too tight. Has dinner been served? I think I'm hungrier than I thought."

I don't know how I laugh and listen to the two of

them the rest of the night. I don't know how I chew and swallow without gagging. I refuse to look toward the kitchen and I even change my seat, claiming a draft. I only think of Rodney and the broken riding crop in the woods. Why do I feel guilty even though I didn't do anything? If I can't convince myself of my innocence, how do I ever expect to convince Grant?

The weeks before Christmas fly by. I make sure I'm never alone.
Never.
I leave when the last bell dismisses the children. No more lingering to correct papers. I take them home and do it while Mom gets dinner. I shop with my mother. I call at her friends' houses with her or I stay home with her. I see her looking at me strangely now and then, but she doesn't question my sudden devotion. Being with her so much has opened my eyes, and I begin to realize just how lonely she is.

I see the wistful expression on her face when we're at friends' houses and husband and wife make small loving gestures to each other. I see the longing when someone excuses himself to attend to the need of a spouse. I notice my mother looks through the photo albums more and more as time passes. Her expression is one of such sadness, such profound longing. More than once I've seen her hastily blink away tears when I enter a room unexpectedly. I hadn't realized how small her world has become. I hadn't realized how much my father had made up her world. And I feel helpless to do anything about it.

My suggestions of new clubs or community dances fall on deaf ears. I try to think of ways to keep her occupied but fail time and again. The spark is gone. She has no purpose. No one to dote on. To cook for. To love for her own reasons.

Selfishly, I'm glad my mother realizes I'm grown and expects me to leave when I find a man to settle down with. I couldn't bear being doted on so lovingly. I'd end up feeling smothered.

Polly is busy with her duties as minister's wife and has little time to spare. The grandkids live too far for a casual visit and Mom doesn't drive. Why do I feel guilty?

I wake to the insistent ringing of the telephone. Who the hell would call so early on a Saturday?

"Hello," I croak. I clear my throat and try again. "Hello."

The connection is lousy. Static crackles in my ear. A faint whistle whines first high and then low. "Tessa? Tessa, it's me, Louise. Louise Franklin."

"Louise?" I blink and struggle to an upright position. I have to wake up. I must have misunderstood. I haven't heard from Louise since high school.

"I can't talk long. Listen, I've gotten a whole bunch of the old crowd together, and we're meeting at a lodge in Quebec. Please say you'll come. We'll ski and gossip and have a great time over the Christmas vacation."

"Next week?" I can't seem to clear my sleep-filled head. I must be missing something with all the noise on the line.

"Yes. We're all meeting on the twenty-seventh at the lodge. Please say you'll come. Everyone is!"

"But I'll never get reservations!" I sit up even straighter and try to think clearly. This isn't a joke.

"My dad was able to use some of his influence.

There's a seat reserved for you for the 9 A.M. flight. Just pay for the ticket when you arrive and be on the plane. Someone will meet you when you land. It won't cost you another nickel. Everything is included!"

"But Louise…"

"I can't talk any longer, Tessa. Please come. Everyone is…" Her voice fades in and out, the crackling becoming too loud to listen to. I hold the receiver away from my ear and wait, hoping it will clear, but I get a dial tone a minute later. Had I heard her correctly with all the interference?

Skiing in Quebec! I do have some money saved, and it would be wonderful to see the old crowd. Louise was always the planner in our group. Heart thumping, I'm now wide awake. I can't help but chuckle. Leave it to her to wait almost twelve years and then arrange an impromptu get-together as if we'd all seen each other just the other week.

This is an answer to a prayer. Always being with someone is starting to drive me crazy. I still can't shake the feeling that Grant knows of my almost, indiscretion and wouldn't approve. This way I'll be away and free for a few days. How long? I haven't asked. Has Louise made reservations for round-trip tickets? I dial the airport and get a prompt reply. The flight leaves at 9 A.M. the twenty-seventh. Return is January 1, 5 P.M. The price is within my budget. I'm going to go, no matter what.

Mom takes the news well. In fact, so well I almost wonder if she isn't as happy to be rid of me for a while as I am her. A quick call to her sister and it's decided she'll probably visit with her for a few days while I'm gone. It's always so nice when things fall into place.

Tessa's Holidays

The flight is uneventful, and I'm grateful after the high excitement of Christmas with family and friends. My young niece and nephew have boundless energy at the best of times, and Christmas is worse. I think they go on sugar overload. The two demure darlings become whirlwinds of nonstop activity from morning to night.

The quiet murmurs of the other passengers and the gentle humming of the engines are very soothing, and I sleep for a good part of the journey. Every time I close my eyes I see Grant in some form. And the deep-down longing begins. And grows till I open my eyes. I never can completely block him from my thoughts, and I don't know if I like the feeling or not.

A man with a sign bearing my name is awaiting me. I climb into the backseat as he stows my luggage in the trunk. He gets in the front and we're off.

It takes me only a moment to find he doesn't speak any English. All my curious questions will remain unanswered so I content myself with watching the world of white pass by. We drive for almost an hour and then enter a small, quaint village that looks as though it could have been moved directly from the French countryside. We pass through it and the cab stops behind a horse-drawn sleigh at the edge of town.

The men exchange greetings. The trunk is opened, my luggage transferred to the sleigh, the back door opened and I'm helped from the backseat. Unfortunately, the sleigh driver is also only proficient in French, and I have no choice but to allow him to help me up into the back and cover my legs with a heavy lap robe.

A click of his tongue, a snort from the horse and we're off. We leave the village behind at the first bend of the road, and I'm surrounded by a world of tall white mountains that are speckled here and there with dark pine trees and firs. The snow is deep all around us. The air is bitter cold. The silence is only broken by the jingle of the bells on the horses' harness.

Grant would love this. My mouth becomes suddenly dry. Could Grant have arranged this? Was I positive it was Louise's voice I heard? The connection had been so bad. Do I dare to hope?

How convenient that each driver doesn't speak English. It is so like something Grant would arrange. I ride in mystery, unable to ask questions or demand answers. Did Louise's father work for the airlines? It's been so long it's hard to remember.

I'm both excited and reluctant to hope. Would Grant want retribution for Godfrey? Would five days with Grant make it worthwhile? Oh, God, I can't make up my mind. Thoughts race from Rodney to Grant to hope to despair.

I try to speak to the driver. I keep pointing at my watch but he ignores me and stays bundled to the eyes in his many scarves and layers of clothing. I smell the sweet aroma of his pipe. The air bites into my flesh. I pull the robe high and huddle beneath it, my frozen fingers between my thighs for warmth. I hope I packed warm-enough clothes.

We travel a long distance and then suddenly turn to the right and the house is before us. It's large, completely of logs and A-framed. Two outbuildings are behind it. Smoke is pouring out of the chimney. I thought Louise had meant a skiing lodge with hundreds of people and bars and nightclubs. This is a private home. My heart quickens. It must be Grant.

The sleigh stops, the front door opens and Louise

rushes out. Squeals of joy, exclamations of delight, luggage brought inside, driver tipped, and then we're alone. I'm a mass of conflicting emotions.

"You look marvelous, Tessa!"

"So do you," I say sincerely. Louise is tall and slender. Her breasts are firm and large. She has the most beautiful hands I've ever seen. Long, slender fingers and nails that never break no matter what she does. I look around. "Where are the others?"

"Most will be here first thing in the morning. It was hard arranging all the different flights from all over, but Dad came through for me. An early birthday gift." She turns and grabs a suitcase. "Follow me and we'll get you settled, and then we can spend the time till the others arrive catching up on all the news. This is going to be such fun!"

I follow her, smile real, but I can't shake the deep-down disappointment. I won't be seeing Grant. I'd been so sure when I'd seen the isolated house. I force myself to listen to Louise's steady chatter as I unpack my suitcase and answer her questions.

We make our way downstairs and I drift to the fireplace. My hands are still cold, and the heat feels wonderful. Louise keeps up a steady stream of chatter about the girls I haven't seen in too many years. Helen is married for the third time. Joyce never did marry but lives with a steady boyfriend. Tara is coming all the way from Germany where she now works. And on and on.

We talk and sip wine. I tell her of my life, such as it is, minus the part about Grant. Louise commiserates about Greg and adds more logs to the fire. I take my sweater off and drape it over the back of the couch. Louise brings the bottle over and pours me more wine.

My head is becoming a bit fuzzy and I demur, but she insists and toasts good friends reuniting. She adds more logs and then sits next to me.

I sip the wine and a feeling of unreality creeps in. It's hot. Too hot. Everything seems to have slowed to a crawl. I fumble with a button to loosen my collar. Hands are there to help me. I can't seem to focus. Louise is looking at me. She smiles and leans toward me. I feel her lips. So light. So gentle on my own. I lean back but she seems to be glued to me. Am I floating? My blouse is opened. Soft hands. Dainty fingers stroke and caress my breasts. My nipples seem to harden in slow motion. Where's my bra?

I can't seem to clear my head. A tongue on my nipple. Then my other. I shake my head but nothing stops. My arms are leaden. Hands remove my skirt. My underpants. My blouse is removed. A hand behind my back keeps me sitting up.

I'm so limp. I feel breasts against my own. Soft. Cushiony. Turgid peaks rub mine till they too respond and pebble up.

Louise is astride me. A breast brushes my lips. "Suck me, Tessa. Use your tongue." The voice is hollow sounding as if it's far away. I hear it over and over and open my mouth to protest. It's filled with a full breast. I feel the tumescent rubbery tip on my tongue and lick it slowly. Moans vibrate in the flesh I taste.

I don't seem to have any will of my own. The voice whispers to me and I do as it says. Lick. Suck. Rub. All is hazy. All is slow motion. All is so dreamlike.

I'm urged off the end of the sofa and onto the thick fur rug. Hands roam over me. It's so soft. So nice. I'm turned. I feel a tongue run over my cheeks. Along my crack. Soft fingers follow. I'm turned and the tongue starts at my forehead and works its way down. Temples. Eyes. Lips. Neck. Breast. Belly. Swirling, licking, laving every square inch. I sense, rather than see, her turning as she makes her way lower.

My body is a mass of floating, wonderful sensations. Skin touches my nose. "Lick." I put out my tongue and she lowers herself further. I feel her tongue on my slit at the same time I realize it is hers I lick. I feel the stubble on her shaved mound. I feel the swollen outer lips and then the soft silky inner lining as she opens up to me. Her clitoris is hard and engorged. "Suck it, Tessa. Think of it as a tiny penis."

I do, drawing it into my mouth. It is at the opposite end of the scale compared to Grant's. I hear her moan of pleasure and answer with one of my own. Her tongue is practiced, steady, and driving me wild. My breath is tortured as I try to breathe and suck. I follow her lead, my moans and slow humping quickening with each stroke of her frantic tongue. Her legs tense, her tongue pauses for the briefest of times, and then she devours me, taking me over the edge as I feel her moisture coat my tongue in return.

I wake up on the couch, dressed and covered with an afghan. My head is clear, my thoughts confused.

"Hi! Boy, you must've been exhausted. One minute you're talking to me, the next you're sound asleep. Feel better?"

"What?" I sit up, completely disoriented. Louise is looking at me strangely.

"You're not ill, are you?"

"No. No, I guess I'm not awake, that's all." My mind

is whirling. Had it been a dream? Hadn't it happened? I feel myself blush, and I turn toward the fire to hide my confusion. It had seemed so real.

I hurry into the bathroom to gather my thoughts. I open my blouse and look at myself. What do I expect to see? Teeth marks? I'm not wet. There are no stains on my underpants. I've never had such a vivid dream in my life. I would've sworn I'd orgasmed.

Was it frustration at finding Louise and not Grant? Was it wishful thinking? What is the matter with me?

Louise calls me into the kitchen. A hearty, mouth-watering lunch awaits and, shaking off the strange feeling, I dig into it with gusto.

We talk and laugh during the early afternoon. There is so much to catch up on. So much to remember. Louise opens another bottle of wine, but I'm wary. Only when she doesn't push it on me and drinks from it herself do I finally accept a glass a little later. What do I think she's going to do? Kill me? Rape me? I just can't quite shake the strange feelings my dream caused. I still can't believe it's a dream even though I know it was.

We take a walk later on, the bitter cold air forcing us inside all to soon. The air in the house seems hot and stifling compared to outside. It's starting to snow.

"I doubt if the others will get here tonight. They'll have to stay in town till daylight." She turns a bright smile my way. "What should we have for dinner?"

"Whatever you want."

Her smile widens and she shrugs. Do I see a glint in her eye or is it only the reflection of the fire? "We'll see when the time comes."

The snow comes down harder and we turn on the lamps early. The living room is cozy, bathed in soft light, the fire flickering and sending out its welcome warmth. Our talk has dwindled to almost nothing. It's so peaceful. The world seems so far away.

Louise gets up and goes upstairs. I hear her call to me to come help her with a box.

I'm reluctant to leave the warm refuge of the couch. I haven't been this relaxed for too long. Louise's voice calls again and I unwillingly get up. I enter her room, feel a pinch, and then know nothing.

I wake up on her bed. Nude. Stretched out. Tied to the four posts. She's shaving me. I hear her humming a popular tune. She peeks up at me without lifting her head. A slow, malicious smile curves her lips. "You were out longer than I expected so I thought I'd entertain myself."

"Louise." My voice cracks. I'm frightened.

"Did I fail to tell you I'm a veterinarian? Wonderful thing knowing which drugs will do what and being able to get them when I need them."

The bonds are tight. I can barely move. The razor glides over my mound. I swear I can hear it moving through the soap. Her fingers spread me. I feel her long nails. The razor grazes. I see her wipe the soap on a towel.

"Please." I tense my thighs against her touch. The quick slap she gives each makes me suck in breath.

"Please. Please," she mimics jeeringly. "You were always such a prude, Tessa. The whole crowd was experimenting and having fun but you were so caught up in getting good grades you never even knew, did you?"

Louise reaches up and grabs a nipple hard. Her

expression frightens me. "I've always wanted to fuck you, sweetheart. All those times I tried to climb in your sleeping bag with you. All the times you pushed me away and told me to stop acting stupid. What did you think all that giggling was about at the pajama parties after the lights went out? Didn't it ever occur to you that something was going on?"

"No!" The whisper carries no conviction. I feel the razor continue its journey. What were we at the time? Thirteen? Fourteen? Was Louise telling me that Helen and all the other girls were fooling around when the lights went out? I remember the muffled giggles, the quickly suppressed high-pitched squeaks. I'd thought they were telling each other jokes. I'd been thinking of upcoming tests and they were experimenting with sex.

She smirks. I hear the contemptuous snort. "Don't worry about it, Tessa. Apparently I'm the only one who found it better than men." Her smile is so cold. "And you're the lucky one who will get the benefit of my years of expertise."

Her movements are so sure. So quick. My skin is crawling. I swallow. "The others?"

"Are busy getting on with their lives. You always were a trusting soul, Tessa." Her fingers open me wide. I'm so exposed. Her thumb circles my clit. Her eyes never leave mine. "You've turned into a hot little number haven't you, Tessa? Even in a daze you responded to me this afternoon."

I knew it had happened. I knew I couldn't be so terribly wrong, and I was now in trouble because I hadn't listened to my instincts. Will Grant punish me for this, too?

"I can tell you've been shaved before, Tessa. Why?"

I panic. I can't tell her. I feel a pinch on my nipple. "I...I wanted to see what it would be like."

"And did you like it?" The poised razor looks so menacing. Instinctively I know what she wants to hear.

"No."

"Tck, tck, tck." The pleased smile belies the sad clicks of her tongue. It makes sense. Louise was always the organizer. The one in charge. The one who had to be in control.

How many times did we all end up going where we didn't want to because Louise just went ahead and made plans? How many times did she put us in embarrassing situations and then just laugh them off. She'd been taking pleasure in our discomfort. She was ridiculing us even then, and none of us had realized it. Had she?

"You were always the smart one, Tessa. How smart do you feel right now?"

"Louise, I..."

"No, Tessa. I call the shots. You do as I say. And you don't open your smart mouth unless I say so." Her matter-of-fact tone sends chills through me. Is she mad? Does she tread that thin line between sanity and derangement?

"All done!" Her smile is tight. I can see the excited tension in her movements. "Would you like to get up?"

I nod, not quite sure whether to fight her or give her what she wants.

"Well, you be a good girl and we'll let you up."

I watch her run her finger over the blade lightly and then put the razor down on the bureau. Her movements are so slow and casual. So calculated to frighten. Her hands slide down her body, fingers tweaking her own nipples. I see their outline as they thrust forward and strain the fabric of her thin blouse. Why hadn't I noticed she wore no bra? Her eyes never stop watching me.

She kicks off her slippers. Slacks are inched down slowly, sensuously. Her smile is evil. She's doing a striptease for me. Am I supposed to flinch? To stare in horror? To pant and declare I want her? Her blouse peels from her body and she stands before me naked, long-nailed fingers gliding lightly over herself.

She's shaved. She thrusts her pelvis forward and walks to the edge of the bed by my head. "Take a good look, Tessa. You will know it intimately before we're through. Now let's see how much you want to get up."

Her taunting crooning makes the gooseflesh crawl over my body. More so when I hear her pleased chuckle as she observes my reaction. She climbs up and sits on my breasts.

"Not much to cushion my ass, Tessa. I don't like a hard seat. Let's see if I can find something softer."

Her slit is above me. Slowly her legs widen and she lowers herself down. I obediently extend my tongue.

Her scent is strong. I can taste the oiliness of her excitement. She rubs herself back and forth so I reach from her anus to her clit. I hear her breathing quicken, the tension in her legs growing. Her movements are jerky and quick. She mashes down into my face, rubbing frantically against me. I can't work enough saliva into my mouth quickly enough. My tongue is dry. I stab at her, trying to hurry her along, and then I hear the high keening moan of bliss. Her movements slow and then cease. I can barely breath as she rests, my mouth and nose buried in her wetness.

I gulp air when she rises. Not a word is spoken.

Louise dreamily walks to the bathroom, her finger lazily tracing a path down my body. I hear the shower. I hear her humming. I think I'm going to start screaming and never stop.

She emerges a long while later, steam trailing out the door after her. Her smile is languid. "Want to get up?"

Is she tormenting me? Should I tell the truth? I see her eyebrow raise questioningly. I nod.

She picks up something from the bureau. I can't see what's in the palm of her hand. Her look dissects me. "It'll only be a moment." The whispered words are followed by a pinch on my upper arm.

Objects seem to split and move in slow circles. I see Louise above me seeming to hover, but then she too starts a slow lazy circling. Can she fly? Is this nothing but a bizarre dream?

My body is so heavy. She pets and plays with my breasts, but I can't seem to lift my arms to push her away. I know the pressure she exerts on my nipples should hurt. Why don't I feel anything? Why is everything moving so slowly? Louise is crooning soft words, but they blur and merge and I can't understand them.

I'm turned on my stomach. I feel like a beached whale. Heavy. Slow. Unable to move. I flounder and flop uselessly. My hands are drawn back. I want to move, to push off the bed, but things spin and whirl around me. My arms refuse to obey my confused mind.

My head is lifted. Leather encases my neck. I feel it tighten around me. Soft leather sits on my back. My hands are drawn onto the top of it. My head clears as Louise pulls the last of the lacing tight. My arms are bound behind me in a single laced leather glove from elbow to hands.

"Is that too tight, sweetie?" The voice mocks me lightly as she takes pleasure in my predicament, my discomfort. I remain quiet. Her fingers lightly trace circles on my buttocks.

"Do you like to be fucked, Tessa?"

I'm terrified to answer. Suppose I say the wrong thing? She has to be unstable. Normal people don't make such elaborate plans for revenge after twelve years. Why does she feel such contempt for me?

"Cat got your tongue?" Her light, amused voice teases nastily. "Let's find out, shall we?"

My legs are swept off the bed and I'm yanked to my feet. I totter a few steps before her hand steadies me. My arms pulled so tightly back make my chest thrust itself out. A glint of silver catches the sunlight, and I hear the snap of a chain on the collar that encircles my neck. She pulls me forward and kisses me deeply. I try to remain calm. Her fingers grope and maul my breasts, and her tongue almost chokes me.

Lips nibble lightly along my jawline. "Kneel, Tessa."

I follow the pull of the chain and land on my knees hard. Her mound is mere inches from my face. "You know what to do."

And I do it. Tentatively at first but harder and deeper as I hear her impatient sighs, feel the cold metal of the chain snaking suggestively along my spine. Soon she moves under my ministrations, her small, febrile jerks turning to hard pumps. She holds my head in a death grip when her climax hits her.

Louise steps away and I stay still. I don't look up. This is one time I'd rather not know. Her eyes terrify me. They seem obsessed. Manic. Calculating. I don't want her to read the fear in mine. I'm afraid it will make her power over me seem even more exhilarating. I wrack my brain to remember some of my abnormal psychology. I wish my mind would work better under pressure.

The chain pulls my head to the floor. My ass is high. I feel her fingers at my slit and gasp when she shoves a dildo into me. She mistakes it for pain. "Poor baby. Not used to a good-sized cock, sweetheart? Did your poor hubby have a baby-sized prick?" The malicious crooning goes on, and I groan again to make her believe she's right.

"If this is bad, wait till you see what this is like." The dildo is pulled out and unceremoniously shoved into my rectum. I squeal for real this time, panting with pain as the thing buries deep in my bowels. It eases quickly but I still pretend agony. Little does she know what I'm used to with Grant.

Another is pushed into my vagina and she giggles when I moan. "We'll just slip this chain through these hooks on the ends and attach it to your hands. Now isn't that nice?"

I'm pulled to my feet, and the chain tightens between my legs, burying the hard tubes deep inside me. The chain cuts sharply into my vaginal lips. I pretend anguish and writhe, only to stop an instant later. Every time I move my arms I feel real pain from the strain on the chain.

"Never been plugged up the ass have you, studious Tessa? Did you ever dream you'd experience twice the fun? Did you even know such things existed? I don't think this is the type of thing you used to read about." Her giggles border on the edge of hysteria. The sound is too shrill. Too high pitched. The hair stands up at the back of my neck.

"Now you do as you're told and you'll feel a lot less pain."

The walk down the stairs makes me perspire. Each step is pure pain. The chain digs mercilessly into me, more so as she tugs on it with each step. I feel the hard, unyielding plugs rub together. Halloween was an erotic orgy next to this.

I'm told to kneel and she begins a discourse on all the hateful things I did when we were growing up. I look at the floor and listen.

I got better grades than her. Did she think it just happened? Didn't she realize how hard I studied for them?

I was prettier than her. Like I had a lot to do with that.

I got asked out more than her. What, twice? Once to the junior prom and once to the senior prom. Actually it was my cousin who took me to the junior prom because my parents insisted I go, but I never told anyone his relationship. I don't try to explain now.

I ignored her advances. I didn't even know or care about sex with boys at the time. Why would I think about girls?

The reasons become more bizarre as she rambles on. I stay absolutely still. Louise imbibes of the wine freely as she rattles on and on about my shortcomings. Every time she paces, she stops in front of me and I obediently attend her. I try hard to avoid her sneering, glaring eyes. She grabs my hair and pulls my head back. "When I think of all those frustrating years about dreaming of you doing this. This opportunity was a gift from heaven. I wanted your mouth, not Helen's soft fingers. I wanted to feel those lips that pursed so provocatively when you read something interesting. I wanted that warm, soft tongue that peeked out of your mouth so delightfully when something puzzled you." She throws back her head and crows. "All good things come to those who wait!"

The obvious disdain she feels for me apparently doesn't apply to my tongue. Each time it's harder to bring her to a climax. Her body must be exhausted, her mind dulled. My tongue aches. My neck aches. My arms are screaming. I know I can't endure five days of this.

"Damn, look at the time!" Her screech makes me jerk and I groan with pain. Nails dig into my arm when she yanks me abruptly to my feet. She ignores my whimpering as she hurries me upstairs and into the bedroom.

I can't make out her mumbling. She seems to be driven by time. Almost panicked. The chain is unhooked from my hands, and I scream and almost collapse as she yanks out the dildos. Nails dig harder and I remain on my feet. Her eyes glitter with malice but still she hurries. The leather collar is unbuckled and removed, and then she turns me. I feel her fingers on the laces but they suddenly stop.

"No. This is too perfect." Her whisper chills me to the bone. My hair is grabbed and I'm pushed forward. I hear the chink of the chain. It clips onto my arms again and then I hear it hit wood. My arms are pulled up behind me. I have to bend at the waist or my arms will snap. She's thrown the chain over the rail that connects the four posts of the bed at the top. My head hits the foot of the mattress. I'm lifted by the hair.

"Keep your head down and bite the pillow. I don't

want to hear a sound. Not a sound," she snarls, twisting my hair in her fingers. I nod, tears spilling from my eyes.

I bury my face and bite the pillow and wait. My shoulders scream. My arms will surely break. Is she going to whip me? Is there someone else in the house?

Hands touch my rear. I swallow the gasp and bite the pillow harder. Is she tormenting me before she whips me? Is she going to arouse me and then leave me wanting?

My ass is felt, molded, squeezed, as if all the contours must be mapped and remembered. My cheeks are pulled apart, I feel something slick rubbed into my sphincter and then the pressure of something large.

I try to relax, try to do as Grant taught me, but still I barely stifle the grunt. Oh, God, what is she using? Her movements are slow and steady, not vicious and hard as I'd expected.

"Ah, Tessa. You're always such a delight. What a lovely surprise for you to welcome me like this. Did Louise spoil the surprise and tell you?"

It takes a full minute for me to realize it's truly Grant's voice. He's moving in and out of me steadily, his hands beneath me on my breasts. A wave of horror mixed with excitement zings through me, and then I take one lungful of air and give in to my sobs.

"What's this? What's this?" he croons lightly. The chain is unhooked, and I hear the chink of it fall over the wood. His strong arm under my breasts keeps me from falling forward. Still he moves within me, but so slowly. Fingers release the laces and my arms fall uselessly to my sides. I can't stop crying as I hang over his arm limply, his massive penis still buried deep within me. Great gulping blubbers wrack my body. His other arm wraps itself around me and pulls me back and up. Still he moves within me. Slowly. Steadily. Fingers lightly caress my breasts, pull the nipples. Lips on my neck. My shoulders. My ear.

"What's wrong, Tessa?" The sweet caress of his voice saying my name starts my tears all over. I can't speak. Can't explain. Can't utter a sound through my clogged throat.

Hands are light, teasing, toying. His lips are so warm. So wonderful. His arm around my waist keeps me tight to him as his movements increase in rhythm and strength. Hand on my belly. I feel the surprise as it wanders over my shaved pubis, and then his incredible thumb is where I need it and my sobs shift to a higher note, the cadence quickening as white-hot fire engulfs me and then fans out slowly to every nerve ending within my body. I lean back against him limply and feel the last deep plunge before his low grunt of satisfaction reaches my ears.

When he pulls out of me, I turn and hold onto him tightly. I can't explain right now. I can't answer his whispered questions. I just want to hold onto him and never let go. He holds my shaking body tightly to his own, and when still I don't respond to his questions I'm picked up, cradled in his arms and laid down next to him.

I snuggle into his body. I want to feel all of him against me. I need to know it's really him. Arms surround and protect me and finally I begin to relax. I fall asleep with the feel of his light kiss on my brow, the sound of his steady heartbeat in my ear.

"Hi."

I hear his voice before I open my eyes, and smile happily. This is not a dream.

"Hi." Ice blue eyes twinkle at me and I snuggle closer to him. The coarse gray hair tickles my cheek and I rub against it happily. It's so wonderful to be held in his arms again. I fight the tears of happiness that threaten to fall.

"I've missed you, Tessa." His whispered words soothe and excite me as no others can.

"I've missed you too, Grant." I can't quite stop my voice from catching. His arms hold me tight, and then we roll over and he's looking down at me. My nipples harden against his chest. A pleased smile teases the edges of his lips. His wonderful strong fingers frame my face, thumbs lightly strumming my jawline. My breath is quickening just with the promise of what is to come.

I raise my hands to stroke his cheek but he shakes his head slowly. "Just lie still and let me love you."

"But I want to love you, too."

The pleased, tender smile makes him look so much younger. "Not right now. This is for you only."

I force myself to lie quietly under him, hands by my sides. He kisses my eyes closed, and I leave them that way as he explores my face with fingers and tongue. His voice is rough, yet gentle. I sense his urgency but feel nothing but calm control.

"It's been too long, Tessa." The beloved caress of my name on his lips. "I want to scout out every part of you. I want to renew my acquaintance with every curve and hollow of your body."

His hushed breath wafts over my face. Gentle, soft kisses rain over my eyes, cheeks. His soundless exhalation whispers in my ear. My nipples ache and pull. I raise my arms but he takes them lightly and kisses a path along one, lingering in the sensitive inside of my elbow, his tongue making light circles till I curl my toes in delicious torment.

My mind spins under the steady, gentle probing of my body. Sensation after sensation washes over me. My breath is ragged, almost frantic. His tongue licks, laves, circles, and finally sucks on a swollen peak. I hear my whimper as if from a long distance. The other tumid tip is tormented, teased, caressed. I'll surely go insane from wanting.

My hands are lightly held to the bed as he travels further downward. I arch up but he slows down. Swirling, probing tongue in navel. A bolt of electricity shoots to my clitoris.

"Please. Please," I beg, beyond caring about anything but finding my release. His elbows keep my legs together. His lips travel lower, circling, skimming but never touching. A warm flick on my thigh. I arch desperately. My other thigh. I strain to open my legs. A tongue traces the crease where my two legs meet. Higher. Yet higher but not high enough. Moans of pleasure are turning into whimpers of torment. Over and over he skims, brushes, nears but never touches. I feel tears of frustration leak from my eyes. His breath is warm on my mound.

"Grant, please," I whisper desperately. My legs are released and he moves up, his mouth covering mine, his tongue caressing my own. His penis is huge. I feel the pulse throbbing through it as it lays heavily between my legs.

"Welcome me home, Tessa," he growls softly, and I do, flinging my legs wide and up. My netherlips open as if blossoming to receive a bee wanting to pollinate, and I rasp out my pleasure as he sinks into me slowly.

His expelled breath rushes past my ear, tingles of pleasure shoot through me, and with only one long stroke of his mighty weapon, I'm there. Screaming. Gushing. Crying. Coming.

I can't hold him close enough. I can't hold him tight enough. My body heaves and trembles beneath his as he seeks his own release and then, too quick even to anticipate, I'm there again with him, the feeling weaker but so much more exquisite to be sharing the moment with him.

Grant rolls from me a short time later. I hear his ragged breathing. His hand takes mine. Strong fingers curl around my own. His thumb brushes small circles in my palm. Raising it to his lips, I hear his sigh. "I really have missed you, Tessa."

Explanations follow. In learning about me, Grant had learned about my friends as well. Apparently Louise does nothing to hide her sexual preferences. A few discreet inquiries and he'd learned about her always having wanted me. Studious, unattainable Tessa.

An anonymous letter, an untraceable check and Grant had made the arrangements so I'd supposedly spend the afternoon before his arrival happily in her arms as a reward for making the trip possible. Louise would realize her dream. I would spend a pleasant afternoon and he would be able to spend five days with me. By the tightening of his lips and the steely glint in his eye, I begin to doubt Louise is going to think her long-awaited time with me was worth it. It's snowing hard. I watch the heat from inside war with the cold outside on the panes of glass. Slowly, inevitably, the cloudy fog that covers the window gathers and forms drops which glide down, making zigzag paths till the moisture drips from the bottom. One by one, others follow till the windows are filled with watery, clear paths etching crazy patterns down the panes. I lightly trace the markings and stare out at a white world.

Arms wrap around my waist from behind. "Why so pensive?"

I shrug slightly. "I was wondering how my mother is. She's seemed so lost lately."

"When it stops snowing we'll go into town and you can call her."

I nod but can't seem to shake the sadness that clings. I feel so guilty. She's rattling around an empty house or probably arguing with her sister. I'm here with Grant having a wonderful interlude.

I'm led to the couch and snuggle up against him, pulling my feet beneath me. "Tell me."

I watch the fire and slowly try to explain the things I've noticed lately. It's hard to put into words the expressions, the tiny little things that tell me she's just existing. Pining. Longing for more but feeling a traitor for feeling that way.

"It sounds like it's time for your mother to be dating again."

Dating? I sit up and look at him. "She's too old to date."

I blush when I hear his roar of laughter. What an incredibly stupid thing to have said. "And how old is your mother?"

"Mom's fifty-four."

"I'm sixty-three." His eyes are twinkling at me. He squeezes me back into his arms. "Are you telling me you don't think I could make your mother happy?"

"Well, of course you could but I mean, well, Mom, I mean…"

"You think of your mother as an asexual being. A mother. And mothers don't do things like that, do they?"

"Mom and Dad had a very happy life…."

"As I did with my wife. But life goes on, Tessa. You yourself know that." He rubs his chin in my hair. "You just don't want to think of your mother as being a living, breathing, sexual being."

I lower my eyes and fiddle with the button on his shirt. I feel uncomfortable suddenly. "I didn't know you'd been married."

"For thirty years. And very happily. But when Maryanne died my life continued, and I found that work wasn't enough to lose myself in. As much as I want to cherish her memory—and I still do—I have needs and feelings, too." His arms tighten around me. "You know and satisfy those needs very well, don't you, Tessa?"

I nod my head but can't quite shake the feeling of betrayal I feel. "Do you have children?"

His amused chuckle rumbles under my ear. "Four. All older than you. And before you ask—" he lifts my chin and makes me meet his eyes. They're twinkling. "Three sons and one daughter. Eight grandsons and four beautiful granddaughters."

I can't equate the image of my grandfather with Grant. Mine was a real grandfather. Old. Bent. Shaky voice. Napping after every meal. Grant is a vibrant, energetic man. It's very easy to forget how old he is. I do all the time.

I can't help the feeling of jealousy that rushes through me and quickly push myself away from him. He lets me go and that upsets me further.

Tessa's Holidays

"I expected better than this from you, Tessa. What is it that you don't like?"

I hear the beginning of annoyance creeping into his voice. I shrug, not even sure myself why the thought of his having a family bothers me. Do I want to believe I am everything to him? Can I honestly be so stupid? So shallow? Why do I resent that he has people who love him? Why is it any different than me having Mom and Polly?

I turn to the window and watch the snow. A warm feeling suddenly crawls through me. This was why Grant didn't seek me out at Thanksgiving. He'd spent it with his family. Jealousy and resentment melt away, and I turn sheepishly toward Grant.

"I'm sorry. I don't know why I acted so stupidly. Maybe it was just the shock. I guess I never thought about it before." I can feel the tinge of heat lingering in my cheeks.

Grant smiles and I feel better. "Did you think I was Scrooge? Working my way through the remainder of my days?"

I toss him a saucy smile and turn back to the window. "Well, you did tell me in the beginning that you were sick and tired of doing nothing but working. That you wanted something more from life."

Arms wrap around me from behind. His breath tickles my ear. "But the something I wanted and still do my family can't provide." His nuzzling sends thrills through me. "Do you know anyone who might care to provide it, Tessa?"

I can't stop the giggle but adamantly shake my head. "No, sir, I do not."

I shriek with delighted laughter when he scoops me

up in his arms and heads for the staircase. "Well, then, I'll just have to make do with you."

We take a snowmobile into town. The air is so cold, so clear, it hurts and dazzles even with the protective helmet on. I'm happy to bury my head in Grant's back and hold on tight as we speed along, the countryside an indistinct blur. We make better time than the sleigh did, and I realize that what had seemed like twenty miles is in reality only two or three. The village is charming. Just like a scene from an old Hollywood movie.

The telephone rings forever at home, but I finally locate my mother at my aunt's. It doesn't help my mood to hear the two of them are arguing and Mom is going home today. She's so upset she barely inquires if I'm having a good time.

Grant pushes a large bill in my hand and urges me to shop while he checks on some business deals. I stuff the money into my pocket and wander away to browse.

The store is delightful. Quilts hang on the walls like tapestries and each part of the store holds different things. One section is foods, another warm clothing, still others various sundries and knickknacks.

I finger the soft scarves and mittens. Unbidden memories of Iceland drift though my mind. Ingrid. Thoughts of Louise follow. Two women left alone with me and both treated me the same.

Why?

Godfrey, a stranger, propositions me with a bizarre offer and had expected me to take him up on it.

Why?

And Grant. Grant, a stranger at the time, offered me, no, threatened me is more accurate, the chance to accept his proposal of a trip around the world providing I would help him fulfill his fantasies or face ruin.

Why?

What is it about me that draws such people? I'm not statuesque. I'm not outstandingly beautiful. I don't have the type of figure that drives men crazy. I'm not world famous. I'm just me, Tessa Duncan, a twenty-nine-year-old widow who teaches the tenth grade in a small town.

"Do you want to buy that, Tessa?"

Grant's words startle me out of my reverie and I drop the scarf I've been unconsciously holding. "No. I guess I got lost in my thoughts." I give him a tight smile and walk away.

We spend the day seeing the stores and boutiques the town has to offer. People are friendly and gregarious, and we learn a lot about the area and its history. The restaurant in the center of town offers a wonderful meal. We eat heartily, our conversation light. The waiter inquires if we'd care for dessert.

"I'll have a cup of English tea." Eyes bore into mine. Had he emphasized the word English? "How about you, Tessa?"

My lips are dry and I shake my head. Is it just guilt that is making me think he knows something?

"Do you have scones?" I feel myself pale. The waiter replies in the negative and Grant shrugs. "Just the tea then and make it strong." He turns back to me and smiles. "I find the English do some things very well, don't you?"

My breathing is shallow. "What?" Is that tortured whisper really mine?

"I like their tea. It's strong. Is something the matter, Tessa?"

I shake my head and play with my spoon. I keep

telling myself it's just coincidence. I've never seen Grant linger over tea so long before. It isn't until dusk begins to settle that we head back to the house.

I can't stop thinking of Godfrey or my mother, and I feel Grant's impatience rising. The more I try to relax, the harder I find it to do just that. Buttons are released, blouse spread, fingers, so firm, so strong, caress and stroke, and I try to respond. He senses the strain. I can feel it in his touch.

"Tessa." The word isn't a caress this time.

"I'm sorry. I just…"

"You need something to take your mind off other things." Even as my brain screams a warning it's too late. He stands and flips me over on the couch in one easy movement. A knee in the small of my back, the whisper of leather sliding out of loops, the ripping of the seam in my skirt and then pain.

White-hot fire leaps across my buttocks and then burrows deep. Again and again as I scream my promises to try harder. To be better. To do anything. My breath hisses out with another blow. Another hits me before I can take a breath. I feel the rage within him as each lands harder than the one before and know this is retribution for the almost rendezvous with Godfrey even if he doesn't say so.

I'm humping madly against the couch, trying to alleviate the sting that radiates down and up and out, over and over. My legs are pulled over the side, I hear the leather belt hit the wood floor, feel him behind me.

My legs are spread with his knees. The rasp of a zipper. Hands on my hot, jerking cheeks pulling them apart and then pressure against my sphincter. Incredible pressure and foolishly I fight it.

Tessa's Holidays

The scream rips from my throat as he sinks into me, and I grab and clutch the cushions beneath my chest. I'm filled, in agony, and yet I keep humping against the burning heat that bubbles and throbs within my sore ass.

I muffle the moan of pain in the soft cushion. Tears start, and I begin to tremble yet still move in a useless attempt to cool the heat in my aching cheeks. And Grant lets me. He doesn't move but lets my own febrile movements pleasure him until they ease too much and he takes over. His fingers are cruel on my neck, keeping me tight to the couch. His movements become stronger, deeper, faster, and I bite my lip to contain the pain, but only for a moment. My muffled screams seem to spur him on, and it's a long time before I hear his roar of pleasure and feel him drop from me.

I slump to the rug and cry, but no strong arms embrace me. No tender fingers soothe me. No lips lick away my tears. I'm alone when I finally rouse myself and get up. I'm cold. I can't stop shaking. I need to be comforted. I need to be held.

His door is locked. I know he won't open it so I don't try to knock. My bed is cold. And too big. And the night seems never to end.

Grant is sitting on the couch in front of the fire sipping coffee. I feel a light heat skim over my cheeks when his eyes bore into me as I descend the stairs.

"Feeling better?"

"Yes." I pour myself a cup of coffee from the pot and watch the back of his silver head. I'm not quite sure what to do or say. Do we ignore it? Discuss it? Pretend it never happened? I leave it up to him.

"Would you like breakfast?"

He shakes his head but doesn't look at me. "I ate."

"Oh." The word barely makes it out of my mouth. He doesn't react. Probably didn't even hear the forlorn utterance. I pick up an apple and bite into it. His back is so forbidding. Damn it, I hadn't done anything. It isn't wrong to have a conversation with someone. No matter what the topic might be, a conversation is an innocent event. I sit at the table in the kitchen and chew slowly. And my anger begins to build.

"I've never known you to pout, Grant." Is that aggressive voice mine?

He turns slightly sideways and stares at me. His eyes never leave mine as he takes a sip of coffee. I see the steam from the hot brew escape his mouth. He hasn't said a word. My frustration mounts.

"Well?" My voice is taking on a strident note.

"Well, what, Tessa?" His voice is so low.

"Aren't you going to answer me?" I demand, standing and placing my hands on my hips.

He rises slowly and places his cup on the coffee table. His studied movements finally penetrate and make me falter. I don't trust the casual tone. "Number one, you didn't ask me a question, you made a statement. In my opinion a fairly stupid one no less." He raises his hand to still my outburst. "Number two, I am not one of your students that you can talk to that way."

Grant walks slowly toward me and it takes all my willpower to stay in my place. "And number three," I'm pulled into his arms, held tight to his chest, fingers under my chin making me meet his flashing blue eyes, "you know what I expect when you're with me. We shouldn't have to renegotiate each time, Tessa." His eyes narrow. "Unless you wish it to be that way?" An eyebrow quirks up. "Is that what you've been trying to tell me?"

My heart is thumping wildly in my chest. I can't tear my eyes from his. I shake my head and swallow. "No."

I feel the tension leave his arms and I almost sag. Fingers chuck me lightly under the chin. "Then behave yourself." A light kiss on my lips, and he releases me and returns to the couch. "I have a surprise for you after lunch."

I gather my wits and shakily reach for my cup of coffee. "Will you tell me what it is?"

He stirs the fire for a moment and then turns. The old wicked twinkle is back in his eye. "Then it wouldn't be a surprise, would it?"

The morning passes slowly. Grant is polite but slightly remote. He looks over the outbuildings, putters in the different rooms, reads a few business briefs and basically ignores me. I'm getting more nervous as lunchtime approaches.

I set the table and see the glint in his eye as he watches me. My hands start to shake. Grant's silence during the meal doesn't help my peace of mind. The food is tasteless. He has no trouble downing a large portion.

"When you're done eating, I want you to put on what's on your bed."

"What is it?" My throat is tight.

"You'll see when you get there. Put it on exactly as it's laid out. I'll meet you at the front door when you're done."

I watch Grant stand up. A finger gently traces my cheekbone, and then he goes to his room. I sit staring at the empty staircase and shiver. Excitement? Fear? Anticipation?

I linger over the dishes, partly to provoke him in retaliation for almost ignoring me this morning, partly in trepidation at what I might find, and partly to make the anticipation last longer. Finally, I acknowledge I have to climb those stairs. I can't put it off any longer.

I open the door slowly, almost in fear something will jump out at me. A jumble of furs sits on the bed. It's only when I move closer that I realize they are individual garments.

A vestlike piece lies first. The outside is soft leather of some type. My hand slips inside and feels fur. Next to it is a pair of pants, again with leather outside, fur inside. A hooded parka of fur is next. The inside is as smooth as the outside of the other. Larger fur pants rest on the bed next to it. On the floor are thick mukluks, two pairs of woolen socks lying on top of them.

I undress quickly and pull the pants on. The fur is both soft and slightly prickly at the same time. It tickles my mound when I move. The pants are loose except for the ankles. I tie the leather ties snugly. The vest pulls over my head. The fur brushes and teases my nipples as it slides down my body.

I pull on the two pairs of wool socks and then the looser pair of pants. I can already feel how warm I'm becoming. The heavy, thick parka goes over my head. It's beautifully decorated with a panel of beads down the front. I yank the mukluks on and tie the laces.

Catching sight of myself in the mirror, I gasp. I look to be about forty pounds heavier. Everything about me looks round, even my angular face once I pull the hood up. My heart is pounding. It's only the intolerable heat that makes me grab the mittens off the bed and go to the front door.

An Eskimo, dressed in warm furs like myself, is waiting for me. The figure turns, ice blue eyes crinkle at me, and I relax.

"Grant this is beau…"

"Let's go." His abrupt words cut off mine, and I watch him step outside into the pristine white world. He lowers his hood further when the wind picks up the new snow and swirls it about him.

I do the same and close the door behind me. I can't shake the feeling I'm not Tessa anymore and I've entered another world.

Grant hands me a bundle when I reach him. Then he helps me into a pair of snowshoes and shows me how to walk in them. I feel clumsier than ever before as I try to master the different gait. It's more like a shuffle than a walk. Grant slips on his own and motions me to follow him.

"But Grant, I won't be able to go far in these," I protest, laughing.

Serious eyes turn and pin me to the spot. "Eskimo wives obey their husbands, Tessa. They never question their decisions."

Eskimo wives. Grant is acting out another fantasy. Last time it was the fires of hell. Now it's to be the ice floes of the North. I certainly can't complain about boredom.

I trudge awkwardly after him, the wind-whipped snow stinging my face. The bundle seems to increase in weight with each step. When I call to Grant, my voice is carried away by the wind. Efforts to increase my speed fail as I flounder on the snowshoes.

Breathing is hard and I suck in air through the fur of my hood. The bitter cold hurts my lungs. My eyes sting and I squint into a world of pure white. I can't go on. I shout once more but Grant continues on as if he doesn't hear me. Does he?

Panic settles in my belly when I turn around intent on returning to the warm house. A blanket of white greets me. Nothing is distinguishable. Nothing stands out. Nothing but white greets my narrowed gaze. I turn, frightened, and almost trip as I start off quickly after the figure that is fast blending into the whiteness ahead. If I lose sight of Grant I'll be lost forever and freeze to death.

I'm completely disoriented. Near complete panic, I spy the vague outlines of Grant's tracks. Keeping my head down I hurry forward as quickly as possible, the small indentations in the snow my only link to Grant. I have to hurry or they might be obliterated with the new snow that falls and whirls around me.

The wind whistles and I look up. A few lonely pine trees are ahead in the distance. I glimpse Grant's figure outlined against them and feel a surge of happiness. I'm not alone in a no-man's-land.

I catch up to him easily once he stops. Proud of my achievement, I grin at him, my heart turning over when he smiles in return. He bows slightly and holds out his hand to the left. "Welcome to your new home, Tessa."

I glance that way but see nothing and turn confused eyes to him. He nods, smiles, and again motions to the left.

I squint harder and peer into the endless white. Slowly I discern a shape. An igloo. An actual igloo.

It's round and about fifteen feet in diameter. A smaller round dome abuts it and in turn has a straight tunnel-like projection running from it. "Do you honestly mean we're going to spend the day here?"

"The next two." I hear the determination in his tone.

He'll not tolerate any objections. "Go inside and unpack your bundle."

I ignore his penetrating stare and walk to the entranceway. It's only about three feet tall so I crouch and do a sort of crab walk in. The tunnel is about five feet long and then opens up into a small circular space that is slightly taller and wider. A few bundles line the walls. I crouch lower and, pushing aside a skin curtain, enter the last low doorway.

It's surprisingly spacious. The middle is about eight feet high and the room is about twelve feet across. A platform is covered in thick fur blankets and another holds a hollowed-out rock that is burning. I get a whiff of oil and see the fire is exactly that. Burning oil in a hollow rock. A small air vent is above me. A clear block of ice serves as a window. The only heat is provided by the rock and my own body.

I place the bundle on the platform and move to the window. Distorted green and brown shapes are the only things I can make out. Everything else is white.

Pulling off my mittens, I realize how surprisingly warm the house is. I toss my hood back and open the bundle. Dried fruit, vegetables, and meat are wrapped in waxed paper. A lightweight aluminum pan with leather strings attached lies on the bottom. I place everything on the platform and then wonder what I should do next.

It's so strange to feel warm while surrounded by snow and ice on all sides. The floor is snow. The platforms are snow. The walls are snow and ice.

A wooden pole sticks out from one wall over the stone lamp. I notice no stove, no form of light or heat except for the oil that burns. Now the leather strings on the pan make sense. Suppressing an excited giggle at my own cleverness, I grab the pan and wiggle my way outside to scoop some fresh snow into it. Grant is nowhere to be seen.

Tying the strings to the pole, the pan hangs a few inches from the fire. I empty a few packets of dried food into it, and the delicious smell of stew permeates the air a short while later. And then I have nothing to do.

Sitting on the platform, I move my hands lightly over the thick, heavy furs that cover it. I remove my outer pants and one pair of socks and place them neatly at the foot of the platform. A short while later I remove the outer parka. And I wait.

Had Grant said this was my home for the next two days? Only me? Has he gone back to the house? Is he so angry with me he doesn't want to be with me?

A trickle of fear curls up my spine. Can I find my way back? Would he do this to me? Why go to all the trouble of arranging this if he doesn't want to be with me?

A scrabbling noise makes my heart skip a beat. Something is coming. It's not footsteps but a scuffling noise. I rise to my knees and look around. The only thing I can defend myself with is the stone lamp. Quickly I grab up my mittens and prepare to seize the lamp and hurl its fiery contents at the intruder.

A bag is pushed into the opening, and Grant's silver head follows. I let the mittens drop when I see his brow crinkle questioningly. "What's wrong?"

Controlling the tremor that threatens to take me, I swallow quickly. "I didn't know it was you."

He stands, takes off his outer parka and gloves, and purses his lips. "Who did you think it would be?"

Feeling foolish, I busy myself stirring the stew.

"Smells good."

I nod but don't turn. I hear Grant moving on top of the furs.

"Tessa, put on your parka." Grant is sitting cross-legged on the platform. I reach for the heavy coat and pull it over my head. His hand reaches for mine and I take it, letting him tug me gently before him.

"I wish your mouth." The words are low and soft. His eyes are sparkling in the dim light. His hands reach out and pull my hood snugly around my head. I have to pull my eyes from his.

Grant lies down. I ease down his fur pants. He's hard. I lean down and start to push the hood back but his hand stops mine. "Go on, Tessa," he urges quietly.

The hood will lend the illusion to his fantasy. He'll see nothing but fur. I take his engorged penis. The pulse throbs beneath my cool hand. I kneel between his legs and lower my mouth to him. As always, Grant allows me to remain in control when I do this. His size spreads my lips wide. I run my tongue up the length of him, swirl it around the rim, the vent, the ridge. I feel his legs tense as his excitement builds. I slow down, relishing the feeling of power I have over him when he will feel satisfaction. I tease him, covering him and sucking hard, stopping the minute I feel the tension build. My tongue traces paths up one side, down another. I look up through the fur and our eyes meet for an instant. I watch him watch me, and then I return to my ministrations.

My fingers play with his tight sacks. I rub his heavy penis with my cheek, the fur on the hood tickling the tip. I can't help smiling when I hear his gasp of pleasure. I lean further over and lave him with my wet tongue, the fur barely touching his sensitive skin. Gooseflesh rises along his muscular thighs.

I love knowing I can make him pant with need as he does me. I love knowing he is under my control no matter how fleeting that time may be. I love the feel of his sturdy thighs beneath my arms, the solid pulsing thickness of his shaft between lips and fingers. I love the taste of him when I finally allow him to explode. I love being pulled up into his embrace and cuddled, the sound of his heartbeat slowing beneath my ear. I love being with Grant.

We eat a quiet meal, both wrapped up in our own thoughts. The house is amazingly snug and cozy. The oil lamp lends a soft glow and softens the unending whiteness of the walls and floor. The furs are soft and thick beneath us as we sit and eat. I scrape the pan and rub snow into it and place it in the small domelike storage area.

Grant is naked in between the furs when I return. I hastily shuck my clothes, all too aware of his eyes on me. Shivering, I join him. The fur is soft and warm. It tickles and soothes. Caresses and excites. Delicious.

Grant reaches for me and also tickles and soothes. And excites. And kisses. And nibbles. And caresses. And takes me time after time to that wonderful sphere of bliss. Delicious.

We dine elegantly on rolls with jelly and a cup of steaming coffee as we stay snuggled up warmly in the blankets. I can't move without being caressed. Fur tickles and pets me whenever I stir. The feeling against my bare mound is incredible.

Tessa's Holidays

Grant takes me on a hike outside, and I find myself in a world of startling white. The sun is bright, too bright, and I squint even behind my dark glasses. It's windless. Cold. And so silent it's spooky.

Mountains rear up on all sides of us, overpowering in their bleakness. White walls with faint outlines of brown, the trees' bare tops looking like they've been dusted with confectionery sugar by a chef gone mad. Only a few lonely spots of green disturb the starkness.

We trudge along on the snowshoes, Grant laughing at me whenever I fail to remember I wear them and try to turn too quickly. My muscles let me know quickly just how unused they are to the awkward shoes. Grant laughs at my decreasing pace and lends a hand to tug me along.

"I have something to show you, Tessa." His voice is casual but I hear the underlying tone of excitement. Blue eyes crinkle at me when he removes his sunglasses for a moment. "Come on. It's not too far now."

We continue on. I keep sucking the frigid air through the fur of my parka. My nose is now beyond cold. I watch the tracks Grant makes in front of me and try to make a game of putting one snowshoe exactly where he placed his. His stride is too long, too far spaced, and I end up facedown in the snow when I reach too far. I lie exhausted in the cushioning snow. My breath puffs out and I watch it form and crystallize before evaporating into nothing. My chest is heaving. My throat is dry. Tiredly I trickle some snow into my mouth. Iciness turns warm and bathes the dry, arid tunnel.

"Are you trying to entice me, Tessa? Couldn't you have found a warmer place?" Grant is smiling down at me so tenderly, his eyes twinkling with merriment.

"I just couldn't wait any longer, Grant." My striven-for sexy huskiness sounds like just what it actually is—breathlessness due to exhaustion. Grant removes his snowshoes and sits in the snow beside me.

I feel him remove my snowshoes from their bindings. Hands run over the double layer of fur slowly. "You'd never be able to tell if you were man or woman from the back, Tessa."

Mittens trace the outlines of my body. It's almost a removed feeling, not quite real. Grant's eyes are invisible beneath the dark glasses. I know what they would look like, though. I've seen the speculative gleam too many times not to sense when it's there. I wish I could fathom what he's thinking about.

I feel the slight beginning of cold penetrating through my clothes and start to rise. Grant moves back and lets me. For no reason at all my skin prickles with warning and I turn around.

Grant is watching me steadily with piercing blue eyes. I know intuitively he's no longer Grant Davis. He's entered into his fantasy again. I can't stop the shiver that ripples through me.

"You were raised by the Eskimos far in the north. You speak no English. You are a good, obedient, Eskimo wife and do as you are bid with no hesitation. Do we understand each other?"

"Why?"

"Tessa." I hear the warning. What do Eskimos do? They hunt seals and whales. They live in igloos. They travel by dogsled or snowmobile. They rub noses. They have blanket tosses up in the Arctic. They fight to keep their right to hunt whales for sustenance.

Nothing terrible. I certainly hadn't suffered last night by pretending to be an Eskimo wife. I could try eating whale or seal if that's what he wants. I nod and reattach the snowshoes at his imperious gesture. He's no longer Grant, but an Eskimo.

We trudge through the snow for almost another hour. I can barely suck in breath I'm so tired. The air seems to sear through my lungs. I feel as if I've been walking for days as opposed to a few hours. I'm panting heavily when Grant stops beneath a few tall pine trees.

"Catch your breath and then we'll go on." I nod, too tired to argue. Leaning against the trunk of a tree, I watch Grant survey our surroundings, his eyes taking in everything at once. They roam the distance and I see them narrow. I can't see anything when I follow his glance. Serious blue eyes turn and pin me with their intensity. They almost seem to glitter. I swallow quickly.

"You speak no English. Not one word. When we reach the cabin I want you to remove both pairs of trousers and the inside vest. Just keep your mukluks and outer parka on. The cabin will be warm enough." Mittened fingers take my chin. "Remember, I expect you to acquiesce in all things, Tessa."

He's already moving before I can think of anything to say. Why the ominous warning? The landscape has suddenly lost some of its beauty as I trudge along behind his fast-departing back.

I smell the smoke before I see the cabin. Nestled amongst towering pines, majestic mountains forming a backdrop, the wood structure looks like something out of a painting. My heart beats faster. What a charming place for an interlude. The images fade a moment later when I hear Grant call out a greeting to whoever is in the cabin.

The door opens and a man appears. A rifle is held

loosely in one hand. The other takes a smoking pipe from his mouth. Narrowed eyes watch our approach warily.

"I saw your smoke," Grant says by way of greeting.

The man's eyes swivel to mine. I see the surprise flick in them. The interest. His tongue moves slowly around the perimeter of his lips.

Now I remember something else. Eskimo men supposedly share their wives.

We're welcomed into the cabin grudgingly. The man's eyes constantly flick to me.

"Where you from?"

Grant shucks off his parka before answering. "Up north. Had to go to the bay area for a few days." Why didn't I notice he hadn't shaved this morning? He looks older. Craggier. Almost disreputable.

Dark eyes flick back to me. I see Grant's warning look of raised brows and remember his words. Without looking at either man, I turn. The cabin is one room, a curtained-off area holding a bed. I'll have to undress in front of them.

I pull the outside parka over my head. "Wife?" The simple question can't hide the interest the man feels.

"Yes. I got her on a trip to the Arctic. She was raised by a northern Eskimo tribe."

I can feel the weathered eyes boring into my back as I slowly remove first one layer of pants and then the other. I hear a sibilant hiss of indrawn breath. I pull the vest over my head and hastily don the hooded parka. The mukluks protect me from the cold floor. Nothing protects me from eyes that seem to look through me. The cabin is warm and still I erupt in gooseflesh.

"She don't look Eskimo." I keep my eyes on the floor. The man is fucking me with his eyes. I swear I can see his hips slowly swaying back and forth. I like being able to affect a man like this. I can't help the thrill that rushes through me.

"She's not. They found her on a piece of drifting ice when she was young and kept her." Grant has placed his outside clothes on a low table by the wall. I walk over and add mine to the pile. His arm around my waist keeps me next to him.

"Quiet, ain't she?"

"She doesn't speak English. Rarely speaks at all, in fact." His hand is traveling lower. I stay still and keep my eyes down. My heart is pounding and I struggle to remain still. Cool, strong fingers brush along my thigh. I know the hem of the parka is high enough to let the man get just a glimpse of my ass before Grant motions me away from him, and it once more falls into place at midthigh.

I see the other's tongue flick out. It reminds me of a snake waiting to strike. I sit by the fireplace and add a piece of wood. The man can barely cover his excitement.

"I hear those northern Eskimos have some strange customs."

Grant smiles and winks. "Makes life with the women easier."

"Is it true all the things you hear?" His grip on his pipe is so tight I wait for it to snap in two.

"Depends what you hear." Grant is playing it as cool as a cucumber. I'd almost forgotten how much pleasure he gets out of watching me with others.

They sit at a makeshift table and lower their voices. I

can only hear an occasional word or two. The man is leaning toward Grant, intent on his every word. I see his tongue swiping his lips now and then.

He's anywhere from forty-five to sixty-five. His face is like old leather, cracked and stiff. About five foot nine, he's slender but the whippy kind of thinness that belies the strength inside. His hands are small, almost gnarled. His teeth are decent, his features rough but not repellent. His body is tense. Poised. I wonder how long it's been since he's been with a woman. By the glint in Grant's eyes, it won't be much longer.

The man stands and offers lunch. Suddenly it seems he's happy to have company. Grant waves him down. "The girl will prepare the meal, Dan."

"Tessa." Grant beckons me to him. He's clipped the word so it almost sounds like "Chetta." I rise and stand before him. My legs shake slightly. The gleam is brighter in his eyes. He loves to watch my reactions. I try to remain in my role and passive. Grant makes a few gestures like cooking, and I nod and turn back to the fireplace.

"That's her name? Chetta?"

"She answers to it."

"Unusual, ain't it?"

"I don't know too many Eskimo names." Grant shrugs and changes the subject.

I rummage around and locate fixings for a simple meal. Dan has some canned goods so he must go into town now and again. I throw everything into a pot and start it simmering over the grate.

I can feel Dan's eyes on me as if they were actually stroking me. A shot of deviltry takes me, and I stand and bend deeply to stir the food. I feel the tickling of the fur hem riding high up the back of my thighs. I hear his quick hiss of appreciation. I know he can just barely see the pouty lips between my legs. Stirring the pot, I let my buttocks rotate with the movement. I love being the tormentor for a change. It hardly matters that it won't last long.

I serve the men. Grant pulls me down by the neck and gives me a long kiss. The stubble on his chin rasps my cheek before he claims my lips. My ass is bared not inches from Dan's eyes. I feel a tentative touch on the back of my thighs. There is wonderment in the touch. Grant releases me and I docilely return to the fireplace.

I hardly taste the meal. My eyes wander around the room. It is surprisingly neat for such a rustic abode, in fact the man is surprisingly neat also. His hair is longish but clean and shiny. I return to perusing the room when his eyes stray to mine.

Traps and skins hang from one wall. The bed is handmade but neatly made up with a warm fur skin. The shelves are precisely lined with jars and tins. Another rifle is cradled on a rack above the door. Various ropes and tools hang on another wall. The man is grizzled and weathered but looks clean enough. I don't know if I'm more nervous or excited about what might happen.

Grant approaches me an hour later and whispers in my ear to behave as he tugs me onto my feet. I nod but avoid both men's eyes. Gooseflesh creeps along my arms when I hear the click of the door shutting. I stand in the middle of the floor and don't move or look up. I sense his presence behind me. The man is catlike in his movements. He makes no sound.

And I wait.

I hear his breathing, shallow but quick. I can hear him swallow. I sense him leaning closer but still he doesn't touch me. Is he waiting for permission? Should I turn? Should I remain as I am and let him set the pace? Where is Grant?

The lightest of touches on my leg. A harsh indrawn breath. I can actually feel the nervous tremor in his fingers. Is he afraid I'll scream? Didn't Grant make it clear how he felt about this? Is he wondering if I'll go along with it, or is it just nervousness because it's been so long since he's been with a woman?

The touch becomes firmer and skims along the back of my thigh. The fur hem tickles the backs of my legs as it raises slowly. I stand still and look ahead, my own breathing quickening with anticipation. It is strange to be touched and stroked by someone unseen.

My ass is stroked, squeezed, and molded in small but strong hands. He steps closer and lightly rubs his body against mine. I feel the hard tube of his desire inside the roughness of his trousers. Hands lift the parka and I raise my arms and let him remove it. Again the sibilance of a quick intake of breath.

Hands roam the contours of my body so lightly it almost tickles. I feel the awe, the wonder of the touch. And yet he still stays behind me. Hands travel forward and take my breasts lovingly. I know he relishes the weight of them in his hands, lifting, stroking, pulling so softly on the turgid peaks. My own breathing is quickening. I want to turn and face him, but the lure to let an unknown make love to me is too strong and I remain facing the fire.

I feel breath on my neck and shiver as he moves from

one side to the other. He's taking in my scent. I know it instinctively. Rough sandpaper hands continue to wander at will over my body, the very roughness exciting in itself.

I feel him kneel and then the breeze of his breath bathes my buttocks. He rubs his cheek against my own. I hear his light sniffing as he traces the curves of my backside. Hands part my legs slightly. I'm sucking in air. A finger traces the outline of my netherlips. Lightly, wonderingly. A tongue follows the length of my crack to my spine. I hear the rasp of a zipper, feel him rise. His hardness rubs between my legs, and then with a groan I feel the stickiness coat my thighs. I'm devastated.

He staggers to a chair and pants lightly as he composes himself. His excitement had been too great and it's over. I wash myself in a small bowl of water and pull my parka over my head. He still sits on the chair, a contented smile on his face, his penis flaccid on his thigh. I return to the fire and wait for Grant's return.

The man dozes—I hear his light snoring. What am I supposed to do? What had promised to be different has been nothing. I don't have to wait long.

"Chetta."

My Eskimo name. I meet his eyes for the first time. They're dark, the color indistinguishable. He still sits on the chair but his penis is no longer flaccid. He beckons to me and I rise slowly. I remove my parka when he motions me to. I turn slowly at his silent request. His excited, pleased smile makes me proud, and I thrust out my breasts more. My nipples harden and bud out. His smile widens. He hardens. He's long and thin. Nothing like Grant.

I follow the motion of his finger and pirouette

around. He beams with pleasure. Raising my hands I stretch languidly. I close my eyes and sway slightly. I love having my body so appreciated.

He sweeps me onto his shoulder, across the room and onto the bed in one swift motion. I have no time to react and he's in me, stroking long and deep in rapid thrusts. Again I barely start to respond and he's done. Our groans mingle, his of ecstasy, mine of frustration. He flops to the side and his snores sound seconds later. I want to cry. Where is Grant?

I wash myself and wander around the cabin. I add wood to the fire. I stare at the man in the bed. Where is Grant? Am I to be left here for the next two days? This isn't usual at all. Grant likes to watch me with others, not just give me to others.

My eyes make a slow study of the cabin. I can't locate any cameras. Grant wouldn't stand out in the cold and watch for this long. I can't understand why he's left me here with this man. It is obvious it wasn't planned. The man had had no idea we were coming. But Grant always has a reason for the things he does. I'll just have to wait to find out what they are.

Dan wakes and motions me to him. He's hardening already. I pull the parka over my head and stand before him. His hand shakes as it reaches for me, and then he slowly pulls me down next to him. I'm trying to remain removed. I don't want to be disappointed again. I lie passive on the bed. He kneels and, never taking his eyes from me, slowly undresses. His body is thin but tight.

Dan straddles my body at the knees. My breathing is quickening despite my resolve. His eyes stroke and caress me from the neck to the knees. Rough hands reach out and stroke my thighs so incredibly softly. As if in a trance, he travels higher, only his fingertips touching my skin.

Light fluttery circles are made over and over. The texture of my skin seems to enthrall him. I try to lie still beneath him, but my bud is starting to throb and I can't help the small febrile movements of my hips.

Fingertips lightly circle, stroke, caress my shaved mound. I strain to raise my hips so he'll touch me in the right place. His knees tighten against my thighs and I'm held tight to the bed. I can't help myself so I raise my arms. He takes them and places them at my sides and then begins his journey of discovery all over again.

His head lowers and I wait eagerly for a swipe of his tongue. I feel warm breath instead. He smells and sniffs along my thighs, the crease between them, up around my hips, my sides. He lightly lifts my breasts and sniffs the undersides of them. I moan. His nose lightly circles the engorged peak. I have to grab handfuls of fur to keep my hands at my sides.

My body is screaming for him to touch me. To lick me. To stroke me with real feeling. This light caress, this bathing of warm breath is driving me insane with desire.

He leans forward and begins on my neck. I feel his hardness against my belly. His breath is in my ear but inhaling, not exhaling. Along my neck, collarbone. My arms are raised above my head, his weight shifts and he turns me over and begins again.

Every curve, every contour is sniffed, explored with the lightest of touches. He lies on me fully and rubs himself into me as if trying to take my scent. His penis is rock hard but still he does no more than to rub himself against me. He turns and lies with his back on mine, ass to ass. I feel him breathing deeply. Is he trying to prolong the moment? To compose himself?

He turns once more and then his tongue starts the same route of discovery, but always missing where I want it to be. I'm turned over and he starts on my chin and works his way down my body. I moan in exquisite agony. His tongue flicks my armpit, and my clit throbs. It circles the roundness of my breasts over and over but nothing but warm breath touches the turgid peaks. My moans of need are ignored and he continues on his journey.

Hot breath, coolness after his tongue leaves to continue further down my body. He shifts his weight once more. My legs are allowed to open and I hold my breath. Please. Please. I feel the tip of his nose skim my hairless mound. I try to raise my hips but his hands keep me still. And then he moves on and concentrates on my thighs.

My breathing is ragged, and I continually whimper with need. Why is he driving me insane this way? Why doesn't he want to have me, to use me, to plow deep within me? I'm going to go mad if I'm not allowed to finish.

His weight shifts and he turns, straddling me in reverse. His penis is above me. My thighs are pulled open and up, and his mouth covers my source. My gasp of pleasure is muffled when he fills me, stroking deep in my throat. His tongue is relentless between my legs. His penis is hurting the back of my throat. Everything shifts between the sensation of pleasure and suffocating. I feel the retch building. His thrusting is becoming savage. I try to grab his hips to lift him, but he lets more of his weight descend.

I'm so close to orgasm. The door bangs open, his head leaves my mound. I scream with frustration. I feel his organ swell and throb, and then I'm desperately swallowing mouthfuls, trying not to choke.

"Finish her off, will you? She's terribly cranky when she doesn't come."

Grant's voice is so calm. I feel the tension in Dan's body even as his heart slows with each receding spasm. His penis is now flaccid within my mouth. I sense his hesitation and then feel a tentative touch of his tongue. I know he must be watching Grant for his reaction. What man wouldn't expect a husband to be furious if he walked in and found another man in his position? He laps tentatively and then harder. His hips relax and his penis still muffles my rising whimpers of need. Teeth nibble and I explode, muted screams of pleasure echoing in the cabin.

Dan rises and hastily pulls on his clothing. I lie on the bed, spent. Grant smiles at me when I catch his eye. He's placed a small ventilated duffel bag on the table. Inside a large grommet I see the wink of a lens opening and shutting. I had forgotten about his photo albums.

Dan is uncomfortable and leaves the cabin a few minutes later. Grant approaches me and sits on the edge of the bed. His fingers lightly stroke my breasts. "I think you've made Dan a very happy man, Tessa."

I remain silent. What is there to say? Grant is the one I always want, yet I can't deny I do have pleasure with some of the others. I shiver with cold and he immediately pulls a cover over me. Still his hands roam and stroke. I sigh, a small tingle of excitement beginning to build. His hands are so sure, so capable of arousing me.

"Turn over, Tessa. You'll be warmer."

I know what he wants by the look in his eye. I turn slowly and stretch my arms high above my head. I'm still so relaxed, but my insides are tightening with the first twinges of anticipation.

Cool air bathes my back as he lifts the cover. I hear the rasp of his zipper and then the sound of cloth moving over skin as he pulls his pants off. The bed shifts under his weight. Strong fingers pull my hips up. My stomach is stroked. Hands cup and squeeze my breasts. My breathing quickens. He pushes his hips into my ass, the hard tube fitting perfectly within the crease of my ass. He strokes it up and down. I moisten. Fingers pull and squeeze my breasts. My mouth opens and I gulp in air. My insides itch with need. A hand caresses my hip, belly, stomach. Fingers seek and find the pulsing bud. My ass contracts, holding him tightly. His breath tickles my ear as he leans over me.

"Do you want me?"

"Yes."

"How do you want me?"

"Inside of me."

"Where?"

"Everywhere."

"Ah, Tessa." His sigh whispers over me as he slowly fills me. I don't tense against him. I welcome him and move with him. His hands reach under me and stoke, pull, pinch, so lightly, so tormentingly that my movements become faster, harder. He strokes deep up my bowels and I meet him willingly, aiding him, encouraging him. Sensation after giddy sensation races through me, and then the cabin is filled with my high keening as I reach the top and peak. I hear his grunt, feel the pulsing deep within me and heed his pressure to sink down prone on the bed. He lies on me, supported on his elbows, still deep within me. I cradle my head in my arms. His lips nibble on my ear. I smile happily. He takes me places no other can.

"Still cold?" His tongue traces the outline of my ear. I shake my head lazily and hear his satisfied chuckle. A hesitant cough makes us both turn. Dan is by the door, his expression a mixture of embarrassment, excitement, and something close to awe.

Grant rises and slowly pulls on his clothes with no sign of embarrassment. "How's the weather?"

Dan's eyes remain riveted to my ass. "Starting to snow."

"Would you mind if we spent the night? I think your bed is large enough for the three of us."

"Huh?"

"I wondered if you'd mind if we spent the night. I hate to travel in bad weather."

"Oh, sure. Sure, no problem," he hastily reassures Grant. His eyes bore into me as I pull on my parka. He seems to be having trouble swallowing. His hands grasp and ungrasp each other. Finally pulling his eyes from me, he goes to the fireplace and busies himself with building a roaring fire.

We eat dinner and I do the dishes. The men talk to each other about different things and then Grant motions me to him. He unzips himself and I kneel between his legs. His massive weapon grows before my eyes. I hear Dan's breathing quicken, his small gasp when I run my tongue along the length of Grant's penis. Grant lays his head back and sighs.

I love this feeling of control I get when I do this.

Grant never forces me when I suck him. I remain in control. I determine when and how and how much. I love it. And so does he. And apparently so does Dan.

Out of the corner of my eye I watch him rise and move toward us as if in a dream. He's mesmerized by the action of my tongue on Grant. I see his chest heaving, his fists clenching at his sides. Grant remains relaxed, eyes closed, hands loose at his sides, head laid on the back of the chair. Only the tension in his thighs beneath my hand lets me know how much I affect him.

My parka is lifted, hands grasp my hips. I don't miss a beat. I feel the thin, long tube between my legs and then Dan slips it in. Compared to Grant he is nothing. I receive no sensation of being filled. My muscles tighten but still don't feel friction. His movements are slow and steady. I hear his deep breath expelled as he sinks into me. He holds my hips and stays still for one long moment and then begins to move. I see Grant open his eyes and smile at the man. Dan's movements quicken. So do mine.

Thighs tense behind me. Thighs tense under my hands. I suck harder, deeper. Dan's breathing is loud now. His fingers grip tightly to my sides. I swallow as much of Grant as I am able. I hear the hiss of breath drawn in both above and behind me, and then Dan lets out a roar and I'm swallowing Grant's copious liquid.

I bathe in a large round tub filled with hot steaming water in front of the fire. I remain in my role: obedient, quiet, and ignorant of English. It's a strange experience for me to be so silent. I love to talk, love to discuss all aspects of any subject and debate its many sides. To sit here in the hot water and pretend I cannot understand them, never mind actually join in, is frustrating, and yet oddly it's sort of nice. I need not take any responsibility. I need not defend my opinions. I only need to enjoy the luxury of hot water, a bar of soap, and four very appreciative eyes.

Delicious.

Dan and Grant discuss my pros and cons. Grant tells him absurd stories of past encounters with other men, and the man almost drools as he listens. This is a side of Grant I've never seen before. His imagination is incredible.

Dan's lived here for twenty-five years, twenty-one of them alone. His girlfriend couldn't take the isolation and left him one day without a word of explanation. Dan claims he'd forgotten what he was missing and is determined to seek out a woman who would be willing to stay with him.

When we leave the next morning my insides are tender from the multitude of ways Dan felt the need to try during the night. Grant's words must have inspired him. Sometimes Grant pretended to be asleep. Sometimes he joined in. Sometimes he lit the oil lamp and blatantly watched. I'm just happy we're returning to the lodge.

I do nothing but remember on the plane ride home. The last day had been one of tender loving, avid conversation, and sadness at the thought of parting. Grant would make no promises about future meetings before the summer. He still hasn't told me how he will arrange it but suggested I might want to acquaint myself with oriental foods and customs. He'd say no more than that.

It was enough. My imagination takes flight and I

envision wonderful weeks of touring the Orient. Where? Hong Kong? China? Bangkok? The possibilities are endless.

Mom is at the airport waiting for me. She seems different somehow. Happier? More optimistic?

"Did you make up with Aunt Helen?"

"Oh, that was never a problem. We're just too much alike to spend too much time together. It always blows over quickly. How was your week?"

"Fine. I had a lot of fun. Louise ended up being the only one to show because of the weather, but we did a lot of reminiscing and had a good time."

"Did you ski?"

Mom can spot a lie a mile off, and I try to stay as close to the truth as I can. "No, but I learned to snowshoe." I watch the passing landscape for a while and then turn back to my mother. She has a lightness about her. A small smile seems to curve the edges of her lips.

"Anything exciting happen while I was gone?"

"No, not really." I don't believe her for some reason but am at a loss about how to pursue it.

Polly and the kids are at the house to welcome me home. The children make pests of themselves until I finally unpack and give them the small gifts I'd bought them. We leave them to play and go into the kitchen for a cup of coffee. I breath in all the familiar aromas. It's good to be home.

Polly brings me up to date on all the happenings in the town. Mom slices pieces of cake and brings them to the table. I reach for one and stop.

"What's that?" A man's hat sits on the corner cupboard. My mother blushes and both Polly and I gape at her.

TESSA'S HOLIDAYS

"It's a hat," mother says and starts fussing with the forks.

"Whose hat?" I demand.

"Mr. Brewster's. Would you like a large or small piece, Polly?" Mom asks, changing the subject.

"Who is Mr. Brewster?"

Another blush. Mom drops a fork, flustered. "Honestly, girls. Mr. Brewster had car trouble and asked to use the telephone. I didn't let him in, at least not right away," she protests at our outraged looks.

"Go on," Polly urges.

"Well, I called a tow truck for him and it took so long in coming I felt I just couldn't leave him freezing outside."

"But Mother..."

"Would you both stop! I'm not a child. The tow truck was on its way, and besides, you could tell right off he was a nice, respectable man."

Both of us still stare at her and again a deep red spreads over her cheeks. "Well, he was," she protests a tad too adamantly. "The poor man was freezing so I invited him in for a cup of coffee. He was a perfect gentleman."

"And he left his hat here?"

"I didn't notice till after he'd gone. I called the towing company and got his business number but his secretary said he'd be gone for a week."

"Is he local?" Polly looks more excited than upset and I resent it.

"Yes. He owns a real-estate business in the next town."

Why do I feel threatened? "Then why didn't you get a ride and just return the hat?"

117

Another blush and Polly absolutely beams. "Why, Mother, I do believe you want to see this man again!"

"What?" I cry, but Polly's enthusiasm overrides my indignation.

"I think it's wonderful. It's been far too long for you to be alone. Why, you're still a youthful, vivacious woman." Mom blushes more. Polly takes her hand and smiles. "Why, I bet Mr. Brewster left his hat here just so he could come and see you again."

"That's ridiculous." As soon as I utter the words I regret them. My mother's face fills with doubt and unhappiness. I see her bite her lip before lowering her eyes. I hate myself, more so when I hear her next words.

"Of course, it's ridiculous. No one would want an old lady like me."

"Mom, I'm sorry. Please don't talk like that." I can feel tears pricking my eyelids and desperately search for a way to atone. "You're not an old lady. Polly's right and I just never realized it before." I try to smile but my throat is tight. "I guess I don't want to think about you being anything but my mother."

The edge of excitement is gone from her face. She smiles at me but it doesn't reach her eyes. "Well, we'll just forget about it. You take the hat back to the real-estate office for me tomorrow, Tessa, and that'll be the end of this nonsense."

Polly is glaring daggers at me and I feel terrible. "I have to work tomorrow, Mom. Maybe later in the week I can get it there." She nods and clears the dishes. I only hope the man comes before I can get to his business. Polly's look of disappointment only makes me feel worse.

The week passes slowly. The students are reluctant to get back into the swing of things after their long

Tessa's Holidays

Christmas vacation, and I find my heart isn't in it either. Mom is back to her quiet existence, the hat moved out of sight into the hall closet. I keep putting off taking it back but as the days pass I begin to think Polly was wrong and I unfortunately was right.

As soon as I enter the house I sense the change in the atmosphere. Mom is humming happily in the kitchen. The house seems brighter somehow. It's filled with the delicious aroma of fresh-baked apple pie and perking coffee. I hear Mom's laughter and the deeper tones of a male voice as I make my way to the kitchen.

Mom is in a fitted skirt and blouse with low-heeled pumps on. Her hair is brushed attractively off her face, a bright red lipstick on her lips. The reason for this change is sitting at our kitchen table.

He sees me enter and rises. Mom turns, blushes, and hurries forward. "Tessa! I'm so glad you came right home. I want you to meet Michael Brewster. Mr. Brewster left his hat here a while ago when he had car trouble, and he just came to retrieve it. Mr. Brewster, this is my youngest, Tessa."

His smile is charming. I hold out my hand to the compact man. His grip is firm, and his eyes twinkle at me. "Call me Michael, please."

"It's a pleasure to meet you, Michael." He must be close to his mid-fifties. His full head of hair is just starting to turn gray at the temples. It lends him a very distinguished air. His movements are confident, and I easily see why he has so thoroughly charmed my mother. I watch him sit down only to spring up immediately and take the tray from Mom. Her eyes are sparkling. I suddenly feel like a spare wheel and hastily excuse myself and go upstairs.

Grant is right as usual. I don't like thinking of my mother as a sexual being. She's Mom. My mom. It's impossible to think of her writhing on a bed with a man, moaning and needing him as I need Grant.

I pace and finally admit the truth to myself. I'm jealous. I can't have Grant here. I can't flirt openly with him. I can't invite him for coffee and cake. I can't date him when I feel like seeing him. I always feel like seeing him.

I hear the door closing a while later. Mom's happy humming climbs the stairs and enters my room. The clatter of cups and saucers being washed and dried reaches me, and still I hesitate to go downstairs. I don't wish to spoil her happiness and I know she'll read me like a book. I have to get myself composed before I face her.

What is the worst thing that could happen? My mother could be happy again. Emotionally I don't want to deal with it. Intellectually I know I must. And after a long time I really am able to be happy for her. She deserves a good man to hold and care for. She deserves to find someone who can make her happy as my father did.

Her beaming smile when I enter the kitchen does nothing but reassure me, and I smile happily back. "He's a dream, Mom."

She's almost breathless. "Yes, he's quite handsome, isn't he?"

"Has he asked you out?"

Her cheeks pink becomingly. "As a matter of fact, he has."

"And?"

"And what?"

I swallow my frustration. "And are you going to go out with him?"

"I told him I'd think about it."

I'm flabbergasted. "Why?"

"Because I don't want to appear too eager." She looks at me and giggles. "You should have seen his face, Tessa. I don't think he gets put off too often."

"But Mom, suppose…"

"Just let me worry about it, Tessa. This is my life. I don't interfere with your love life. Don't crowd mine."

I can't believe this calculating flirt is my mother. I'm speechless for one of the few times in my life. Mom flashes me a happy smile and goes back to her humming. I take a walk in the frigid air to clear my mind.

Twice more Mr. Brewster stops by. My mother flirts and charms in an unassuming way but still declines actually to go out on a date with him. I can't figure it out but she refuses to explain herself.

Three weeks later I come downstairs early on a Saturday morning and find Michael standing at the stove turning bacon. He throws me a smile and a shrug. "Your mom's in the cellar looking for a jar of preserves."

He seems so comfortable, I can't help but ask. "Isn't it a little early to be calling?"

Another shrug. "It's hard to find time to spend with a busy woman like your mother. I figured if I pled starvation she'd give in and feed me. Do you think if I ask her to a community dance she'd go with me?"

Busy? Mother? I can't quite take in his words, and then Mom is coming into the room. "Good morning, darling," she coos, placing a kiss on my cheek. She is absolutely glowing. "Thank you, Michael," she says, taking the fork from him.

"Millie, would you like to go to the community dance this weekend?"

Mom turns and gives him a rueful smile. "I'm sorry, Michael, but I've already accepted another invitation. Maybe we'll see each other there."

My head is spinning. Mom is going to a dance? With someone? I watch Michael trying to be gracious about this turn of events. His frown isn't quite gone when Mom turns back to him. She flashes him a brilliant smile and puts breakfast on the table. I eat automatically. I think Michael does, too.

As soon as the door closes behind him I pounce. "Who are you going to the dance with?"

"Mr. Potter from the bank."

Mr. Potter is a confirmed bachelor and lady's man. The way he looks at women makes me shudder sometimes. "But why?"

"I have my reasons, darling. Are you going?"

"No, I hadn't planned to."

She pats my cheek and walks away. "You really should date more, Tessa."

Saturday night Mom arrives home with Michael Brewster instead of Mr. Potter. I sit on the sofa and watch the picture on the television without actually seeing it. I hear their low murmurings on the porch, see their shadows meet and hold for a long moment, and then Mom lets herself into the house.

"What happened?"

A Cheshire grin spreads her lips and she shrugs. "Not too much. The band was exceptionally good this time and played a large selection of very romantic music. Mr. Potter got a little out of line and Mr. Brewster just happened to be near when I needed assistance. Good night, dear," she calls and then breezes out of the room. I don't think I know this woman any longer.

Mom insists we go to a restaurant so she can wear a new dress she's bought. Her heels are higher, sexier than I've ever seen her wear. The dress is low cut and shows plenty of cleavage I never knew she had. This stunning woman seems to have risen from my mother's body. She brushes her hair onto the top of her head, and I can't believe this gorgeous, sophisticated woman is my mother. Where has she been all these years? I find myself searching my wardrobe desperately so she doesn't outshine me.

We arrive promptly at eight fifteen and tell the maitre d' our names. He bows slightly and leads us to a table. I can see eyes turning to watch our entrance. A pair of ice blue ones catch and hold mine. My breath quickens and my steps falter. His companion turns, brows raise in surprised delight, and then Michael is heading toward my mother. He neatly intercepts her just before she is being seated.

"Millie! What a delightful surprise. Hello, Tessa. Are you two alone?"

I nod numbly. My heart is pounding. I hear his words asking us to join them. My mother demurs quietly, but Michael is insistent and she finally agrees. I walk as if in a dream. Nothing exists except for the pair of ice blue eyes that watch our approach.

Grant stands when we reach the table. "Millie. Tessa. This is my friend Grant Davis."

"How do you do," Grant says with a bow. He holds my chair and I sit as if dazed. They all have to hear my heart pounding. It's hard to concentrate on words. He's talking to me and repeats his words.

"Would you care to dance?"

He's already moving my chair back, and I rise and look stupidly at my mother. She's in conversation with Michael and doesn't even realize I'm there. Grant's hand takes my elbow and then we're moving smoothly around the floor.

"Tessa, smile. You look like you've seen a ghost." His voice is low with a hint of laughter in it.

I try desperately to clear my mind. "Did you arrange this somehow?"

He chuckles and shakes his head. I feel the slight pressure of his hand on my back and wish it were covering my breast. "Just the fate of the gods or, if my guess is correct, your mother's planning."

That snaps me out of my daze. "What?"

"Now I know where you get your intelligence from. Never have I seen a man more skillfully maneuvered than your mother is doing with Michael."

I defend her instantly. "I don't know what you mean. Mother isn't planning anything. She's just enjoying herself for the first time since father died."

"Oh, yes, she is," Grant insists with a smile. "Michael is a man about town. He never has a problem getting women. In fact, they tend to fall all over him."

"What's your point, Grant?"

"My point is your mother knew that and didn't fall into the same pattern. She has seduced him in an entirely different way, and Michael has no defense against it."

"My mother didn't know Michael Brewster before his car broke down."

"I know. But your mother is an astute woman and recognized his type immediately. Michael is not used to being turned down. Your mother's superb looks attracted him immediately. He told me he left his hat at her house on purpose just so he could go back and ask her out. Instead of her falling all over him, he received a warm, cordial invitation to coffee and cake, and she ignored his attempts to flirt with her as if she didn't see them. It intrigued him, especially when she kept declining his invitations. He'd call and ask her out now and then, but she was always polite but busy. The other night at the dance brought out all his protectiveness, and it's just made him more determined to conquer her."

"Conquer her?" My anger rises. "If he thinks he can…"

"Relax, Tessa. Your mother knows exactly what she's doing. Michael is a gentleman. Your mother is safe with him, and she knows it even if he doesn't."

"Did you know she was my mother?"

"As soon as he said her name." He smiles and my heart skips a beat. "I think your mother would be wonderful for Michael. He needs a stable influence in his life. I know he's tired of the constant social whirl, and while he doesn't know it yet, he yearns for the stability of a home life with one woman." Those wonderful eyes crinkle at me. "And if I'm not mistaken, your mother is determined she is going to be that woman."

I can't take it all in. I open my mouth but then snap it shut. His arm tightens around my waist. "Remember the last time we danced, Tessa?"

Time shifts. Halloween. My wicked devil. I nod happily. This is sweet torture to be with him yet unable to have him. The dance ends and reluctantly we return to the table.

Michael is holding my mother's hand on the tabletop

and talking low but earnestly to her. I watch his thumb slide up and down her knuckles. I clench my legs with need for Grant. I wish he could hold my hand. I wish his fingers were on my knuckles. He meets my eyes and I know he knows just how I feel.

The conversation is light and general during dinner. I try not to let my eyes wander to Grant's too often. I know I won't be able to hide how I feel.

"How about going to a club for cordials and dancing?" Michael's eyes never leave my mother's though he's included Grant and me in the invitation.

"I'm afraid I have an early plane to catch tomorrow."

Disappointment rushes through me. We might have been able to dance again. I swallow and remain quiet.

"I'd like to, Michael," Mom says wistfully. I see his hand tighten on hers.

"Maybe you could drop us off, Grant, and I could pick up my car. "Oh," he says, suddenly remembering me. "We'd love for you to come with us, Tessa."

The tight smile is so strained. He is a nice man and a gentleman. "No, thank you, Michael. I have some things to do at home. I didn't expect to be out late."

"If Tessa doesn't mind she could lend you her car and I could drop her off on my way home. You can always take a taxi back to your place, Michael."

"That would be great." Eager eyes turn to me. "Would you mind, Tessa? I promise to take good care of it and your mother."

His smile is so charming I have to smile back despite the roaring in my ears. Leave it to Grant to figure out a way to be together.

"I don't mind in the least, Michael."

We part outside the door of the restaurant, Michael's desire to get my mother alone hardly hidden. Mom takes her time and prolongs his agony with inconsequential conversation until he finally takes her arm firmly and bids us good night. I stand amazed when Mom throws me a victorious smile over her shoulder.

The limousine pulls up and Clive opens the door. "How are you, Mr. Davis?"

"Fine, thank you, Clive." Grant removes his jacket and helps me into the back.

"Just drive around, Clive."

"Yes, sir."

The interior is dim. I watch the dark panel slide into place between us and Clive. For some inexplicable reason I feel suddenly shy. Strong fingers take my hand. Warm lips nuzzle my palm. An itch begins deep within me.

"I've missed you." His low words thrill me.

"I can't believe we're together."

I hear the automatic locks snick into place. The itch builds. Soft music floats over us. His arm pulls me close but he makes no move to kiss me. A thumb lightly traces the contour of my collarbone. And I wait.

The thumb glides along the same piece of skin over and over. I want to feel it on my breasts. I try to raise my shoulders slightly but the weight of his arm stays me.

"Grant..."

"Be quiet, Tessa." We sit side by side and his thumb continues its roving. Neck to shoulder. Neck to shoulder.

I don't understand. I watch the lights pass by the tinted windows and wait. The thumb moves infinitesimally lower and my breath quickens. The feel of his skin is so light. A mere inch of flesh roving small trails over my neck, shoulders, and almost but never quite touching my breasts. I'm almost dripping with anticipation.

Time moves slowly, and I finally give in and begin to squirm under the remorseless tracing of his finger. His pleased chuckle only ignites me more. I reach for him but he brushes my hands away.

Fingers deftly unbutton my dress. I love the feel of the cloth sliding over my skin when he pulls it over my head. Such a wicked feeling of freedom. I can see people walking along the sidewalks. Here I am stripping for my man and no one but us knows. It lends a deviltry to the simple act. I love it.

A slight pursing of his lips is the only sign of his disapproval when he sees my underwear. The bra is removed; my nipples crinkle when the air brushes them and then they pulse with want when I see his hungry expression. Panty hose and underpants are skimmed off my body. He pulls me to him and kisses me so thoroughly my head swims. The buttons of his shirt dig into my breast when he holds me close.

His tongue roves, ravages, strokes and caresses the insides of my mouth. I can't think clearly. Everything seems to center between my legs at this moment. I twine my fingers through his thick hair and return his passion. He pulls me over his legs and I sit astride him. The rough cloth of his suit both tickles and torments the insides of my thighs.

Grant's hands roam over my body. My hips gently grind into his lap. My buttocks are stroked and molded, his strong fingers digging and squeezing the flesh, the tips just brushing my netherlips. I push down to feel it more. They enter me and I move on them. His thumb seeks and finds my pulsing bud. His hand holds my head still as he continues to ravage my mouth. I can't breath enough air. My head swims, my heart races, my insides are turning to liquid fire. I'm mewling with need, desperate to have more, to have him deep inside me. My insides ache, swell, and then the lightest of pinches on my clit takes me over the edge. My screams of ecstasy are swallowed by him and then I'm released.

I slump against his strong chest and fight to breathe as my heart slackens its furious pace. My hips are still fluttering with the last sensations of passion. Grant holds me loosely, his warmth welcome in the coolish air. I shiver slightly and his hold tightens. Hands rub my back, caress my backside, explore my thighs. Over and over.

I'm turned and lie over his lap. I feel his need but he does nothing but stroke and caress my back, thighs, buttocks. His fingertips are so light, so tantalizing as they skim along my skin. My need is once again building.

I want him to be happy as I am. I try to rise but a light slap on my ass keeps me still. His hands are hypnotic, more so when he turns me onto my back and begins the same stroking on the front of my body. I lie under his ministrations and let sensation after sensation roll over my body. The buildup is so slow. So intense. So wonderfully compelling.

My breathing is becoming strained. Fingers lightly circle my shaved mound. Closer. Closer. I tense, waiting. Please. Please. I'm going to scream and then I do, but in bliss, not torment. The intensity takes me by surprise and I shake uncontrollably. Strong arms lift me and cuddle me close. I can't seem to stop shaking.

Warm lips brush my temples, skim my cheekbones,

and then claim my lips in the softest of kisses. I take a shaky breath and snuggle deep into his embrace. Grant places his jacket over me and I sigh with repletion.

The low hum of the engine and the warmth of his clasped arms lull me and I doze. I wake to his fingers stroking my nipples. His lazy smile makes me tingle.

"Are you going to sleep the rest of the night away, Tessa?"

Again the soft caress of my name on his lips. I smile and shake my head, sitting up straighter. "No. I don't want to waste a moment of it, Grant."

"Then help me."

I do, eagerly. Shifting to my knees I straddle his legs and begin to unbutton his shirt. I let my lips linger on his neck. I love the smell of his skin. My lips follow my fingers, each piece of exposed skin beneath a button kissed, licked, nuzzled. I rub my cheek against the coarseness of his chest hair and breathe in his scent. I love it and now begin to understand Dan's fascination with mine. I spread the shirt wide and rub my breasts against his skin. Large, turgid peaks brush and caress small, equally hard nipples. I love the feeling. Straightening, I feel the moistness of his tongue glide over first one peak and then the other. I have to clench my legs.

Sliding to the floor, I pull off his loafers. I peel the socks off his feet slowly and kiss the soft instep before sucking his big toe into my mouth. I hear his quick intake of breath. I love being able to excite him. To surprise him. My chin rubs up his trouser leg and I release the button and zipper. He's hard and ready. I work around his huge shaft without touching it in any way and take my time. My clit is throbbing.

My tongue follows the pants down his right leg and

then back up his left. I linger at the back of his knee, my fingers lightly rubbing along the tops of his thighs. When I glance up I see his penis rising off his flat belly. Ice blue eyes twinkle when they catch my pleased expression.

Grant's hands reach to pull me up, but I shake my head and he lowers them to his side. They're clenched. I love it. Taking my time, I let my tongue trace a path through the hairs on his thigh till I reach the crease where hip meets leg. His legs tense and I smile to myself. His scent is stronger here. I lick the crease from thigh to hip, blowing lightly against the moist path. I know the rubbery peaks of my breasts are teasing his thighs lightly. I know my hair is tickling his penis. Lowering my head, I rub my nose against the twin sacks, breathing in his wonderful male scent. His thighs tighten imperceptibly against the sides of my head. My tongue touches the hard, taut skin at the base of his tool and lazily makes a zigzag path upwards. Ice blue eyes glitter as they watch.

Slowly I swirl my tongue over the tip. It pulses at my touch. I suck and lick, relishing the feel of power, the knowledge that I can drive him just as crazy with desire as he does me. I'm pulled up suddenly and sit poised above him, his hands under my buttocks suspending me directly above the pointed tip of him.

"You are a witch, Tessa. A very sexy witch," he whispers. My body tingles. My vaginal muscles clench with anticipation and then slowly, so terribly, tortuously, painfully slowly, he lowers me down upon his throbbing manhood.

Exquisite torture as the thick member slowly slides an inch within me, pulling, stretching, titillating the thousands of nerve ends that line the spongy walls. Up again and then down but only an inch lower than the last time. He is making the journey last and last. An exquisite payback for torturing him. Heat flares, pulses, eddies out, and then focuses on a pinpoint of skin. Up. Down. Lower and lower until the touch of his belly rubbing against it as I end my downward journey shatters my determination to wait for him, and I whimper and then burst.

Warm lips suckle at my breasts, keeping time with the waning pulsations within me. I clasp his head tightly to me. Will it ever end? Do I want it to? Can they go on and on forever? Can you die from ecstasy?

Two hours later I'm so weak from his constant attention that Grant carries me to my bedroom. His prodigious control is both a pleasure and a torment for me. I don't even notice that my mother still has not returned home.

Mom is a different person. She smiles constantly and hums all day long. Never have so many men called. Never has my mother had so many dates. Never has one man arrived at our door more than Michael does each week. Mom goes out with him only once a week but always makes him welcome in our home. I can see how well her strategy is working. Michael is eaten up with jealousy.

I like him. He's confident, except where Mom is concerned. I think determined is a better word for his attitude about her. He doesn't mind lending a hand around the house. In fact he seems to always find the time to be fixing something just as Mom arrives home from another date. I have to smile at his tenacity at never leaving them alone. He joins right in their conversation or helps himself to a cup of coffee until the man finally gives up and leaves, usually without a chance to ask for another date or get a good-bye kiss. I always wonder what the men think about him being at our house so late sometimes. He's polite, well mannered, and just about at the end of his patience.

I wasn't surprised when Mom mentioned one Saturday that Michael had asked her to accompany him on a business trip to Hawaii.

"Are you going?"

She shook her head and sighed. "No. I would love to but it wouldn't be the right thing to do."

"Don't you think that's a little puritanical for this day and age? No one thinks twice of going off for a fun weekend anymore. Not even people of your generation."

Mom throws me a rueful smile and takes a sip of coffee. "It's not that, Tessa. If I went with Michael now, he'd lump me in with all the other women he's dated. I want him to want me, as a person, as an individual, before we get intimate. You must have had that special something with Greg that makes you want to be with just that person. Well, I want Michael and me to develop that special something so that he thinks of me as me and not just another quick weekend. I really like him, Tessa. I want him to really like me, too."

"But I know he likes you, Mom."

"Yes, I know he does but right now he thinks of me as a challenge. I'm waiting to see if it changes to something better."

The bell rang and I got up to answer it, not at all surprised to see Michael with a bag of pastries in his hand. "Am I too late for breakfast?"

"Mom's in the kitchen having coffee."

"Would you do me a favor, Tessa?"

"Sure."

"Would you give me a half hour alone with your mom? I want to talk to her privately."

He's edgy and it makes me smile with understanding. "No problem."

Twenty minutes later I hear the front door slam. Tires squeal for a second as a car hurtles down the street. Michael hadn't liked Mom's refusal to travel with him. When I enter the kitchen she doesn't look confident at all. She shrugs and gives me a hesitant smile.

"I guess I'll just have to wait and see."

Valentine's Day arrives and with it a huge bouquet of flowers and a note of apology from Michael. I swallow my jealousy and disappointment when I receive nothing. I hadn't really expected to but deep down inside I had hoped.

The week before winter recess I'm leaving my classroom at the end of the day and am surprised to find a nervous Michael outside in the hall. "Hello. What are you doing here?"

"Tessa, I need to talk to you."

"Is something wrong?"

"No. Well, yes. Well, not exactly." He takes a big breath and gives me a sheepish grin. "I need your help."

"I guess this has to do with my mother?"

"Look, can we go get a cup of coffee or something and I'll explain my problem?"

"Sure, Michael." His relief is so obvious it's almost comical. When we reach the town's one diner he leads me to the furthest booth. I feel like we're conspirators in a spy movie.

Tessa's Holidays

Michael takes my hands in his and looks deep into my eyes. "Tessa, I have to ask an enormous favor of you."

"Okay."

"I realize this is going to be a huge imposition, and I'm really putting you in a very awkward position but I'm getting desperate. Your mother is the stubbornnest woman I have ever met."

I have to smile. The poor man is obviously desperate about something.

"I guess your mother told you I asked her to go to Hawaii with me?" I nod and he gives a small snort of disgust. "I almost blew it completely doing that. I really thought she would never speak to me again."

Foolish man. "What is it you want, Michael? If you want me to talk my mother into going away with you I can tell you right now she would never go for it."

"I want you to go away with me."

"What?"

"No. No I mean I want you to go also so your mother will go with me." He runs his hands through his hair and gives an order to the waitress without consulting me. He's so distraught I feel a rush of compassion toward him.

"I work, Michael."

"That's the beauty of it, Tessa. I have to go to Rio de Janeiro the same week the school is out. That's what made me think of it."

Rio. My heart pounds with excitement. Sambas, beaches, cool drinks, nightlife. And me all alone. The excitement ebbs. I'd be a third wheel. I'd sit and watch them dance and then graciously accept the dances Michael would offer me out of politeness. I'd be with them knowing all the time that they'd like nothing better than for me to be somewhere else.

I shake my head slowly. "I don't believe it would work, Michael."

"Look, Tessa. I know how this sounds, but I'm sure if I could get your mother away from this confounded town I could show her how exciting life could be. With me." He licks his lips and doesn't quite meet my eyes. "Did your mother tell you I asked her to marry me?"

"What?"

"I didn't think she had." He suddenly seems a shell of the confident man I knew only a week ago. "I don't think she believes me that I care for her deeply. I think she's afraid I'd use her and then turn to another."

"Would you?"

"No. Never. I can't explain how I feel about her. I've never known anyone like her before. She's beautiful. Witty. Kind. Gentle. And the most sincere person I've ever met."

"I don't know what to say, Michael. I'd hate to feel like an intruder."

"Well, that's the other part of it. Look, I know he's a lot older than you, and I know you'd both probably like completely different things, but Grant Davis will be traveling with me and he could kinda be your escort."

My mouth is dry. My heart pounding. He misreads my expression. "Tessa, I realize that I'm asking a lot from you but think of it as a paid vacation. I'll pick up all costs, and you'll get to see a lot and do different things. Grant is really an interesting guy and I'm sure you would end up having a good time. Who knows, maybe you'll meet someone while we're there. I mean it's not like you'd have to be with Grant all the time.

He's older and probably would retire early each night. He's a good dancer and easy to talk to. Your days would be your own because we'd be doing business most of the time and…and I'll beg you if that's what it takes."

It takes everything I have to remain outwardly calm. Grant. I'd be with Grant. Could I do it? Could I play the role? Could I fool everyone that I wasn't madly wild about this man? Would we be able to find time alone?

If anyone could arrange it, it would be Grant.

"Does Mr. Davis know of your plans?"

"He said it's fine with him if you can cope with being with an old geezer."

An old geezer. I can't stop the smile that spreads my lips. Grant puts many, many younger men to shame. "What about my mother?"

"I wanted to know if you'd be willing first." His eagerness is contagious, and I let the smile spread my lips fully.

"If you can convince my mother, you've got a deal, Michael."

He lets out a bark of excitement, jumps up from the table, and grabs me into his arms and spins me around. Shocked eyes swivel from stools and booths. Tongues will wag steadily for the rest of the day. Michael places me on my feet, gives me one more big hug and then stands there grinning at me. "Now to convince your mother."

He almost looks terrified.

I dally away the rest of the afternoon and early evening. I don't want to walk in on Michael before he can convince my mother to go. I don't know if I could cope with being so close to spending time with Grant and losing it.

The stores offer an array of clothes in their windows. A bright red lace teddy catches my eye. Would Grant like it? He doesn't care for any undergarments at all. Would he appreciate it if it was all I was wearing?

I pass by all the sexy lingerie. No sense in spending the money if I won't find anyone to appreciate it. Would Grant like to see me in leather? Latex? I wonder briefly if Godfrey sells things like that or if he only sells restraints.

Jack was big on bondage. And if I'm honest with myself, sometimes being bound makes the waiting more bearable. To keep one's hands at one's sides voluntarily when someone is driving one to distraction with his tongue is infinitely harder than being bound and helpless to fight it. There is a certain slick thrill to being at someone's mercy.

I wonder if Martine is still with Jack. He spoke so easily of selling her into permanent slavery. He thinks nothing of giving pain, in fact by the quickness of his actions I'd have to surmise he enjoys it immensely. I know he likes having people under his control. Helpless. Frightened. I think if Jack becomes bored with Martine it will be for that reason alone. Martine began to love being a slave. She thrilled to the punishments. The demands placed on her. When Jack ran out of new things to torment her with he'd lose interest quickly. He wanted her fear, not her compliance.

He still frightens me. I don't think Jack has any limits. He likes to keep you on edge constantly. I hope I don't see him again.

I'm in swimsuits. Rio is a place where everyone wears string bikinis whether they should or not. Memories of the scrap of material I wore on Long Island float through my mind. The bottoms had floated out to sea when Grant ripped them from me.

Had a boater found the torn scrap of material and wondered at the meaning? Had he conjured up wild fantasies of his own about how the unknown girl might have been captured and abused? Had he gotten an erection substituting himself in the unknown villain's stead? What had he visualized?

A young girl bound and gagged and hustled onto a boat to be used at his will whenever he wished or not? Did he wish to beat her? To cause her pain? To pump his hardness into her vagina till she swooned, or into her ass till she screamed in surrender?

Or was it her mouth he craved? To feel her lips soft and warm around his shaft. The moist tongue gently licking the vent and ridge as he pumped in and out?

Or did he visualize a harsher scene? Was she tied, stretched to her limit and totally helpless before him? Did he wish to crush her breasts with the weight of his body as he sat on her helpless flesh? Did he wish to use her mouth viciously? Hard and cruelly? To pummel his thickened shaft into her till he bruised the back of her throat?

Or would maybe a younger man find the scrap of material? Would his visions be about lying on the beach with the girl of his dreams? He would overwhelm her with his kisses, his hands and their knowing ways. Would he see himself infallible in his approach to overcome all her whispered protests? Did he daydream about sliding the tiny piece of material over her hips and off her legs? Did he push himself into her in his fantasies or slowly enter her and entice her to join his special dance? Did he wish to be her master either willingly or unwillingly? Or did he only wish to reach his goal?

What are a young man's dreams? Are they so very different from a young girl's?

"Hi, Tessa."

I jump, startled out of my reverie by the sound of my friend's voice.

"Hi, Kathy."

"Getting a jump on the new swimsuit styles?"

I look at the piece of material in my hand and feel my cheeks pink. "No. I guess I was just wondering how someone could actually wear so little. I don't think I'd feel comfortable."

Kathy looks down at her very ample figure and grins ruefully. "I don't think it would cover me. I'd end up arrested!"

We laugh and then agree to a hamburger at the diner for our dinner. Kathy and I have been friends since grade school, but even though we're two of the very few who never left town after graduation, we rarely seem to see much of each other. Reminiscing helps the time pass quicker, and then I head for home.

My mother is pacing up and down the living room. "Where have you been?"

"I met up with Kathy and we had dinner at the diner. I thought you'd want time with Michael, Mom."

"So you know."

"Yes. He thought it better to see if I would agree before he spoke to you. I think it's a wonderful idea."

"You do?"

I've never seen my mother so unsure of herself. "Don't you think it would give you a good chance to see Michael in different situations? Right now you don't know much about him because you've purposely kept him at arm's distance. This way you'll see him morning and night. Good days and bad days. It's a great way to get to know him, and Mom—Rio!"

My mother clasps her arms around herself and takes a deep breath. "I know. I've thought of nothing since Michael left here this afternoon. I've never really traveled. Your Dad and I went to Niagara Falls on our honeymoon, but that's really all I've done." She chews her lip and raises tentative eyes to me. "Do you really think it's a good idea?"

I have to keep the desperate need for her to agree to this out of my voice. I almost choke with the effort and cough to cover it up. "I think you couldn't ask for better. As I said, it's a great way to get to know him without becoming too intimate if you don't wish to. You and I will share a room and so will he and Mr. Davis. You'll see him for breakfast, possibly lunch, I assume dinner and at night. Maybe you'll meet some of his clients, and then you'll be able to judge him that way, too."

My mother stares at the floor for a long moment and then lifts her head and winks at me. "I'll call him now."

We're on the plane by ourselves. A last-minute matter came up, and Grant has sent Mom and me ahead. The men will follow later tonight. I don't by so much as a blink of an eye let on that I've been on this plane before.

Mom's cries of surprise when she sees the bedroom do nothing but remind me of my cries of pain and wonder that I experienced in the bed. I meet Bill's eyes steadily with an effort, and he does the same with no effort. Rodney has trained him well. Mom's excitement seems to have wiped out all her normal "Mom knows all your moods and thoughts," and I'm eternally grateful. I'm not as well trained as Bill. Is that what I'm becoming? Trained?

I don't like the thought. I love my independence. I love being my own person. But I also love being with Grant. I love the sights and sounds and smells I've experienced with him. I love the long, slow sessions of making love. I love it when our hot, slick bodies move as one. I love the quick, frantic couplings. I love the heady nights of primal, animalistic pleasure.

Sometimes I even like the pain.

I peer out the window and sigh. The thought both excites and frightens me. If I begin to love the pain then I become dependent on him. What would the average man say if on a date he asks to spend the night and I say, yes, of course, but only if you'll torment me both sexually and physically? I could just imagine the reaction I'd get. And truth to tell I doubt I'd ever trust anyone as I do Grant. And trust is the one essential that allows me to put myself into his hands as I do whenever we're able to get together.

Grant never seems to lose control. He always seems to sense when I've had enough. And he doesn't seek to give me pain. He'd rather torment me with the tips of his fingers and his exciting tongue and his prodigious penis than use the belt or flat of his hand. Those I seem to bring on myself. I wonder if subconsciously I do it on purpose. I don't think so. But still I can't quite bury the thought.

The flight is long but the time passes quickly for us as we talk and read about Rio. Mom and I change out of our warm woolens and into lightweight dresses. I hold my breath when Mom peeks into the closet, but only men's clothes hang on the hangers. I'm not surprised. Grant always takes care of everything.

Bill is quiet but attentive, and I keep the smile on my face when my mother suggests that I might want to get to know such a handsome, well-mannered man. Little does she know how well I know him. Little does she know what he prefers to do to women. Little does she know that he belongs to another. And Rodney is a very jealous lover. I wonder what happened to Miguel?

The airport is crowded with milling people and we both stand off to the side, a little overcome by the hustle and bustle of the mass of humanity. I hear first one language and then another and my head is whirling. Suppose we can't find a cabdriver who speaks English? And then Clive is directly in front of us.

"Mrs. Duncan. Mrs. Fortuna. My name is Clive and I'm Mr. Davis's chauffeur. Please follow me and I'll take you to the hotel."

My mother sighs with relief and flashes me a slightly weary smile. "Thank God, Tessa. I don't know how we would have managed. I never thought about getting to the hotel. Suppose the cab drivers didn't speak English?"

Another well-trained servant. Clive hadn't batted an eyelash. My mother stops just before entering the limousine. "How did you know it was us, Clive?"

I hold my breath. "Mr. Davis faxed me your pictures and names, ma'am."

"Well, wasn't that thoughtful of him. He really does seem to be a very nice gentleman, doesn't he, Tessa? I hope you find his company pleasant. I can't tell you how much I appreciate you doing this for me. I mean, he's even older than me and probably won't be too much for the lively nightlife I've read about."

"Don't give it a thought, Mom. You know me. I'd just as soon visit the museums and such as go dancing all night. That could get boring very quickly."

"Oh, Tessa, I wish you'd loosen up a little. You've always been so studious. Let loose and live a little for a change. There's more to life than school and books."

"We'll see," I answer vaguely and turn to look out the window and hide my smile.

Ipanema is a mixture of charming private homes and luxurious high-rises. Lush tropical vegetation peeks out here and there between buildings and seems to spill down from the mountainsides almost to the beach. People stand under the shade of the many palm trees as they wait for buses to arrive. Vendors at the colorful corner stands sell tropical fruit juices, and cafes abound. And the beach stretches out wide and beautiful, the many people enjoying its beauty seeming to enhance its allure instead of detracting from it.

I watch the palm leaves sway in the breeze, and I tingle wondering what exotic, mysterious scents they will convey. I love the breezes of foreign lands. They promise so much. They entice and lure one to seek more. Grant has taught me to want more. To anticipate. To revel in. To open myself to new adventures.

I can't wait to start this one.

The hotel is beautiful. The room is light and airy. A balcony shows us the length of Ipanema and some of Copacabana. Sugar Loaf rises majestically in front of us. The ocean sparkles beyond. It's breathtaking. I want to breath it all in at once and learn its essence.

Tessa's Holidays

Vitality throbs and shimmers through the air. People, very scantily clad people, from all walks of life, seem to burst with energy on the beach. They swim, run, chase, play ball, and some just lie still and have a quiet, passionate affair with their god the sun.

Music drifts up to me. The air vibrates with the sound of the samba and then slowly drifts away as the car playing it moves along. I can still feel the beat within me. It calls as if daring me to let go and move to it. I want to. I want to be in the midst of it and let it hum along my naked body till I move as it wants me to. Alone. With Grant. Skin to skin. Hot. Slick. Pulsating.

"Isn't this lovely, Tessa?" Mom's excited voice breaks the spell. My mouth is dry. My breathing rapid. I have to swallow twice before I can answer calmly.

"Beautiful." I turn back into the room. A maid is unpacking our suitcases. "Shall we get some sun so we have a little color when the men arrive?"

"Good idea."

I go into the bathroom to change, and when I come out I stare in surprise. My mother has on a one-piece suit that is so low cut I swear she'll fall out of it. Her figure is good and the suit ensures that any part of her that isn't perfection will be missed. I cannot imagine anyone being able to look away from her neckline. Neckline? The top of her suit is nowhere near her neck.

"Too daring?"

"Not if you want to see Michael drool."

"That might be fun," she giggles and then slips her feet into a pair of sandals. Her cover-up is sheer cotton, very feminine and almost see-through.

As I slip the lightweight robe over my own skimpy suit I can't help but feel that Michael doesn't stand a chance.

The sun is hot. Almost too hot but the breeze makes it more than bearable. The scenery makes it all worthwhile. The statue of Jesus looks down lovingly at us, and Sugar Loaf juts out of the Atlantic before us. Two sentinels watching over man.

Beautiful women seem to be everywhere. Handsome men abound. Young couples walk hand in hand along the warm sand. I wish it could be me and Grant. The thought of being so close to him and unable to hold him or reminisce makes me tremble. How will I keep from slipping and saying something wrong? How will I restrain myself from touching him? How will I keep the yearning I'll feel out of my eyes? This will be more tortuous than anything he's ever asked of me.

The sound of a band in the distance lends a backdrop of heady excitement to the quiet, steady cadence of the small waves. Palm trees sway. The breeze gently kisses my skin, and I shut my eyes and listen to the sounds around me.

Different tongues swell and ebb with the breeze. It seems that people from every country are passing by my towel. I hear the babble of one replaced by another. Over and over. I try to guess where each comes from without opening my eyes. The change is too quick and too often for me to guess, and I give it up.

The sun is so very hot. Mom strolls down to the water to cool off. I sit and rub suntan oil onto my skin. It's so slippery. Immediately I imagine Grant and me here together. I feel his strong fingers spreading the slick unguent over my body. Over and over. My nipples harden with want. I have to swallow and clench my legs tightly together. I'll never get through this week.

I watch my mother in the surf. A middle-aged man

approaches her and tries to start a conversation. Even from here I can see his eyes ogling her deep cleavage. She's polite for a minute and then tries to move off. His hand stays her. I can see she's becoming frightened and I rise to go to her, but then a tall, well-built young man intervenes and the older man's hand is slowly but deliberately removed from her arm. Clive returns with my mother.

"I can't thank you enough, Clive." My mother is almost breathless. She's upset.

"My pleasure, ma'am. I'll move my towel beside you so no one bothers you further."

"Are you all right, Mom?"

She gives me a shaky smile. "Yes. Of course. I guess it startled me to be set upon like that. He just wouldn't take no for an answer. I'm not used to dealing with men like that."

Clive places his towel down and promptly lies on his stomach and closes his eyes. I should've realized that Grant would never leave me alone when I was away from home. I'm glad now he hadn't.

I can't resist taking an inventory of Clive's body. He's big. Probably at least six foot three or six foot four and burly but muscular. I've never seen him in anything but his uniform. I can't help but wonder why Grant hasn't included him in any of our scenarios. He must know. How could he not? Maybe he wasn't interested? How couldn't he be?

All too soon it seems we must return or our too-white skin will be too red the next day. Clive escorts us back and we're delighted to meet the men in the lobby. My heart picks up speed when I meet Grant's twinkling eyes. My belly twists with yearning, and my nipples harden. Grant's eyes crinkle with the knowledge and it just makes the wanting worse.

Michael's eyes are bulging at the sight of my mother's suit. His eyes swivel around to see who else is watching, and my mother chatters away happily as if totally oblivious. By the twinkle in her eyes I realize she knows exactly what she's doing. Michael almost sweeps us into the elevator in his haste to remove her from public view.

Michael's room is down the hall. Then Clive, Rodney, and Bill's room. Then ours. Then Grant's.

We shower and dress and then meet in the lobby for drinks and dinner. Clive is at the limousine door, and we enter the cool, luxurious interior of the car. Drinks are poured and general conversation passes between us. I scrupulously avoid Grant's eyes. I want nothing more than to be beside him, holding his hand, feeling his strong body next to mine.

We enter one of the many *churrascarias* and the aroma of grilled steaks hits us at once. Mom and I can do nothing but laugh when our dinner arrives. The portions are huge and the little we consume is ludicrous indeed. Even the men have trouble finishing the meal.

We linger over cordials. The balmy night is so soothing. Lights on the many boats docked in the harbor twinkle at us. I can't stop my sigh of contentment.

"It is a lovely sight, isn't it?"

I nod to Grant's observation. "It is indeed." I wish I could take his hand and hold it as we share the beauty around us.

The day has been a long, exciting one, and I can't suppress the yawn that takes me. "Tired, Tessa?"

I hear the tinge of regret in Mom's voice. "A little. Why don't you two go on and maybe Mr. Davis would escort me for a moonlit walk along the beach back to the hotel."

"Call me Grant."

I smile and try to keep the eagerness from my voice. "What say you, Grant? Would you mind a slow walk and an early night?"

"It would be my pleasure."

Michael and Mom make no protest, and we leave the car and Clive to them to use to explore the nightspots. The beach is almost deserted. Only a few couples seem to linger, unwilling to let the night end their happy moments on the beach. Grant and I are silent for a long time.

Strong fingers curl through mine and I look up and smile. "Clive told me what happened at the beach. I don't want you or your mother being alone. Take Bill or Rodney or Clive with you from now on."

"If my mother and I are together we'll be fine, Grant."

"I wasn't asking you, Tessa." The no-nonsense, determined voice that is always so low and quiet. I resent it somehow.

"This is not your trip, Grant. We don't have to follow your rules this week."

"You're absolutely right. This is for Michael and your mother." His lips on my fingers distract me. I wish it could be more. I wish he would at least kiss me, but we have no idea how long Michael and my mother will be gone. Maybe it would be harder if he did kiss me?

I never should let his actions distract me from his words. I should know better than that by now. How can such an intelligent person as I fall into the same trap twice and not learn a lesson from it?

The day dawns bright and sunny as usual in Rio, and we join Michael and Grant on Michael's terrace for a leisurely morning meal. The sky is so blue, and the breakfast portions are so enormous. Is it all the dancing everyone does down here that gives them the appetite to eat such huge meals?

Mom and Michael can't seem to look at anything but each other. Jealousy and envy spoil what little appetite I have. I hate myself for feeling this way.

The men leave for a business meeting and, after watching Rodney and Bill run across the street to the beach, I turn to my mother. "How would you love to be daring?"

"What kind of daring?"

"I was speaking to the maid this morning, and she told me of a secluded cove where we could go bathing in the nude."

"Tessa!"

"Oh, come on, Mom. Haven't you ever wanted to swim naked?"

"Well…"

"Let's do it! Why not? Who's to know?" I see her faltering. "You might never get another chance, Mom."

"All right. As long as it is secluded. And deserted. And you're sure no one will come. No one!"

I check to make sure Bill and Rodney are still on the beach before we leave the room. We giggle and grab our gear and get into the taxi like two naughty schoolgirls cutting school. I relax completely when I see Rodney and Bill not looking toward us as the taxi leaves the hotel. Clive is driving the men to their meeting.

We give the driver the instructions and he knows immediately where I mean. He drops us off and agrees to pick us up in two hours.

Tessa's Holidays

How do I explain this place? It's a small stretch of sand behind a small hill of lush vegetation. The flowers are indescribable. I almost feel as if Tarzan will swing out of the jungle at any moment. I wish Grant would. The water is gorgeous. The sand pristine. The air is clean and clear. The sun is hot. The place is isolated and we're completely alone.

We look at each other and shrug. "Well?"

Mom drops her towel and cover-up. "Why not?"

We both hastily drop our suits before we lose courage, and then run splashing into the water. It's warm and calm. It's silky and absolutely delightful. We swim and float. Mom isn't a strong swimmer so we stay close to shore.

"Oh, Tessa, this was a wonderful idea!"

"It is nice, isn't it?" I murmur and float on my back, the sun warm on my breasts. The time seems to fly by and then the impatient sound of a horn calls us away from our idyll.

Dinner is again delicious. And too much. We leave the restaurant too full to sit so we decide to stroll along toward another part of the city. Clive follows at a discreet distance behind us. Mom and Michael walk in front of us.

"Did you have a nice day?"

I think back to the morning and smile. "Yes, very nice. Mom and I went to the Museum Nacional de Belas Artas this afternoon. It was fascinating."

"Yes, it is." We walk a little further and then Michael and Mom are starting back to us. Michael lifts his hand and Clive pulls the car up immediately. A group of young street toughs are coming down the opposite side of the street. We quickly duck into the car and pull away before any trouble can start.

"Since Rio is sometimes known as the street-crime capital of the world, I see no reason to invite trouble."

"I agree with you, Michael. Maybe it would be wise if either Rodney, Clive, or Bill accompanied the ladies while we're unavailable."

"I think that's an excellent idea, Grant. You wouldn't mind, would you, Millie?"

"No. Not at all. In fact I think it's a great idea. Thank you, Grant."

I swear I can feel his Cheshire-smug grin.

We join a throng of people on line to enter a huge place that is more like a stadium than a dance club. The stage is filled with percussion instruments. Excitement ripples through the air. The band is going to rehearse for Carnaval, and the people are eager and waiting to move to its beat.

I count ten tambourines, ten snare drums, ten bass drums, and two of the largest drums I've ever seen in my life. The music begins and without thought everyone starts to move to the incessant, hypnotic beat. The sound vibrates inside of you and seems to take over your body. My pelvis actually throbs, and a perverse need takes me while I stand gyrating in the midst of hundreds of people.

It is a living thing, this beat. The people become almost as one no matter what their age or shape. Fat people seem to become graceful. The old take on new vitality. And the young just let go and enjoy, enjoy, enjoy.

I become separated from Grant and my mother and Michael. The beat is wild, insistent. Hands and weaving hips seem to propel me further and further from where I started. I feel no fear. Nothing but the need to move. To grind my hips—and I do. I'm looser, easier in my movements than ever before in my life. The sound invades my soul and my body responds with a will of its own.

The music is loud, all-encompassing. My chest vibrates with the percussion. A woman faces me and catches my eye. Her head is thrown back but she maintains eye contact. I've never seen such sultry eyes. They're liquid, huge, and so inviting. They almost suck me in with unspoken promises. I can't drop my eyes from her and feel as if she's making love to me across the mere two feet separating us. Her hips move and sway. The gentle mounds of her breasts bounce seductively beneath the thin material of her dress. The way the material hugs her I know she's naked underneath, and I feel a sexual thrill streak through my body. Her smile is mesmerizing, her movements nothing but pure eroticism. As if in a dream, I take a step toward her but am blocked by a thrashing, gyrating, male form, and then when he moves she's gone. I can't describe the feeling of loss that fills me.

"Ah, there you are, Tessa. We got separated in the melee." Grant is smiling at me, his words barely audible above the music. I smile, still thrown by my reaction to the woman. His strong fingers on my lower back slowly but skillfully guide me back to my mother and Michael. They're caught up in the movements of the samba and have no eyes but for each other. I don't think my mother realizes just how far gone she is on this man. Whether they know it or not they are making love to each other. If Grant looked at me the way they are looking at each other, I don't think I'd hesitate to rip off his clothes right in the midst of this pulsating crush of humanity and have him then and there.

But Grant has too much control to lose himself in the moment.

We share a last nightcap when we finally drag our tired, heated bodies from the crowd and let Clive bring us back to the hotel. My mother takes quite a long time saying good night to Michael. I'm almost asleep when I hear her entering the room. Her huge yawn only reminds me how tired I am, and I drift off immediately.

I'm awakened by a hand clamping over my mouth, hard. I struggle to clear my sleep-drugged mind, one part refusing to think, the other silently screaming in terror. A thick piece of tape covers my mouth, a piece of cloth my eyes. I'm flipped and my arms stretched up. Leather encases my wrists. I'm bound to the bed. My ankles are held motionless by strong hands. My hips are lifted and pillows wedged tightly beneath my stomach. My nightgown is pushed up around my waist. My muffled screams seem to go unheard. I feel two strong hands clamp down harder on my ankles, and my legs are pulled apart and held down tightly to the bed.

The pain is so unexpected. Five slashes of something viciously thin. One on top of another. And then I'm filled. No preparation. No help. Just pain and stretching. It has to be Grant. I'm almost choking on my tears as my ass bucks and humps against the pain that is now both inside and out. His fingers are cruel on my hips.

I hear his grunt only after a long time and then he pulls out. A hiss sounds as if from a distance and then more pain directly on the same spot as before. My ass is on fire, screams ringing in my ears but hardly heard above the tape. Why doesn't my mother wake up?

Again I'm penetrated. It only takes a second to realize it's Bill. None other would be so vicious in his movements. He takes pleasure in grabbing and digging his fingers into the welts on my ass. He's done. The pain again. Again in the same place. Right across the fatty parts of my ass. It must be a riding crop.

And then again I'm penetrated. I don't know by whom. He's long and thin and stabs more than pumps. I can't take any more. I can feel myself starting to let go. A quick hiss of indrawn breath and he's finished. But Rodney isn't. Five more vicious swipes. Again right where he'd done it before.

Hands release my hips and I collapse on the pillows, squirming and wriggling in torment. I'd forgotten how much it hurts. My wrists are released and I hug my own body tight, trying to fight the waves of pain. The tape is removed. I feel a breath on my ear.

"Let's see you parade that ass around naked tomorrow, Tessa."

And then nothing but my muffled sobs. I don't hear them leave. I don't care about anything but my fiery ass. I look across the room and see the still shape of my mother in the dim light. When I hold my breath I hear her steady breathing. How could she not have heard my muffled shrieks?

I pull in a couple of shaky breaths and ease out of the bed. I let the cold water of the shower lightly hit my ass for fifteen minutes. The pain is now tolerable. Just.

I don my nightgown and reenter the room. Curious, I go to my mother's bed and shake her shoulder. She gently snores on. I can't wake her. Detail-oriented Grant has taken care of everything as he usually does so he could get his own way.

How had he found out?

I am so stiff the next morning it is an agony for me to get dressed. I remain in the bathroom with the door locked so my mother can't walk in on me.

A quick tap on the door makes me hurry. "Tessa, do you want to go back to the lagoon like yesterday?"

"No!" My answer is too quick and strident. I take a deep breath and continue. "No. Let's try not to do the same thing twice, Mom. There's so much out there to see."

"Oh. Okay. If that's what you'd like." I can hear the disappointment but don't care. Grant doesn't care that this isn't his trip. He's stilling playing by his rules and I can't afford to anger him after last night. I couldn't take another like it.

My ass is actually hot to the touch. A bathing suit is out of the question today. Anything tight or clinging is also out. The weals are still raised and puffy. Actually, it's more like one thick one. Rodney has only covered an inch-and-a-half area across the width of my ass. I would rather have had them spread over my entire body.

I wish I could smack off the bright smile Grant flashes my way when we all meet for breakfast.

Sitting is a new experience in pain. I quickly suggest a long walking tour to my mother and almost cry with relief when she agrees. Grant and Michael still insist we be accompanied, and it's decided Rodney will escort us because he's proficient in Portuguese.

My mother is completely oblivious to my pain and Rodney's silent enjoyment of it. He constantly leads us to benches to take a break from our walks. I know he seeks out the steepest steps. He tends to walk directly behind me as we climb and descend. I can feel his eyes on my ass. Probably gloating. Probably wishing he could see the weals. If it didn't throb so much I'd wiggle it to make him angry. Thank God there's no breeze to lift my flared skirt and expose my nakedness to the world.

Mom is tireless in her pursuit to see as much as possible. We walk amidst the old colonial buildings in the downtown area of Centro. The modern skyscrapers that intersperse the older buildings seem unexpectedly right. We stroll along the wide boulevards, the side streets so narrow it seems unlikely cars could travel them but do. We linger in the grand public plazas and marvel at the many movie theaters that crowd the area. People seem to shop in waves, first one group of one language passing, then another. It's wonderful. It's exciting. It's fascinating. And my body is screaming.

I don't know how I manage to make it to late afternoon. A cooling shower helps only slightly, and I finally stop trying and plead a massive headache so I'll be left alone. It doesn't take much to convince Mom to leave with Michael and Grant for dinner.

I wait a good half hour to make sure she won't change her mind and return, and then and only then do I give in to my tears of self-pity and pain. The letting go is such a relief, and after a long time I finally feel calmer, more able to cope.

A quiet knock on the door arouses me. "Your dinner, ma'am."

Grant follows the waiter into my room. "Your mother ordered you something to eat, Mrs. Duncan. Are you feeling better?"

"Yes. Thank you, Mr. Davis. The worst of the pain seems to have eased."

I hand the waiter his tip and he bows once and takes his leave. I feel awkward suddenly being alone with

Grant and hug my robe tighter to my body. My ass seems to start tingling all over when I see his penetrating stare. I lift the cover of the chafing dish for something to do.

"I love your attempts at insouciance, Tessa."

His half-mocking, half-chuckling sentence makes me smile despite my resolve. "I should be furious with you, Grant Davis."

"Why? You know by now what happens when you defy me." His fingers lift my chin. "I really do wonder if you don't ask for it sometimes, Tessa."

I pull my chin from him and walk to the balcony. "I can't go swimming. I can't enjoy the sights. I certainly won't be able to dance tonight or tomorrow."

"And whose fault is that, Tessa?"

I absolutely hate it when he becomes condescending. "I am not a child, Grant! I am certainly capable of making decisions about my own welfare."

"The very seclusion you sought could have become your tomb, Tessa. This isn't downtown Iowa. Did it never occur to you that the very people who urge you to go to these out-of-the-way places might have an ulterior motive?"

"A maid in the hotel?"

He leans against the corner of a table and folds his arms across his chest. "Was she?"

"Well, of course she was! Why else would she be dressed as one and be here?"

"Was she here in your room? Was she cleaning up? Making your bed? Did you ask her about a place you could skinny-dip?"

I can feel the blood leaving my face. She'd been in the hall. Now that I think of it, she was almost standing around as if waiting for someone. And she had approached me. All smiles. All eagerness to make suggestions.

Grant's arms wrap around me from behind. "Now do you understand?"

His breath is so warm, so tickly against my neck. Reluctantly, I nod and pull my hips forward away from contact with him. "Who watched us?"

"Clive. I didn't trust your acquiescence so we took a cab to the meeting. After having to watch you cavorting naked all morning I thought it only fair that you relieve some of his frustration that night."

Clive had been the last to use me. I shiver and feel my face flush. I need to get away from Grant's nearness. It makes thinking hard. "But we weren't disturbed."

"Of course not. The sight of Clive with an automatic rifle was more than enough to turn the three men away."

Reality crashes down on me and I begin to shake. "Relax, Tessa. It's over. Nothing happened."

I'm turned in his arms and held gently. Warm lips kiss my terrified eyes closed. I shiver with reaction and the feel of a moist tongue making its lazy way down my neck. My robe falls to the ground. My nipples harden. I hold my breath, waiting.

And then his lips grab my breast and suck, and a bolt of pure lust streaks to my loins. My body tightens, loosens, and then just throbs with need. His lips are so gentle. So insistent. So provocative. So downright tantalizing I almost sink to my knees, but he beats me to it and traces wet, noisy paths to my belly.

His chin grazes my thick thatch. I almost moan. My clit is throbbing, pulsing, yearning for his touch. Waves of need ripple along my skin and center deep within me. His scratchy cheek lightly rubs my belly. His lips browse along the crease of my hip. Lower. Lower. Lower till I can barely breathe, the anticipation is so great. And then I'm devoured. The is no other word for the feeding frenzy he begins, and I'm lost in a whirling maelstrom of rampant unleashed lust. I grind myself onto his ravishing mouth and barely contain my whimpers of need that quickly escalate to muffled keenings of unbelievable bliss.

I sleep the sleep of a baby.

The men take the next day off and we all spend a delightful day at the beach. My new one-piece suit is a little uncomfortable, but I'm not willing to forego a day of fun because of a sore ass. I think the exercise of playing ball and walking and swimming actually helps loosen the stiffness. Grant and I spend a lot of time alone because my mother and Michael keep wandering off on their own, each time for longer and longer periods. I only wish I knew where they went and how long they'd be gone. I'd love to do more than talk to Grant during their absences. Frustration has to be one of the worst feelings in the world.

I enjoy our conversation enormously. Grant is amazing in his worldliness. He's so well read there are few subjects he can't converse on intelligently, and we hardly realize how late it is, our conversation is so interesting, our arguments defending our own points of view so intense.

I suddenly realize that the beach is slowly becoming deserted. The shade beneath the beach umbrella is no longer necessary. Grant and I look at each other and smile. "I've missed these long talks," he says.

I wish I could hold his hand. I wish I could run my

fingers across his coarse chest hair. I sigh instead. "So have I."

He grins wickedly. "Do we dare return to the rooms?"

I don't think it's funny. I can't quite mask the bitter sarcasm from seeping into my voice. "I guess I know why you two have separate rooms, don't I?"

My jealousy is so obvious, Grant chuckles. "Actually it was my idea, not Michael's. I said I was a loud snorer so Michael would get his own room with the hope of enticing you into my room as often as feasible."

I'm not amused by his cavalier attitude and ignore him as I gather up our towels and paraphernalia. Grant takes my arm and stops my progress toward the hotel. "Tessa, I hope you realize by now that your time with your mother is very limited. I know you don't want to spoil your mother's happiness with your too-obvious resentment, so I suggest you make up your mind to the marriage. Michael is just about at his wit's end. I really wouldn't be surprised if we're asked to stand as witnesses before the end of the week."

"What? That's ridiculous, Grant. My mother isn't some young girl who would rush into anything like this. And...and even if she did decide to marry Michael, she would talk to all of us first. Why, Joe would be crushed if he didn't perform the ceremony."

I hate the sound of my own peevishness. I sound like a spoiled young child and despise myself for it. Why should I deny my mother a chance of being happy? Because I'm jealous. Terribly, terribly jealous. I want to be able to be open with Grant. I want to be able to be with him whenever and wherever I want. I want what my mother has.

I flush when I see him reading me so clearly. Strong fingers lift my chin, and reluctantly I meet his eyes. They're tender, not mocking. "Maybe someday."

I bite my lip and nod. At least he didn't mock my feelings. I wonder if he feels the same?

Thank God for the talk we had, because Michael and my mother are in the lobby waiting for us. Dressed. Suitcases at their feet. Guilty, excited faces beam at us. I know before either one speaks. One look at their left hands confirms it. They're married. They couldn't even wait to ask us to witness their marriage.

Quick explanations, apologies, kisses, hugs, more kisses, more apologies, more hugs, and then Michael is leading my mother away for their honeymoon on a remote island in the Caribbean. By the look in his eye it is going to be a long one.

Grant and I stand silently in the lobby and watch them leave. I'm torn by so many conflicting emotions until it suddenly occurs to me that Grant and I are alone. No Mom. No Michael. No one knows us here.

Our eyes meet. Our smiles match. And we return upstairs without another word.

My skin is alive. Tingling. Goose bumps erupt all over me. His hand taking my elbow makes me shiver with need. He guides me to his room. It's larger than mine and has a sitting room.

"Go shower."

The bathroom is spacious. A sunken tub fills one side of the room. The shower stall is large and transparent. I peel the suit from my body. I feel as if I'm in a dream. We're alone. All alone. We have four days of being together.

The water is cool. My body throbs. Heat is steadily building within me. Four days with Grant. Four tropical days of being together. Had he arranged this also?

The door opens and I don't turn. I raise my arms to the coolness. Warm hands take my breasts from behind and knead them gently. I keep my hands raised, my face to the flow of cool water. Fingertips on nipples and I give in and turn around.

Crinkling blue eyes. Sensuous lips. The touch of coarse gray hair against my nipples sends shock waves through me. Our kiss is so slow. So searching. So wonderful. I'm lifted, poised, and I wrap my legs around his waist. And then I feel it. I open my legs wider. Wider still and feel the full, puffy lips spread to let him enter. Slowly he lowers me and indescribable sensations ripple through me as he fills me totally.

Lifted, lips nibble on rubbery hard peaks, my legs clench, my breathing quickens. I'm lowered. I sigh. I love this. His hands move me gently up and down. Lips kiss eyes, mouth, breasts, neck, and then start all over. I try to quicken the pace but his hands keep me going slowly. The buildup is so slow. So wonderfully tormenting. So exquisite when it reaches its peak.

I'm carried, dripping wet, into the sitting room and out to the balcony. He's still inside me. I rest contentedly against his strong chest. His shaft pulses within me. Grant sits on a cushioned chair, and I lie against him as my heartbeat slowly decreases. His fingertips lightly play over the small ridge of my welts. I finally rouse myself and push up from him. His blue eyes crinkle at me.

I shift my position so I sit astride him more comfortably. "I've missed you."

"I've missed you, too." Our lips meet and I sigh with happiness. He is so tender sometimes. So passionately loving. My hips move slightly and I feel his response deep within me. The breeze wafts over us and I remember where we are. "Won't someone see us?"

"Not unless they can fly."

I straighten up and lean forward. Lips suck and nibble at my breasts. I love this feeling so much. My vagina tightens. I feel his response. I clench and unclench myself to grip him harder. Grant takes my hips but I shake my head no, and he looks at me for a long minute and then lets his hands drop onto the arms of the chair. I love this.

My tongue circles his ear and dips lightly into it. I feel his legs tighten. I love it. I blow lightly and take another lick. His legs clench again. I sniff his neck and make my way to his other ear. My fingers lightly stroke and pull on his tiny nipples. I feel his shaft grow still larger. I wiggle my hips slightly and lick his lobe.

Bracing my legs on each side of him I lean back. I am filled to capacity. I try to wiggle even more. I never seem to get enough of Grant. For all his prodigious size, I'm insatiable and want more.

"Stroke my breasts," I whisper as I take his twin sacks into my palms. The skin is so thin, so soft. So terribly, terribly vulnerable. He groans low in his throat when I squeeze a little too hard. His fingers tighten on my breasts, and I relax the pressure, only to do it once more. His breath is sucked in and then hisses out. He grows within me.

The surge of power is heady, and my hand tightens just a little bit more. My nipples are taken and held, and reluctantly I release my hold on him. He rolls the turgid peaks once or twice and I have to bite my lip as liquid fire streaks through me. My insides are screaming for me to move, but I want to make it last as long as possible. My vaginal muscles are steadily gripping and releasing. I bend low and slide hard peaks up his chest. He takes a swipe at them with his tongue. I love it. Shock waves of lust race though me. My hips begin their instinctive motion slowly, but soon I'm rocking on him wildly, hands clasped behind his head. His hands are on me but letting me set the pace, and it's a frantic one till once again I'm climbing the steepest of trails until I reach that apex of feeling.

"Come on. Come with me," I demand in a ragged, desperate breath, and he does, fingers tightening on my hips till I cry out with both ecstasy and pain, and then there're just the gentle rockings of fading spasms and breathless wonder. It's quite a long time till either of us rouses.

Another almost perfect day greets us the next morning. "Why not take a long sail along the coastline?"

"Sounds lovely."

"You'll be able to wear your string bikini. It will only be us. No one will see your ass but me."

And Jack.

My first instinct is to flee when I see Jack checking the sails on the beautiful ship Grant has rented. Why don't I ever listen to my instincts? Grant's strong fingers on my arm compel me forward. Jack grins and gives me a mock salute. "Morning, Mrs. Duncan."

"Hello, Jack." My throat feels tight and dry. My feet move automatically under the pressure of Grant's hand. I know I'm in trouble when he leads me down into a cabin and leaves me there. Locked in.

My pounding on the door and frantic yelling is ignored. The ship moves and lurches. We're under way. I scramble onto the bed and look out the porthole. The latch is stiff and I can't move it. The land slowly fades into the distance. My heart is pounding. I'm not frightened of Grant. It's Jack that makes me tremble.

My suitcases and Grant's are in the corner of the room. Grant has checked us out of the hotel. Four days on the lonely, empty sea. It's the yacht all over, but smaller. My mouth is dry. My body seems to shrink and expand with all the thoughts and memories that rush through it.

Grant enters the cabin and smiles. "Why are you down here? Why don't you come up and enjoy the air?"

"Very funny, Grant." I stamp my foot. "Why did you lock me in?"

His brow lifts and his eyes crinkle with amusement. "Whatever are you talking about?"

"You locked me in."

"I did no such thing." Grant turns and tries the door. It won't open. My feelings of anger are evaporating quickly. He pulls, kicks the bottom and the door opens only after another tug. I feel foolish when he looks at me.

"I thought you'd locked me in," I murmur, embarrassed.

"And why would I do that?"

"Well...I thought...I mean Jack..." I let my voice trail off, confused.

"Jack stayed on shore. He was just checking the rigging for me to make sure everything was shipshape."

Relief is sweet as it washes over me. "You mean it's just you and me?"

"And the two boys who are sailing the ship for us." He takes me in his arms and kisses me lightly. "Four days of freedom for you and me, Tessa. What should we do? Should we stop at islands and explore uncharted places? Should we just sail in and around Rio? Should we attempt to make Buenos Aires?"

"How far is it?" Excitement is building quickly.

"About two thousand miles." He laughs at my expression. "No, we won't attempt it, Tessa. I never meant it seriously. If we had the summer maybe."

We ascend through the hatch and I breath deeply. The day is perfect. The sails billow and puff out high above us. My short hair is whipped back from my face when I face the wind. The motion of the ship is gentle and steady. I breath deeply and feel a sense of freedom I haven't felt since we'd been on his island. There is nothing but sea and sky and Grant.

And two Brazilian sailors. As soon as I see the speculative gleam in Grant's eyes I know what he's anticipating. I just don't know what or when or where or how. My sense of freedom vanishes. I've been neatly and completely caught in his scheme. Do the men know?

I see them watching me, but it doesn't seem to be a calculating look. Nor an anticipatory look. I glance at Grant and he breaks into a big smile. "I bought lots of film before we left the mainland."

A chill runs the length of my body. Is it fear or excitement? I don't know which is stronger.

We enter the cabin to change into our suits. "Grant I…"

"I've said this before, Tessa. I have no intention of renegotiating our relationship each and every time. Just behave yourself."

"But why can't you and I be together? Just us?"

"We will be, but I think it'll be interesting to see how these two strangers react."

I have to swallow. "To what?"

"Oh, various things."

I remove my clothes and try to open the suitcase. It's locked. "I need the key."

"No, you don't. There's no one out here to see you."

"Grant…"

He opens a small skylight-type hatch above his head and my clothes are whisked away by the wind. His eyes aren't amused. "End of discussion."

I watch him pull on his trunks and meet his eyes steadily. "Are you coming on deck?"

"No."

He shrugs and yanks open the door. "Suit yourself, Tessa."

Two minutes later the door is kicked open and the larger of the two sailors is in the doorway. He's big and brawny, with deeply tanned skin. His eyes are almost black. His naked chest is heaving slightly. His eyes are wide in surprise. I back up and hit the wall when I see the slow grin that spreads his lips. I wish I could disappear. His tongue licks his lips and he takes a step forward. I try to cover my breasts, my mound, but it seems to amuse him.

"Get out of here."

His smile widens. He shakes his head and says something in Portuguese. And then he's on me. His hands grab my shoulders, and I scream and duck trying to escape him. His hands are everywhere, pulling, grabbing, pinching, until I'm finally clasped tightly to his chest and held still. I lift my leg and an instant later scream under the sting of his hand on my still-sore ass. Rough hands lift, turn, and throw me over his shoulder, and then I'm carried unceremoniously to Grant, who is at the wheel of the boat. I'm literally dropped at his feet.

"I'm glad you decided to join me, Tessa."

I can barely breathe, I'm so angry. "That was unnecessary, Grant, and you know it!"

"All you had to do was come up quietly with Enrico, Tessa. I really think you beg for this kind of treatment without realizing it."

I hate him so thoroughly sometimes. This is one of them. My eye catches the delighted grin of the younger sailor, and my blood boils. Without thought, I lash out with my foot and Grant ends up flat on the deck beside me. One look at his face and I know I've made a mistake. I barely start to move and those incredibly strong fingers have me by the back of the neck. I'm pulled straight over his lap and know nothing but pain for the next five minutes. My screeching cries don't move him in the least, and my bucking hips and legs take their fair share of the pain. I'm a thoroughly chastened woman by the time he pushes me off his lap.

He's still livid as he gains his feet. I can hear his heavy breathing above my own whimpering cries. "If that's the way you want to do it, Tessa, I'll be happy to oblige you."

"I'm sorry." I hate groveling but I'm suddenly too aware of how much in his control I am once more.

"You haven't begun to be sorry." His tone is too steady. Too ominous in its quietness. I curl into a tighter ball and continue to cry. All three men ignore me. I wish I had the courage to throw myself overboard.

I'm curled up on the back bench of the boat. Grant won't let me go below. Nothing but sea and sky meet my eyes. Not even another sail in the far-off distance. Paulo and Enrico's eyes have barely left me since Grant's spanking. Paulo's eyes sparkle with mischief.

Grant said he wanted to see their reactions. What is each thinking? How does he know they won't do him any harm? How is he able to control or judge them if they aren't part of the plan?

Paulo is the younger of the two. Maybe twenty years old. I see him licking his lips constantly. What fantasies rove through his mind? What are his dreams? His desires? Will he get a chance to live them with me?

Enrico's stare is bolder. More direct. He knows most of the contours of my body. He'd made a quick but thorough inspection under the guise of subduing me. He makes me nervous. His stare is calculating. I don't think I want to know his desires.

A shadow falling over me makes me look up. Grant is directly in front of me. His eyes are hard. So is his penis.

"I want your mouth, Tessa."

My name is not a caress this time. I'm too aware of the others' stares. I shake my head. My neck is gripped and I'm pulled onto the deck directly before him on my knees.

"A captain of a ship is complete master, Tessa. You should know that because of Jack. I could order you whipped. Hanged. My crew is loyal and obeys all my commands. Stowaways can be treated any way a captain deems fit."

We're in another of his fantasies. I nod and his grip loosens imperceptibly. "Your mouth, girl."

I reach up and lower his trunks. Out of the corner of

my eye, I see Paulo stand up. Grant has us sideways to the front of the ship. Paulo and Enrico have an unobstructed view.

As soon as my mouth covers him, he lets go of my neck. As always, he's letting me go at my own speed with this.

Six eyes burn into me as I slowly lower my mouth over the huge shaft in front of me. The skin tightens and expands under my tongue. My tongue glides down the long length. I keep going and lick Grant's hardening sacks long and slow. My hands rub the length of his thighs lightly. I can feel the tightening in his thighs. I love it.

All others cease to exist, and I concentrate on tormenting him. That's all I desire right now. I know it will end in his pleasure, but I wish it to be the most excruciating buildup possible. Grant has unbelievable control. I intend to see just how much he has. He has his fantasies, I have mine.

I barely touch him as I slide my tongue up one side and down the other. I doubt if he can distinguish my breath from the breeze. My moist tongue touches, leaves, touches, leaves. I suck in the knob. I release it. I exhale long and slow over the now-moist tip. My fingernails lightly glide up and down his leg. I let a finger skim and then linger along his crack. His muscles tighten more. His ass is soft but tight. Tingles of excitement race up my spine. My nipples harden.

I can feel Grant breathing harder. I prolong the agony as long as I can. Licking, sucking, barely touching. I scratch lightly along his scrotum. I hear his breath sucked in. I can feel the shaking of his thighs. My fingers trail up and down his legs, his crack. I know he's going to have to give up soon, and I lower my mouth further than I've ever been able to. I suck. Hard. And swallow in victory a second later.

I can tell he knew what I was doing. I can also tell he's torn between satisfaction and annoyance that I won. I rise and curl back onto the seat, barely concealing my Cheshire-cat grin. Paulo is rushing below while trying to hide the wet stain on the front of his trunks. Enrico's eyes are glittering with lust. His hands are clenched tight at his sides. I see the thick tube in his pants before he turns back to the steering wheel. I can't quite hide the satisfied smirk that spreads my lips. I lay there and revel in my moment of glory.

And probably as an unspoken reward Grant allows me to. We both know it won't last for too long.

The night is so calm. The breeze so cool and refreshing after the heat of the day. The sky is filled with millions of stars twinkling and sparkling like diamonds thrown upon black velvet. I breath in deeply. And wait.

Grant has tied me to the forward deck. I'm spread-eagled and available. At least the tape across my mouth will prevent them from using it. Grant is too aware of my feelings about fellatio. I don't think he's willing to spoil it for himself by allowing another to ruin how far he's brought me along with it.

The breeze brings the salty air to me. The rolled-up sails move slightly with the gentle motion of the ship. It amazes me how much light the stars give off on this moonless night. I hear the slap of bare feet slowly coming toward me. They know I'm here. Grant hasn't concealed his anger toward me from the other men. They think I'm a stowaway. At least that's what he told me they discussed during dinner. I don't understand Portuguese.

Their approach is stealthy. Had they waited till Grant

slept? Had he given them permission or do they do this on their own? It's only Paulo, not both. His still-developing chest is heaving with excitement. His eyes flick here and there. I can see him shaking. Is it fear of being so daring? Of being caught? Of what he plans?

He quickly pulls his pants off and kneels between my legs. He strains his neck to look behind him one more time and then falls on me. Literally. I feel my breath leave in a whoosh. His hand between my legs, a feeling of something, and then he gushes. His breathing is harsh, tortured; he's almost crying with disappointment. He makes no effort to get off me but lies full on me and snuffles into my hair for a minute. And then he's gone. I almost feel sorry for him.

Enrico is no child. No inexperienced boy. He's quiet. I don't even know he's there until I feel his hands on my breasts. Knowing fingers tease and torment. I sense a steak of cruelty in him. I hope Grant doesn't let him explore its limits.

For all his bravado, he's nervous. Grant hasn't given them permission. He's just put out the bait and is waiting to see how they'll react. Is he watching? Or is he filming? Probably both.

Enrico tweaks my nipples and I groan loudly, instinctively knowing that's what he wants. I see his pleased smile. He pushes into me and is done within a minute. And I just lie there.

Grant leaves me there for most of the night. He must really be furious with me. He knows how to punish me. No loving. No being held. No Grant. He knows that's what I love the most. I relish the closeness. I love being with him.

I'm not uncomfortable. My bonds are not too tight. I

lie on a mat. The night is warm but not too hot. The breeze is intermittent and welcome. I just wish I weren't alone. I'm not for too long.

Paulo comes again. He sits beside me and touches my breasts almost with wonder. I see him constantly looking to see if anyone is on deck. He's excited and scared at the same time. I know the feeling well. It's a frighteningly heady experience.

He dips his head and sucks a nipple into his mouth. His tongue touches the hardening tip and then is gone. Paulo shifts position and runs his hands over me. I can hear his breathing quickening. He fumbles between my legs and then slides into me. I hardly feel him. His thrusting is jerky and almost frantic. His breathing is furious. A final lunge and he's done and gone. I felt nothing at all. It's almost as frustrating as if I had.

Enrico is another matter. He delights in tormenting me. Little does he know that I feel nothing with him. I moan and groan and twist and tremble because I know it's what he expects. How pathetic that he needs to cause pain to derive pleasure. He's not happy with being dominant. He wants to make me suffer. He strikes my breast and I scream for real beneath the tape. We both hear Grant's yawn almost immediately. He's been watching. I know it's his way of making Enrico stop, while not interfering. Enrico is still, listening to hear if Grant will come up on deck. When Grant doesn't, Enrico pushes into me and foolishly believes he causes me discomfort. Hadn't he seen Grant's size? How could he believe he could hurt me after being with Grant?

Paulo comes to me once more. I barely open my eyes. He's so quick it almost seems a dream. The boy has a lot to learn.

Grant releases me just before dawn. We swim in the calm ocean but stay close to the boat. Nothing is said. No explanations. No apologies. He holds me but doesn't make love to me when we climb into his bed. I'm not sure if he's still living his fantasy till the next day.

"Get me a cup of coffee." Gruff. Demanding.

"Don't you th…" His belt hits the back of my thighs and I scream under the unexpected pain. The blue eyes are cold. No crinkling. No tenderness. He's still the captain.

Paulo is in the galley when I enter. He can't seem to meet my eyes. I actually see a flush suffuse his dark face. I don't care. I just hurry to get the cups of coffee. Enrico is in the corridor. His eyes latch onto the red streak across my thighs. His smile is evil. I push past him and hurry back to our cabin. Grant takes the cup from my hands without a word. He cocks a brow at me but says nothing.

Not knowing what else to do, I sit quietly on the edge of the bed and drink my coffee. Grant never looks at me, but studies some papers at the small table. Is this just a fantasy or is he truly still angry about yesterday? I wish he would talk to me. I wish he would explain more, as he had when we were in Quebec. At least then I'd known his intentions. And I had enjoyed it, too. But then Grant had been loving. Not cold, as he is now.

"Stand up and bend over the bed."

There is a nasty glint in his eyes but I do as he says. He's fondling his belt and I bend and tense for the pain. I hear the scrape of a jar opening and tense for another reason. He thrusts into my ass. No fondling. No loving. Nothing but filling and pain. He gives me no time to adjust. I'm just thankful he doesn't prolong it. I don't say a word. I don't look at him. If I don't play the part of the stowaway right, I know I'll suffer for it. I've never seen Grant so cold. So angry.

"Clean up the cabin, then make me breakfast." His words are hard and low. And then he's gone. I stand there and pulse. With pain. With need. And, if I'm honest, with a little fear. I don't know who this man is.

I bring Grant's breakfast topside and he literally grabs it from me. He's completely into his role of rough captain. He's unshaven and rough looking. His voice is harsh and demanding both to me and the men. He yells out orders without thought. And we all scramble to obey him.

I'm mauled. There's no other word for his hands on my body. He takes delight in seeing the men's reactions to his pawing me. Paulo lowers a sail and almost knocks himself out because he can't take his eyes from Grant's hands on me. Grant yells and pushes me roughly away from him. Thank God the seat in back is padded.

He berates the boy sternly and then shoves him at the wheel. I'm lifted, turned, and penetrated. Grant's hands on my neck keep me pinned down. He uses me without emotion. With nothing but a desire to finish. I can't stop the tears. I don't like this at all. I don't want to be a part of this. I wouldn't dare tell him with the mood he's in.

He shouts Enrico's name and when the man approaches pushes me toward him. Strong hands and arms catch me easily. I don't understand the words but I do the surprised delight in the man's expression. I'm lifted and carried to the cabin. Enrico kicks the door closed behind us. I'm really nervous now. None of this is playacting. Has Grant lost his mind?

Enrico grins evilly at me and removes his belt. I can't seem to breath. He speaks but I have no idea of what he's saying. He motions me with his finger to turn around. Ice seems to fill my veins. I shake my head but his smile just widens. A hand snakes out and before I can guess his intent my hands are pinned behind me and tied with his belt. The thick leather cuts into my flesh. I'm pressed up against his thighs. I feel the length of his growing cock against my cheek. He's breathing hard.

My hair is grabbed and I watch his hand fumble with his zipper. Now I am afraid. The tube lifts and springs out at me. The eye seems to stare at me. He forces my head forward and I grit my teeth. Cruel fingers on my nipple compel me to open my mouth. I'm panting, braced, terrified, but he merely places the tip within. I'm rigid with apprehension but he moves ever so slowly back and forth. He unbuttons his shorts and they fall to the floor along with his underwear. Still he doesn't move. And then I understand. He wants me to do what I did with Grant yesterday. But he doesn't trust me not to hurt him so he's tied me.

I cover him more with my mouth and then begin the slow descent down the length of his penis. Up. Down. Sideways. His smell is musky. More pungent than Grant's. I lick his balls and make my slow way up his length. I breathe and blow, lick, suck, nibble. His legs are trembling violently. I watch his fists clench and unclench and fear he won't be able to stop from forcing me further onto him. I run my teeth along the ridge ever so lightly. I feel his entire body tighten and then I'm picked up, turned over onto the bed, and he's ramming himself up my ass. Thank God for Grant's stretching.

Thank God for my own saliva. Thank God he doesn't have Grant's stamina.

He collapses a scant minute later after a roar of victory. He lies heavily over me. My arms ache from his weight crushing them into my body. His breathing is harsh but slowing. I want to get up. I want my hands freed.

I get neither.

He shoves me further onto the bed and with a meaningful push on my neck tells me to remain on it. I hear him tug open the door and then his heavy tread ascends the stairs. My arms ache. My ass pulses slightly. I wish Grant would come and relieve this odd feeling I have. It's not desire. It's not pain. It's not want, it's…what? I have no idea. I only know I don't like this fantasy at all. I don't like having absolutely no control.

Even in the cabin with Dan I had had some control. I'd been the enticer. I'd played the seductress, the teaser. And I'd enjoyed his lovemaking once he'd gotten past his initial excitement. And Grant had been there and made sure I enjoyed myself. This is nothingness. No one cares about me or my needs at all. All three of them only want what they want.

And not speaking the language I don't know what they want or what Grant has told them. I only know I am frightened of this man Grant has become. I'd never seen him so totally in character before. And I don't like this character one bit.

Grant enters the cabin an hour later. I've done little but cry in self-pity. He looks at me with disgust, and leaves. I hear his voice yelling but cannot make out the words. He returns and unties me. My sigh of relief is short lived because I no sooner stretch my arms then he pulls them up and ties them to the headboard.

"Open your legs, Tessa." What once sounded like a caress is only harshness now.

"Grant..."

"You'll call me captain or nothing at all." His eyes are so cold. "Open your legs."

I do. Ankles are grabbed and knees bent. He ties my ankles high on the sideboard so I cannot lower them. I'm splayed open like a wanton whore.

Paulo enters. His eyes widen. Grant speaks to him and the boy nods. "If he tells me you said one word—one word, Tessa—we'll beat and use your ass so you won't sit for a week. Understand?"

"Captain..."

"Understand?"

I nod. I have no defenses against this stranger before me. If I'd been blindfolded I would have sworn it couldn't be the Grant I know. How many different people did he wish to be? How many different lives did he wish to live? To experience? The thought is both thrilling and terrifying. How far would he dare to go?

"I can promise you you'll suffer no permanent trauma either mentally or physically." His words of last year echo in my mind. Permanent trauma. It's true the marks will fade. He's never used a whip that scars. It's true the wonderful times remain in my memory and I tend to forget the harsher moments. He's never pushed me too far. But does he know how far too far would be? Do I?

The sound of the door slamming brings me back to the present. Paulo is licking his lips. His eyes are glued to my nether region. I'm spread wide and available. He rubs his hands together. He licks his lips. His eyes rove from breasts to pubis. I bite my lip to keep silent.

He kneels between my legs and I see his Adam's

apple moving as he swallows deeply. He pushes down his trunks and I wait to be stabbed with the hard member. He's nervous again.

He bends and I feel his breath along the inside of my thighs. It tickles the silky hair between my legs. A tentative touch of his tongue. A stronger one. My lips seem to blossom and open as if welcoming him. I hear him sniff. Feel his tongue and then his whole mouth.

I'm to be brought to orgasm. I know it as surely as I know this boy has never done this before. Grant is throwing me a bone. This is to keep me happy while they play with me. But it's only a bone and he knows it. He knows I never enjoy it as much as when I'm with him, but if he did this now he would lose his power over me because then I would know for sure that Grant is still Grant, and he doesn't want that. At least not yet. Not until he has lived his fantasy.

The boy's tongue is inexperienced and he licks me all over. From the bottom to the top. The swipes are either too hard or I barely feel them. I hate it but slowly the feeling of need is building. I wish he understood English. I wish I could tell him what I want. This is why I'm not allowed to speak a word. Somehow I would have conveyed to him when it was good and when not. And Grant doesn't want that.

A form of torture that he can't be blamed for. I won't be able to blame him for the boy's lack of experience. I won't be able to blame him if the boy stops before…the thought sends me into a panic. He couldn't. He wouldn't. How will he know? How much does the boy know? My hips start moving in a desperate attempt to encourage him, to show him when it is good and when not.

Can I groan? Is a groan a word? Do I dare? Is Grant listening? Will he come in and stop the boy if he hears a sound from me?

My breathing is getting ragged as the feeling builds and builds so tortuously slowly. Why doesn't he stay where I want him? He's snuffling and nosing around like a hog in the mud. He hits my clit and I ram myself further into his face. He moves lower. I want to scream with frustration. Why doesn't he understand? I lift myself from the bed and try to make him return to where I want him but he grabs my thighs and continues on his haphazard journey. My insides are churning. I'm boiling. Close to exploding, but he won't go where I need him. I can't take it anymore.

"You stupid son of a bitch," I scream in frustration. He stops in surprise and looks up at me, and then I see the sly smile that covers his face. I've been set up. He isn't as naive as I thought. He'd known just what he was doing. It seems Paulo understands and speaks flawless English.

He moves up and enters me slowly. I tilt my hips. His hands stop me from getting a good position. He slides into me smoothly but I can't feel him. His methods are crude. He is inexperienced but not stupid.

"Will your ass be as hot as your clit is?" His breath is strained as he reaches his release. I can't stop the tears of frustration—and now fear—that form and leak from my eyes.

He lies on me and plays lightly with my breasts. "The señorita will do as I wish or I will have to tell the captain about her words. Her very nasty words."

I just nod. He rolls from me and continues to play with my breasts. He seems to be fascinated with their weight and pushes them up and watches them fall over and over. The nipples are stroked, kissed, licked, pulled. He laughs every time I feel the need to clench my legs. His fingers toy with my slit. He flicks his finger against my clit once in a while and chuckles when I suck in breath.

Little does he know how close I am. I keep my eyes closed and just concentrate on the touching. My clit is engorged and almost there. His lips brush my nipples and I force myself to remain still. He teases the throbbing bud once, twice, and then makes the mistake of sucking in my nipple and flicking the tiny organ at the same time. And I'm there. My body pulses with relief. Nothing earthshaking, but a welcome easement of tension nonetheless.

One look at his eyes and I know Grant will hear about my words. At the moment, I just don't care.

But now I do. I'm tied to the mast. Arms stretched at full length. I've been apprehensive about this all afternoon. Paulo left me shortly after. And I waited with trepidation for Grant's retribution.

But nothing happened. He arrived shortly after and untied me and ordered me to prepare lunch. I did. They dined on the meal I'd prepared. I dined on Grant. I hate the control he has. I hate how he sat there and calmly ate his lunch while I tried every trick I knew to make him choke or come. He did neither. Not until my jaw was aching and he was good and ready.

He tied me to the back railing and ignored me unless he again felt like having me minister to him. The other men always watched with avid interest. I couldn't tell anything from his expression.

I fixed dinner and again Grant made me service him,

but this time he allowed me to eat afterwards. It was only as dusk fell and he advanced upon me with ropes in one hand and his belt in the other that my worst fears crystallized.

And now I wait. They're taking in the sails around me. The cadence of sea being pushed out of the way by the boat's hull is slowly diminishing as we lose speed. The breeze is fading as that special quiet calm descends that usually does just before the sun disappears.

I'm on tiptoe. It's hard for me to look anywhere but straight ahead. One by one they all walk to the front of the ship and I no longer can see them. And he makes me wait.

I hear the hiss, and then pain explodes on my backside. It seems to linger in one spot for a brief moment and then radiates out. He gives me plenty of time to think about it until he swings his arm again. Five times. I feel as if it will never end and I scream with each hit. How can I forget each time how much it hurts?

He's directly behind me. A hand between my legs. A gentle caressing. A soothing motion with his fingers and then my moisture is spread around my anus. My sphincter fights him and I feel nothing but pain for a short while but then my body takes over and I respond to his pounding. I hump back into him, trying to exchange one feeling for another. I'm crying I'm so desperate to find some relief, and then his fingers are where I need them and I'm screaming for a different reason. I'd collapse if not tied.

Grant moves back and then unbelievably the pain returns. He watches my eyes in the dim light. I know he loves to see my expression. "Please, Grant," I beg and then suck in breath under another blow.

Soft fingers stroke my cheek even as another blow sends fire spreading through me. "This is the price you pay for disobedience."

And he's gone. Five hits. All hard and then the grunting body of Enrico behind me. He's nothing compared to Grant and I hardly grunt. I can't keep my mind from dwelling on Paulo.

Reality comes all too quickly. Paulo's hits are lighter but my ass is so sore they could have been the hardest. As usual with Paulo, the excitement is too much for him and he's done before he pushes all the way into me.

Grant comes for me soon after. He bathes me, soothes my tears, whispers words of love to me and cuddles me in his arms till I fall asleep.

We're back in port when I awake. Clothes are laid out on the bed. The suitcases are gone. A quick knock on the porthole startles me.

"Let's go, lazy one. We have a big day of sightseeing and a night of wonder ahead of us. Get a move on!"

I'm sore and stiff but I dress as quickly as I can. As usual I don't have any underwear to worry about. Walking sneakers, white cotton blouse and navy blue walking skirt. And no one but the Grant I know and love waiting for me on deck. Blue eyes crinkle with merriment and tenderness.

"Sleep well?"

"Yes." I feel breathless with happiness. What wonderful things has he arranged? Now that this is out of the way, I'm sure the next two days will be exciting.

And I'm right.

We walk the crowded plazas and wide boulevards. We visit the government houses, the Carmen Miranda

Museum, the multitude of tiny shops, and stop at numerous cafes to sip the marvelous *cafezinhos*. The smell of grilling beef fills the air whenever we pass one of the many *churrascarias*, and my mouth waters every time.

Grant takes me to a small train, and we hop on board with many others to take the ride through the Tijuca rain forest to the mountain summit of Corcovado. Birds sing and screech, their bright colors flashing by occasionally. I laugh at the antics of the monkeys high in the canopy.

Standing beneath the outstretched arms of Jesus, we gaze in awe at the beauty before us. The incomparable beaches of Ipanema and Copacabana spread out before us. Sugar Loaf is directly in front of us and all of spectacular Rio is ours to behold.

I don't want to leave but Grant insists we must return to our rooms and rest for the night's adventure. What that is, he keeps me in suspense about.

The shower feels good but I'm disappointed when Grant doesn't join me. I step out and expect to see him getting ready to go in, but he's just getting out of the sunken bath. "Didn't you want to bathe with me?" I don't think I quite keep the hurt out of my voice.

His chuckle is amused but rueful. "I didn't think we'd get much washing done if I did."

"Would that be so bad?"

I love his smile. I love the way his eyes crinkle with pleasure. "Only if you wanted to miss the sights tonight. We leave late tomorrow night, Tessa."

The caress is back. I feel tears of happiness prick my eyelids. "It would be worth it."

His laugh is music to my ears. "You say that now but on the plane tomorrow you would be ruing the loss.

You've never truly forgiven me for missing the Eiffel Tower and you know it."

"But this is different."

Strong arms surround me and lift me up for a long, slow kiss. "It's only different at this moment. It won't be when you think back objectively."

"Well, if sights are more important to you, Grant...."

I'm scooped up and carried into the bedroom quickly, screeching with pleasure when he tosses me onto the bed and follows me down. I love the feel of him on me. I love the feel of his strong fingers stroking my body. I love the feel of him inside of me. I love the feeling of reaching that special mind-dizzying place together. I love snuggling into his arms and drifting off to sleep knowing he'll be there in the morning.

Another flawless day. Does Rio have any other kind? I'm beginning to wonder.

There is an expectancy in the air. A low-keyed hum of building excitement. Carnaval will begin in ten days. The people are anticipating. Readying. I'm beginning to wish we could be here.

"Have you been here during Carnaval?"

He smiles. "Just once. Many years ago. The crowds were enormous. The music overpowering. I much prefer it now."

"It must be something to see."

"It is if you like being jostled and taken along with crowds. You can't relax during Carnaval. Everything is slightly frenzied. The numbers of people are overwhelming. Believe me, Tessa, when I tell you this is the best time to be in Rio."

I shrug and let it go. I will do nothing to spoil this last

day and night here. We're scheduled to leave at 2 A.M. for home.

What a wonderful day we have. Sunbathing. Swimming. Touring. Bicycling. I love how perfectly the old and new of Rio seem to blend together. The people are happy and hospitable. Every time we hear loud music we find a group of people who have stopped and just started dancing to the beat. It seems to be a part of their life. Their soul.

We dine in a beautiful restaurant overlooking the ocean. Everything is open to catch the night breezes. Exotic smells waft over us, and I'm immediately caught up in trying to define them and imagine where they came from.

His hand is warm and gentle as his fingers curl through mine. "Have you had a good time, Tessa?"

I nod. Already the boat is fading. This is all I dwell on now. "I wish we didn't have to leave."

Lips on my hand. So soft. So moist. So exciting. "The next time we meet will be in a totally different place. To do totally different things."

His eyes are so tender. Mine feel moist with emotion. "When will that be, Grant?"

Such a small smile to make my heart flutter. "Ah, Tessa, that is the question. If I told you, there would be no anticipation. If I told you, there would be no mystery."

"Do you know when the next time will be, Grant?" My throat feels tight with excitement. My voice sounds strained.

"Perhaps."

A light kiss on my palm and then he's signaling the waiter for the check.

The night is delightful. I'm surprised when Clive pulls up with the car. "We'll go to Urca tonight."

"Yes, sir."

"Where are we going? Urca? What's that?"

"It's a section of the town. There is something you must not miss before we leave or you'll never forgive me."

No amount of pleading budges him, and I remain mystified. The ride isn't too long, and then I'm whisked out of the car and onto a cable car to the top of Sugar Loaf mountain. How to describe the view? Breathtaking. Spectacular. Unbelievable.

The city and all its lights are spread out before us. A small collective sigh is heard from the assorted people with us. The sight of *La Cidadu Maravilhosa* protected by the mountaintop Jesus is enough to move the most unemotional.

Turning around, we gaze upon the endless expanse of ocean that is lit by the thin crescent of the new moon. The water shimmers as it undulates gently. It's hypnotic. Mesmerizing. I'm torn between the two sights. One seems more beautiful than the other until you turn once more and are caught up in the beauty that you gaze upon.

It's an awe-inspiring sight and all are hushed and quiet as they gaze from one to the other. The soft rumble of the cable car returning breaks the spell.

"Glad we came?" His voice just reaches my ear. I nod, unwilling to break the spell that is still wrapped around me. Grant seems to understand, and I lay my head on his shoulder and breathe in the wonderful smells till we reach the bottom.

"Do you tango, Tessa?"

"No." I smile and look up at him. "There isn't too much call for the tango in Iowa."

His eyes crinkle and he places his arm around my shoulder. "You'll wish there were after you've been to the Circo Voador."

And as usual he's right. The Flying Circus is in Lapa, one of the older and more run-down areas of Rio. It is inside a permanent tent. Like many places, its sides are open to catch the breeze. There are numerous bars in the open areas and then a tent within the tent. We pass through and are in a huge area with a wooden floor. A large orchestra is playing on a stage, and people from all walks of life are gliding along to the elegant sounds of the tango.

The movements are so perfect, so graceful, so exact. The women's flared skirts spin and twirl around their legs when they execute the quick turn. The men guide and maneuver with meticulous precision. I'm hardly aware of the taste of the Brahma beer I sip as I watch, entranced. I wish I could be so graceful. I wish I could one of them. I can't pull my eyes from the dancers until the music stops and the orchestra takes a break.

Crinkling eyes watch me, and then he smiles and takes my hand. "You're so easy to read, Tessa. I love watching your expression when you experience new things. It always reminds me of the wonder I see in my grandchildren when they see something they did not know existed."

My heart is fluttering in my chest. I love this man so much. I hope he cannot read that in my eyes. I give him a small laugh and lower my eyes. "I'm hardly a child, Grant."

"No. Not your body. Not your knowledge. But still a

little bit of one inside. And that is good. We all need to feel the wonder of things now and then. When the wonder is gone the essence of a person seems to wither and dry up. It's a sad time for any person. There is nothing left to look forward to. Nothing to go on for." His fingers skim along the top of my knuckles. His eyes are sincere when he looks back up at me. "You are my wonder. You are my reason to explore new worlds. I always dreamed of doing what we do but you've made the reality far exceed the fantasy. You never disappoint me, Tessa. You are always a delight."

My throat is almost closed with happiness. His finger traces a gentle path along my cheek and I swallow quickly. I wish the night would never end.

My life is so different now. Mom and Michael returned tanned and glowing from their two-week honeymoon. I don't know why it never dawned on me that they wouldn't live here in the house. After the laughs and hugs and kisses and tales of wonderful times, Mom had excused herself to go and pack her clothes. I'd followed like a puppy dog.

"I didn't realize you'd be living at Michael's."

"He didn't really give me any time to think about it myself. But it makes sense, Tessa. His home is larger and closer to his work." She folds a pair of slacks and looks around her room. I see her sigh. "I guess maybe some of it is he doesn't want to compete with the memories of your father."

"And how do you feel about it?"

"I'm torn. I understand Michael's feelings. I really do. But it hurts to give up this house. I came here as a bride. Raised you girls here. It's all I've ever known."

I can see the struggle she's going through and smile encouragingly. "Dad would be the first one to be happy for you, Mom."

She brushes away the tears and nods. "I know. It's the only reason I let Michael talk me into marrying him so quickly."

She looks around and sighs and then glances back at me. "And what about you? Will you mind living here by yourself?"

"Aren't you going to sell it?"

"No. We talked it over and if you want to remain here it's fine with us. When the time comes to sell the house you'll do the right thing and give Polly half."

"Well, of course, but…"

"No. No buts, Tessa. Michael is very well off and doesn't want or need the proceeds of the house. He's the one who insisted you be allowed to stay. He's the one who suggested it was time for you to be independent, and I think he's right. I've been very selfish wanting you to remain with me. I hope I haven't spoiled your chance of happiness, Tessa."

"Mom, I never felt…"

"I know you haven't but you've never been on your own either. You always lived with me and Dad or with Greg. It's time for you to continue with your life. Look how much fun you had last year on your travels. Think of all the new and wonderful things you experienced. I'm sure if you tried to save you could travel more, and maybe someday you'll meet someone, too."

If she only knew.

So here I am in a house all to myself. Polly took one or two things she really wanted and Mom did the same, but basically it's me and the house. And I hate it.

The first week was wonderful. I changed some furniture around and moved some dishes from here to there. I scrubbed floors, put my feet up on the coffee table, stayed up late—too late—and did whatever I pleased with no explanations to anyone. But I miss having someone to talk to. Cooking for one has to be the most depressing thing there is. I don't do it anymore. I stop at the store and pick up something simple to pop in the microwave.

I quickly gave up the notion that Grant would come to see me now that I'm alone. It's not his style and he wouldn't take the chance of ruining a good thing. And I miss him. Terribly.

The nights are the worst. No one to talk to. No one to help pass the time. Television is awful. People are busy with their own families. And I'm lonely.

Tonight is the same as always. I mark the children's papers, check the teaching plan for the morning, and sigh. The half-eaten piece of pizza stares back at me from the dirty plate. I dump it in the trash. I'm going to have to join some clubs or gyms or something. I can't stand this loneliness.

I linger in the shower and shave my legs and underarms. The steam reminds me of Iceland. My breath quickens. My nipples harden. I want to be back with Grant. It's becoming an obsession. I don't even care about his fantasies anymore. Being with him is all I can think about.

I wonder why Grant never gave me his telephone number. I know he lives alone. Or at least with Rodney and Bill. I don't know if Clive lives with him or not. There's an awful lot I don't know about Grant. There are some things I'd rather not know. Like what fantasy he wishes to live out the next time we're together. But there is so much I'd like to know.

I wonder what his favorite color is? His favorite food? What does he do at night? Does he ever think of me? Does he date other women? Do they do what he wants as I do?

No. I don't think so. I think I'm very special to him in that way. Do I resent it? Not in the least. I love it.

March comes in raw and wet, and my spirits dampen along with the weather. I haven't heard anything from Grant in almost two months. Mom's out with Michael and I roam around the house at a loss for what to do.

Rain lashes against the panes of glass. I hear the wind soughing through the pines out back before it howls around the corner of the house. Even the fire doesn't cheer up the gloom of the day.

I straighten the dining-room chairs and fuss with the flower arrangement in the center of the table. I open and then shut the curtains against the endless pounding of the elements. I can't relax. I can't settle down to something. My insides churn and swirl as each blast of wind rattles the windows.

I go to my room and look around. It's neat and tidy and doesn't need straightening. I look in the closet. It's neat. I fiddle with my pocketbook and take out my checkbook. I hate balancing a checkbook. A card falls from it.

Godfrey York. Leather goods.

My breath catches in my throat. A strange tingling runs up my spine. Do I dare? Do I want to?

I'm so restless, so at odds with myself and my feelings. I pace and try to think clearly. What if Grant found out?

What if he doesn't?

What would it be like to be in total control of a situation? To be tender or harsh depending on one's mood? To be the tormentor instead of the tormented? I like being in control when I suck Grant. Would I like to be in total control? Would I want to strike another? To inflict pain both physically and mentally?

I don't know.

I yearn for something. I know it's Grant but that's impossible. Godfrey had seemed nice and sincere. No pressure. No pursuit.

I reach for the phone and drop my hand. I can't. And yet I want to. I don't know what to do. I pick up the receiver. I replace it. Maybe he's at work? Maybe he isn't? I finger the card. Perspiration breaks out on my brow. I take a deep breath and put the receiver to my ear. My finger shakes when I start to dial. Maybe he won't be home and then I won't have to decide.

He answers on the second ring. "Hello?"

My throat closes.

"Hello?"

I try to clear my throat. A strangled croak escapes.

"Tessa?"

Surprise loosens my muscles. "How did you know?"

I hear his soft chuckle but it's kind, not mocking. "You're not the only one who is terrified of trying something new. I knew you'd ring me up, I just didn't know when. Would you like to come over here or would you rather I came to you?"

"Not here!" I cry out before I can stop myself.

"Like that, is it? All right, I'll give you directions."

I shower and wash my hair. I pace. I change my mind five times and then change it back. I get in and out of the car twice before I force myself to start driving. He lives on the outskirts of a small town about thirty miles from me.

All the time I drive I wonder how he can do the things he intimated without anyone hearing or wondering. I find out when I pull onto the small dirt track and ride down a bumpy, weed-overgrown lane. He lives on a small farm miles from anyone else. There are two small cars in front of the barn. The house stands off to the left. My mouth is bone dry.

I shut off the engine and sit, my heart hammering in my chest. The silence is so complete. The rain has stopped and the day is overcast and dreary in the extreme. Somehow it seems sinister.

A tap on my window makes me scream and jump. Godfrey smiles and apologizes. "Sorry, love. Didn't know you were so jumpy. Ready?" he asks, opening the door and taking my arm to help me out. My heart pounds and I start to stammer some inane excuses, but he grips my arm firmly and leads me to the wide barn doors. I feel as though I'm walking to my own execution.

"I don't think I want to do this, Godfrey," I protest, suddenly terrified. He pulls the door open and pushes me inside. I stumble a step and hear the slam of the door and the click of a key. I'm not in a barn. I'm in a torture chamber.

The walls are padded. The ceiling is about ten feet high. We're in a large room within the barn. A man is standing naked in front of me. His chest and buttocks are heavily welted. His hands are above his head in chains. He smiles at me. I think I might faint.

"Take off your clothes, love." Godfrey's voice behind me makes me jump.

"I've changed my mind." My mind isn't functioning well. I can't take my eyes from the heavily striped man who looks like he's in heaven.

"Too late, love. All those who enter must indulge. Martin here is waiting for his next round of punishment. You can see he's happy you've arrived. Come, Tessa. No nonsense. You know you want to know what it feels like to be the giver instead of the receiver. Now is your chance."

I turn and Godfrey is clad in only a small leather loincloth. His body is thin but solid. He's holding a whip in his right hand. "Please."

"Yes, love, we intend to please you. Come on, now, off with the rags."

"I want to leave." I feel numb and terrified at the same time. My hair is gripped and my head pulled back sharply. I'm staring into the heavily made-up eyes of a huge woman. She has to be six feet tall.

"They all do the first time." Her voice is husky, and her eyes glitter with excitement. She jerks my head back so I'm off balance. I try to hold onto her for support but find my neck surrounded by wood. I hear a lock snick closed and then pressure. It rises and I'm standing on tiptoe, my neck stretched to its limit. I start to panic and claw at the yoke.

"Hands by your sides." A small sting on my ass accompanies her husky command. I just try harder to undo the thick wooden piece. The sting is more pronounced.

Godfrey stands in front of me. "We don't want to hurt you unless you want it, love. Everyone has a momentary fear when they first enter our room of entertainment. This is just to make the beginning easier for you. Hands at your sides, Tessa."

"Godfrey," I protest shakily, his hands brushing mine down and starting to undo my blouse. It's removed along with everything else. Every time I cooperate, the neck stock lowers a half inch. I'm docile by the time my underpants are pulled off me.

The woman, Godfrey calls her Helga, stands in front of me once more. "There isn't too much of her is there?" she comments. My cheeks burn. She runs her hands over my breasts and stomach. She's massive and built like a weight lifter. Her only garment is a one-piece leather tunic that amplifies her voluptuous curves.

My ass is prodded and the cheeks pulled apart. "She's built like a man." A finger tickles my crack and then circles the tight sphincter. Her laughter is throaty, sexy. "She's no stranger to being touched here."

Martin's penis is rising as he watches Helga explore my body. The touch is impersonal, nonarousing. I'm cold with dread. What have I gotten myself into? Why didn't I flee when I saw how isolated the place was?

"Well, young lady, do you think you have it in you to whip another? Can you rule with an iron fist? Can you give Martin pleasure?"

"I don't know." I can hardly speak.

"Let's help her get in the mood, Godfrey." The stock is released and I stand uncertainly in the middle of the floor. Helga goes to a small closet and removes black pieces of leather. I stare at them when she holds them out to me. "Put them on."

High-heeled boots that go to the tops of my thighs. I stagger in them when I try to pull them up. Helga's strong hand holds me steady. A strip of leather continues up each side of my hip, and Helga buckles an attached thick leather belt around my waist. It cinches it in cruelly. My ass and cunt are exposed. Available.

Thin black leather fingerless gloves slide up both arms. Helga places a collar around my neck and attaches the tops of the gloves to it with small silver chains. Strands of silver chains hangs from the front of the collar, and these are wrapped around my breasts so they support them and are then reattached to the collar. She darkens my eyes and paints my lips bright red. I hardly recognize myself when I face a mirror. She hands me a riding crop. Martin is fully erect. His eyes glow with a fearful excitement.

I look from the crop to me to the man. "Go on and make him happy. Martin can take anything you want to give him. He's a good subject for beginners."

I can hardly feel the crop in my hand. The man's penis is wagging in front of me. He's licking his lips nervously but his eyes shine with excitement. A hand nudges me forward. I almost stumble in the tall boots. Helga presses her soft flesh into mine from behind. My hand is lifted.

"Go on, love. Once you get started you'll find it easier. Go on. Don't be nervous. Look at his prick. It's almost upright he's so excited. Go on, love. Give him what he wants. Give him what he needs. Give it to him so you can pleasure both of you. Think of the power you hold. Think of the things you could do to him." She caresses my back lightly and then her hands slip around me and her palms rub lightly over my peaks. Her voice is husky. Persuasive. Hypnotic. "Think of the things you can make him do to pleasure you. Anything you want. As many times as you want. He'll be your slave. Your minion. Yours to do with whatever you like. Whenever you like."

She takes my arm and raises it high in the air. "I'll help you begin," she husks behind me, her voice so close to my ear I feel the warmth of her breath.

I feel as if I'm not really there. It all has such a sense of unreality about it. The man is licking his lips and turning so I can whip his ass. He juts it out in my direction. He turns and looks back at me. His tongue swipes his lips. His eyes shine. Helga is gripping my arm that holds the riding crop and raising it, her other hand gently pulling on my breasts. Her breath tickles my ear. She breaths out, her tongue licks my lobe, the inside of my ear. My clit pulses. My breathing is tortured.

My arm descends and the sound of the crop hitting flesh makes me quake. I can feel the impact shudder up my arm. I see his flesh squeeze together and then hump the air. A vivid red line breaks out across his buttocks. My stomach turns. Helga presses into me. I feel her pubic hair rub against my ass. My arm is lifted again. I try to drop the instrument of torture, but Helga has placed her hand over mine and forces me to strike the man again and again. He screams. I start to shake. She rubs herself against me harder with each stroke she forces me to give.

My mind is spinning, whirling out of control. Each time the crop lands I feel the force of its striking the flesh. Helga strengthens her hold on my breast, and I cease struggling when her fingers take a painful hold of my nipple. My arm rises and descends under the guidance of her stronger one. My nipple is pulled and stroked. My legs are nudged apart by her feet and then a mouth is at my source, licking, sucking, spinning me into a mindless whirl of need.

Her hand leaves, I drop the crop. The mouth is insistent. My body is on fire with need. I can barely breathe. I'm only half aware of the thicker instrument she thrusts into my hand. I can barely suck in air. My thighs are held still by a viselike grip. A tongue delves deep inside me. A finger pushed into my ass torments me more. I can't stop the frantic mewlings of want that escape from my throat and then the mouth is gone.

"No. No!" My scream is a frenzy of unfulfilled lust. Strong fingers grip the back of my neck and keep me still and forward.

"Then whip him."

I'm panting with frustration. Tears are streaming down my cheeks. "I can't."

"Yes you can. For every stroke you give him you'll feel a tongue like you've never felt before."

"No. Please. I can't. Please," I beg and drop the cane. It's placed back in my hand and kept there by hers. Her voice is right at my ear from behind me. A tongue swipes along my slit lightly. I almost sag with desire.

"Do it, Tessa. Do it so you can feel good. Think about yourself. Think about what you want. Whip the man so you can feel better. Go on, Tessa. It will feel good. Think about how good it will feel to come. Think about having the tongue back on your body. Go on, Tessa. Go on."

The voice is so low. So insistent. I raise my arm. The man glances back and smiles at me. I think of Rodney. He has the same dark eyes. They glitter the same way when he thinks he can beat me. My hand descends. Hard. The crack of bamboo meeting flesh makes me flinch, but the man makes a mistake and glances back once more. Rodney. Pain. His pleasure in hurting me. My arm raises and lowers without thought as I beat the man, wishing he were Rodney.

Tessa's Holidays

I'm sucking in air. Grunting with the effort to put all my strength into the hits. His body blurs before my eyes. I can think of nothing but paying back Rodney, until the mouth once again claims my source, and then the cane is dropped and I'm holding Godfrey's head tight to me and keening loudly as pure animalistic joy surges through me. I collapse when my thighs are released.

I open my eyes and stare at the ceiling. Chains dangle high above me. A tongue is slowly caressing me. Nuzzling me into consciousness. Reality returns and I try to rise. My legs can't move. My arms are immobilized. The man I beat is groveling between my legs.

"Relax, Tessa. Now you'll learn the pleasures of having a slave. He can think of nothing but pleasuring you now."

"I want to get up."

"Not yet. You haven't learned how to relax and enjoy your power yet. Let him minister to you."

My legs are spread, the knees bent. A pillow is under me, making me more accessible. His tongue seeks, sucks, licks, nibbles. He makes small animalistic grunts as he grazes along my puffy lips. He lowers his head and works his tongue into my tight tunnel. I grunt in surprise and try to wiggle away. It is such a perverse sense of pleasure. I love it. I hate it.

"I want to get up."

"All in good time." Helga kneels beside me and runs her hands over my breasts. It is the first time I'm aware of my total nudity. I've been undressed. Godfrey stands above me and grins.

"I told you it would be something new, didn't I, Tessa? You whipped into him with a vengeance. What was it that made you suddenly so eager to beat him?"

The tongue is working. I can't quite concentrate on Godfrey's words. "I want to get up." Why does my speech sound slower? Thicker? Helga's mouth descends to my breasts. My toes are curling. The need is building. I pull against the restraints. The tongue licks me, slow and steady. Up and down. Each time it reaches my clit I can feel the quick nips of lust sinking deeper and deeper inside me.

Godfrey sinks down cross-legged next to me. His hand lightly toys with my other breast. His smile is lazy. "Didn't I tell you I could bind you totally and you'd feel good? You're not in pain, are you, Tessa?"

My clit is grabbed and sucked in hard. I'm panting harder. Godfrey leans down and kisses my nipple. Helga is flicking the other peak steadily. The tongue moves deep inside me. "Don't you like being like this, Tessa? I think you're more of a receiver than a giver. I think you like being done to, not doing to. I think you love the feel of so many tongues on your body. I think you don't get enough sex. I think this is just what you needed."

My mind is spinning. I can hardly hear his words. The tongue is swirling around my sphincter. I can feel it responding. It pulses and twitches as if trying to capture the tongue and suck it in deeper. My breasts are so sensitive. My clit is engorged. Painful. Pulsing. Needing.

"Tell Dan what you want. Show us you're a mistress and not a slave."

My head thrashes back and forth. Why can't I vocalize what I need? Why is it so hard to say it aloud? I groan. I whimper but I can't force the words past my mouth. I try to lift my hips so I'll be closer to that wonderful mouth but it's gone. I almost cry with frustration.

"Please."

"No, it's too late, Tessa. You took too long. Now you will only be pleasured when we decide. You had the opportunity to control this session. You chose not to."

I'm humping the air with the minutest of movement. I don't know how I'm restrained but it is total. I feel no cutting. No pressure, but I cannot move.

I'm scared. "I'll do better. I'll make him do what I want."

"No." Godfrey's voice comes from somewhere behind me. "No, I think Helga is right and you're more slave than mistress. But that's all right because Helga is all mistress. I like both but today I'll be a dominant, and this way we each have a toy to play with. Which would you like, Helga?"

"Her."

The word chills me to the bone. The woman says it with absolutely no emotion. The sound of chains chinking together draws my eyes. Godfrey is fastening the man Dan to a pipe that reaches from floor to ceiling.

"Bend."

The man does, sliding his manacled hands down the length of the steel. His fat asscheeks spread when he reaches the floor. I shut my eyes. It almost makes the sound of the lash worse. My eyes open instantly when white-hot fire streaks along my thighs.

Everyone is meeting at Flanagan's Bar to celebrate St. Patrick's Day. I sit and listen to the lively chatter and sip my green beer. Kevin Daly challenges me to a dart game, and we spend an enjoyable half hour trying hard to top each other's move. I happily cede the title of champ to him when he beats me by only two points.

Kelly O'Brien enters the bar to a round of applause and whistles. She's dressed like a leprechaun—a very sexy leprechaun—and the single men in the place hurry to clear a bar stool for her. She gives me a sly wink and begins to flirt outrageously with the fakest Irish brogue imaginable. The men think it charming. I can't help but laugh at her tactics. She's never made it a secret that she wants nothing more than to have fun in life. I'm sure she will this night.

Why is it that she can get away with this behavior but none would accept it from me? Is it because I was born here and she wasn't? Do the townspeople consider me one of their children? Or is it the connection of being related to the pastor of the community church? Either way I think it very unfair.

The music is loud, and before too many beers have been downed the required Irish jig is played on the jukebox and the more outgoing all give it a try while we urge them on with clapping and shouts. The music is now blaring, the jokes getting more risqué, the place smokier. Kevin takes a seat beside me. He has to shout to be heard. "Having fun?"

"Yes. You?"

"Yeah. It's good to get together like this and blow off some steam. I'm really looking forward to summer vacation this year."

The bartender finally lowers the audio and we can hear each other without yelling. "Do you have special plans?"

"I sure do. I'm taking a leaf from your book and going to see some of the world." His eyes are almost glowing. "I'm backpacking as much of Alaska as I'm able to in eight weeks."

"That sound like fun, Kevin."

Tessa's Holidays

He turns and faces me more directly. "It will be. They say it's a beautiful state. Uh, you wouldn't be interested in going with me, would you, Tessa?"

I'm floored and taken completely off guard. "No!"

Kevin blushes lightly. "Don't misunderstand me, Tessa. I don't mean it the way you think. I just thought that you might be the type of person who would enjoy something like that. I mean, here you went off all by yourself and saw so much last year. I don't know anyone else who would have traveled to so many strange places by themselves. I really admire you for it and thought you might be good company on a trip like this. I didn't mean anything by it, honestly."

He's such a nice man. I smile but shake my head. "I know, Kevin. And I appreciate the offer, but I think I'm going to take my friends up on their invitation to visit them in the islands. There's a lot I still haven't seen, and it's an economical way to travel when you have a home base you don't have to pay for."

He nods in understanding and gives me a lopsided smile. "Can't blame a man for trying."

I nod and try to stifle a yawn. "I think I'll call it a night."

"Do you want me to walk you to your car?"

"No, thanks. I'll just visit the ladies' room and then leave. Good night, Kevin. See you in school tomorrow."

It takes a while to make my way to the back of the building. Everyone is laughing and smiling and has something to say. I open the door and enter the tiny hall that leads to the rest rooms and back door. One of my fellow teachers is just leaving the cramped area. We kind of sidle pass each other and both wear slightly embarrassed grins.

I look at my face in the mirror and splash it with cold water. I can't quite define the way I feel. Tonight was fun but it lacked something. I feel somehow incomplete. Almost lost. I stare at myself long and hard but I cannot put a name to my feelings. How can I be in the midst of so much fun and noise and people and yet still feel so terribly alone? I feel weighed down. As if I'm slowly smothering. As if there is no reason to go on.

I need a direction in my life. Teaching isn't satisfying anymore. I want to live on the edge. I want the fearful anticipation of never knowing what will happen next. I want the thrill of being swept from one place to another. I want to experience even more new things. I want Grant.

Bill is at the open back door. He smiles a mocking smile and invites me outside with a sweep of his arm. My heart is pounding in my chest. This is it. Grant does know about Godfrey and he's sent Bill to punish me. For all his hardness, I would have preferred Rodney. I'm shaking as I walk past him. Clive is standing at the open door of the limousine. He smiles and tips his hat.

I swallow and step inside. Strong arms wrap themselves around me and firm, wonderful lips claim mine. The door closes and the car starts forward, and I let myself savor the wonderful feelings coursing through my body.

"Hi."

"Hi," I answer breathlessly. My body is tight with excitement. I tingle under the light kisses on my neck. Strong fingers stroke my back. My thighs. My breasts. My nipples harden and push themselves into his hands. I hear his delighted chuckle. I feel his glorious mouth begin to cover mine.

And I let myself go completely. His hands are so knowing. So able to take me where I want to go in such a short time. It's too fast. Too unexpected, and I moan into his mouth as the spasms lessen and ease. I lean against him happily.

"How did you know I'd go in the back?"

The inside of the limousine is dim. I snuggle deeper into his body. His chuckle vibrates beneath my ear.

"I've never met anyone, man or woman, who can drink beer and not have to go to the back."

"But how did you know when I would?"

"I did. That's all that's important."

A sudden thought makes me sit up. "My car. Someone will miss me."

"I took care of it, Tessa. Relax. Enjoy our short time together."

I snuggle under his arm and lean contentedly against him. My hand has a will of its own, and after stroking his broad chest for a few minutes it finds his lap. His lumpy lap. I have to smile. Lightly I trace my fingers along the length of his thickness. I can't resist toying with the zipper and lowering it as slowly as I can. The button on top almost springs apart, and then I have the wonderful weight of that object of pleasure in my hand.

I clasp it tightly between my two hands. The pulses make me smile. I lean down and rub it lightly along my cheek. I breathe in the scent of him. My mind is whirling with pleasure. With expectation. I love the rubbery feeling of his shaft. The skin is so tight. The knob is swollen. The vent opens at a touch of my tongue.

I kneel beside him on the seat and immediately his hands are easing my skirt off. My underpants follow. I lower my mouth on him and suck lightly. Firm hands skim and stroke my backside. A finger lowers and tickles my slit. I suck harder.

Hands are beneath my bent body. Air touches my chest. My back. The snap of a hook is heard and then my breasts are free and hanging. Hands cup, stroke, and caress their fullness. I trace the length of him with my wet tongue.

I'm lifted and he shifts position. I feel the coolness of leather against my back. My hands are held lightly at my side. And his mouth descends and his lips pull on my throbbing peaks. Streaks of pure lust shoot through me. I suck in air and tighten my vagina. I wish he would penetrate me. I need to feel him inside me. I want him so desperately.

Moist warmth wraps itself around one breast, then the other. His tongue teases, swipes, tickles, circles, and drives me to distraction. I'm humping wildly beneath him but he does nothing but lick and suck and tease.

I try to squirm down so I can feel the mighty shaft against my mound, but he holds me steady. I'm moaning, wriggling, writhing in sexual fever and still he torments me. Everything within me pulses with need. My body almost hums under the strumming of his tongue.

And then he's there. Deep within me. I raise my legs and clasp his hips. My arms hold tightly to his neck. I grind my breasts against his broad chest and move wildly beneath him.

Strong hands take my hips and keep me still. I mewl with need. I clasp him tightly with every muscle I possess, and then he moves. So slowly. So deeply. Every inch of him rubs along the throbbing organ, and I let go and scream with building frenzy till I shatter and begin to sob with relief.

Lips lick away my tears as my breathing slows. Grant pulls out of me and then lifts up. I feel his hands turning me. The leather is cool and damp beneath my cheek. I bury my head in the crook of my arms and raise my hips as he guides me to. His hand is so soothing. He skims my belly. He soothes my still-pulsing clit and then eases into my tight tunnel slowly.

I'm so lethargic. So at peace. He's gentle and steady, and his hand is soothing beneath me. A tingle of desire sweeps through me. Another. And yet another, and I'm slowly returning the pressure of his pumping. I want this to be good for him. I want it to be better than good. I tighten and hear his quick intake of breath. I do it again and again and all the while I pleasure him my own is building steadily.

His fingers are busy beneath me. They tease and tickle and then penetrate further to drive me wild with need. The building pressure is pure torment. I want it to last. I want it to end.

My pumping gains speed. My breathing is rapidly becoming ragged, and I squeeze and squeeze my muscles with all my might. For the first time I hear Grant let out a roar of pleasure instead of his usual low grunt. The sound alone takes me over the edge.

I love this feeling of being close to him, nestled in his arms. We sip wine and just enjoy being together for a long time. The black night glides by us silently. Nothing exists but us two.

"Anything new or exciting happening in your life?" His question causes me to pause. Is it a leading question? His eyes are calm. I sense no tension in his body. Guilt does terrible things to a person.

My smile is almost regular. "No. Not really. It's kinda strange to be living alone."

"I like it myself. I guess it's what you get used to."

"I guess." I wish I could think of another topic to discuss. Where has all my articulation gone? Why can't I think of anything to talk about?

Because I'm wracked with guilt.

"I thought we might go to England this summer."

My heart races with both excitement and fear. Why did he say England? Was it just a coincidence? I thought he'd mentioned the Orient? "That would be lovely. I'd love to see Big Ben and Buckingham Palace."

"There is much more to England than old buildings, Tessa. There are legends and traditions. They have an enormous number of traditions. Why, I do believe England has the best attitude about corporal punishment. They believe in it thoroughly, you know. The schools still allow it. I understand there are even places men can take their wives and have them, uh, let's say corrected or taught better behavior."

My chest is tight with fear. He knows. He's playing with me. I swallow. "Why would you be interested in that, Grant? Besides, not being your wife I've no need to be corrected or taught proper behavior." Does he believe my bravado? "I thought one of the reasons you were attracted to me was you thought I would know how to act with your guests and acquaintances?"

His fingers are firm on my chin. His lips are soft, gentle. A rush of pleasure fills me. "It was only one of many things that attracted me to you, Tessa." Delightful chills rush through me when I hear my name spoken like a caress. "One was the spirit of adventure you displayed. Wouldn't you like to experience all different kinds of things? You seem to me the type that would be eaten by curiosity until you satisfied it by trying something new. Isn't that true, Tessa?"

My head is light with happiness. My skin is crawling with warning. "Not necessarily. I guess it would depend on what it was." I nuzzle my nose along his hard jawline. I breath in his scent deeply. I wish he would change the subject.

"What if I wanted you to go to a man who would show me how to discipline you by the lash?"

Reality crashes in. "I don't like pain, Grant. You know that!"

His hand keeps me close to him. My heart is pounding. "But would you go?"

"Would I have a choice?"

"Perhaps." His fingers stroke my knuckles. They're lifted to his lips, which rove over them slowly. I have to clench my legs. I hate it that he can distract me so easily. One finger at a time is sucked and licked. "Would you like to experience being a dominant?"

My head is reeling. My mind tries hard to concentrate on his words instead of the feelings he's creating inside of me. He has to know. I feel perspiration break out all over my body. I shiver. "I don't think so." My voice is no more than a squeak.

"But wouldn't you want to know?" His voice is husky. Low. Terrifying.

I shake my head and try to pull my hand from his. He won't release it.

"Haven't you ever wondered how it felt to hold a riding crop or a cane and hit someone with it? Try to imagine the feeling of power. Haven't you ever wanted to retaliate for the smacks you've taken? Haven't you ever dreamed about giving Rodney back what he's given you? Haven't you ever wondered why Louise and Ingrid did what they did to you? Wouldn't you like to be able to repay them?"

I start to shake. This is too much to be a coincidence. He's playing me along before he seeks retribution. I take a deep breath and force myself to stay calm. "And what about the smacks you've given me, Grant? Do you want me to seek revenge? Do you secretly wish to feel a cane or riding crop on your bare ass? Is this one of the things you would still like to experiment with? Would you lie down quietly and let me learn the feeling of being dominant with you?"

"That would be most unwise, Tessa. Surely you know that by now?"

I can't quite suppress the shiver that ripples along my skin.

"Are you cold, Tessa? I'm sorry. I didn't realize. Let me help you get warm."

I'm laid back on the seat. I expect to feel pain when he lifts my leg, but warm loving lips make a slow journey up my calf. They linger on the soft back of my knee. My leg is lowered and the moist tongue continues on its travels. Thigh. Other thigh. Crease of hip. Belly. Other crease. Lower. Lower. I'm going to scream. Fear mingles with building need. My frustration grows with each touch of his tongue. The fear is fading, raw animal need takes over. His nose nuzzles through the silky hairs on my mound. His breath bathes my puffy lips and they open at the first touch of his tongue. My mouth is dry. My breathing tortured. I will go mad. I will surely go mad one day.

The tip of his tongue snakes out and just lightly flicks my clitoris. It's pulsing. Needing. Poised on the edge, but he moves up and his tongue is traveling higher. It skims the slight curve of my belly. The underside of my breast is licked, browsed upon. He grazes on my nipples. Lightly. Softly. His whiff of breath sends chills of pleasure through me. The hardened peaks thrust themselves into his mouth. I want him to suck on them. Why can't I say the words? Why can't I tell him what to do to pleasure me? Why do I lay here and let him torment me?

I reach for him but he won't lift his weight from me. His hands take mine and lift them above my head and hold them tightly to the seat. I panic, thinking he means to torment me then leave me. Is this the punishment for Godfrey? Does he know? Oh, God, I can't take the uncertainty. I can't stand the frustration of being so helpless and needing so much.

My hips grind into him as much as his weight allows. I'm crying with the agony of needing to finish. I'm crying with the fear of what he intends. He continues working on my breasts. The pressure in my loins is sheer anguish.

"Please, Grant." My voice is strained and husky, begging.

"Do you want me?"

How can he ask? I can barely suck in air I need him so badly. I nod and try to pull my hands from his tight grasp. I need his body higher on me. He won't budge.

"Do you want me?"

Anything. I will do anything. "Yes! Yes, I want you. I have to have you. Please, Grant. Now. Now!" I scream, uncaring about who might hear.

He lifts himself and roughly plows deep within me. Pain slices all the way to my depths, and feelings shift and merge and split, only to merge again. He's like a pile driver thrusting deep inside me, and then suddenly the pain melds with the need, and I'm keening wildly and holding him tightly to me so he'll continue the agonizingly wonderful act.

How can something so beautiful, so wondrous, be mixed with pain and still be exquisite in its completeness? I have no idea who put me into my bed.

I still don't know for sure if Grant knows about Godfrey. The days pass too slowly. The uncertainty is beginning to show, and I find myself snapping at the children and grumpy with the adults. The news that Michael is taking my mother and Polly's family to an amusement park during Easter vacation doesn't help. I know he took me to Rio. I know I shouldn't feel left out. I know that being alone during vacation should excite me. It means Grant and I might be able to get together.

And the thought both arouses and alarms me. I can't shake the feeling that Grant is trying to lull me into a false sense of security. Everything in my body screams to be extra careful, but then the next instant I'm reliving the wonderful night in the limousine, and I'm sure if he knew he'd have done something about it then.

Unless he no longer cares if I see other people.

Again that mixture of emotions. Sorrow. Hurt. Jealousy. But a quick sense of relief also. And yet I don't really desire anyone but Grant. He's the one who enjoys observing people's reactions to situations. He's the one who demands absolute obedience physically yet revels in my opinions, my thoughts, our arguments for and against everything under the sun. He hates when I agree with him on any subject because then he loses the chance to pit his intellect and reasoning against mine. The memories of the long nights of talk and arguments are sweet. Frustrated beyond endurance because neither one could come around to the other's point of view, we'd tumble into bed and work off the chains of exasperation. Imagine if they could settle world affairs this way?

The kids at school are gritty and antsy. Most are leaving for vacations further south so they can start their tans early. Very few are concentrating on anything I say. It makes the days seem longer. Slower.

On Easter everyone comes back to my house after church. Mom hardly notices the changes I've made. Mom hardly notices anything but Michael.

I try real hard to bury the resentment I feel at their happiness. I try real hard to listen enthusiastically to all the places they'll go to in Florida. I try real hard not to wonder when or if Grant will contact me. I try real hard, and succeed, in not asking Michael where his friend Grant will be during this vacation.

I'm still not completely sure I want to know.

Monday morning I wander aimlessly around the house. I'm on edge. Ready. Dreading. Yearning. Fearing.

The doorbell rings. I stop myself from running to it. Grant would never come here during the day. He doesn't even come under the cover of darkness. It's the delivery truck with a package for me.

My hands are shaking as I pull off the wrapping. The box is taped and I struggle to get it open. Inside lies a beautiful silk black dress. It's simple and unadorned.

Two tiny bows at the shoulders are the only ornamentation. A small card lies beneath it.

> 10 P.M.
> Tuesday.
> The Beat.
> South Street.
> Des Moines.
> BE READY.

I have to clutch my chest, my heart is pounding so hard.

I have my hair cut in a saucy short style. The kind that I know Grant likes. I shave my legs, my underarms, and just for him I trim my pubic hair. I don't like being shaven, but I make it more the way he likes it.

I agonize over whether to wear underwear. I know he detests it but we'll be in a public restaurant where it's more than possible we'll see people he knows. That alone makes my heart start beating wildly. What does it mean? Does this signal a change in our relationship? Does he feel, since we've been introduced through Michael and he's now a friend of the family so to speak, that it will be all right for us to dine together occasionally or attend the opera or such? The thought of being able to see him more often than I do is enough to make me tremble with excitement.

The arrival of high heels, silk stockings, and black garter belt decides the issue of undergarments. I'm not to wear them.

I do my nails.
I pace.
I brush my hair.
I pace.

I put on another coat of polish.
I pace.
I dress.
I pace.
I undress and throw on a robe.
I pace
I make a light snack.
I push the food around on my plate.
I look in the mirror.
I fix my lipstick.
I pace.
I pull the dress over my head.
I slip on the heels.

A final look in the mirror and I grab my purse and open the door.

A limousine awaits me. A chauffeur opens the door and tips his hat. I smooth the clinging dress over my hips once more and enter the back. It's not Grant's limousine. I'm alone.

I hear the locks click into place. My mouth goes dry. The windows are dark. Very dark. I barely make out the streetlights. A black partition separates me from the driver. I push the button to lower it but it remains up. The phone doesn't work. The radio doesn't work. The door won't open. I can barely breathe.

My body is trembling violently. Why am I being kept here? Why would Grant do this? Was it Grant? I clasp my hands in panic. Who else would it be? Who else would invite me to dinner? Why this way though? Why hadn't Grant been in the car? Why hadn't it been his limousine? Why wasn't Clive driving?

I hug myself tightly and rock. Try as I might, I can make out no distinct shapes beyond the black glass. I have no idea of where I am or where I'm going. The feeling of helplessness is total. The feeling of fear is all-encompassing. The feeling of being a fool is complete.

We ride for a long time. I can barely swallow. There is nothing to alleviate my sense of isolation. No drinks. No water. No glasses. No control over anything.

The car slowing down and stopping both thrills and terrifies me. I hear the chauffeur's door open and close. I listen to the sound of his footsteps circle the car. I'm holding my breath and staring at the right-hand door. I only let it out when the door slowly opens.

A gloved hand reaches in, and I take it and step from the car. Everything is normal. It disorients me. I'd expected…what?

The restaurant is directly in front of us. The doors open and I hear light, happy chatter from inside. A couple emerges, laughing and complaining about how they ate too much. The street is a busy main thoroughfare. Cars beep horns and whiz by. People stroll along the sidewalk. I see the lights of a few stores that remain open late.

I suddenly feel like a fool.

The chauffeur is waiting for me to enter the building. I give him a tentative smile of thanks and take a deep breath. The door opens easily. The foyer is decorated in rich, deep colors. I can see the room beyond is filled with happy patrons and I start to relax.

The stiffly erect maitre d' approaches me. "Mrs. Duncan?"

I can't stop the start of surprise. "Yes."

He smiles and bows slightly. "If you'll follow me."

I'm surprised when he turns to the right. It must be a private room. Grant doesn't think it all right to meet in public. The carpeting is thick beneath my feet. The elegance of the decor is rich and quiet. We walk along a wide hallway. I can't help but admire myself in the many mirrors we pass. The dress fits to perfection. It hugs my slight curves and shows off my slenderness. I love the new hairstyle.

An elegant couple join us as we wait for the elevator. The man is dressed in a tuxedo. The woman's dress is exquisite. The doors open and the maitre d' ushers us in with a sweep of his hand. I'm surprised when he doesn't follow us.

The doors close, and a hand grabs my head and pinches my nose. A large ball gag is thrust into my mouth. I'm screaming around the intrusion. My hands claw for a scant second and then are pinioned together by the woman, who is now in front of me.

I'm terrified. The woman has no expression. None. She holds my hands tightly together and doesn't look at me. She's watching the man tighten the gag. I'm going to choke. I'm going to suffocate. The dress hobbles my legs and I can't kick out more than a few inches. She stands just far enough away to be out of reach. The man is the same. All my twisting and writhing is ignored. The pressure on my cheeks is enormous. My eyes are tearing and I'm terrified of choking.

My hands are taken by the man and lifted. The woman opens her purse. A hood dangles in her hand right in front of my eyes and then is taken and placed over my head. I'm blind for only a minute and then they adjust it so only my eyes show. The laces tighten under my jawline. I've never been so frightened in all my life.

Leather slaps against my wrists and then they're tied together. I'm released and reel to the other side of the elevator. My hands rise to feel the hood. My thighs explode with pain. Two elegant people smile coldly at me and shake their heads. I lower my hands and lean weakly against the wall.

My mouth aches and I force myself to calm down and swallow slowly. The mask muffles the muted groans I make. I'm ignored. The man and woman stand and converse quietly as if I weren't there. The lights pick up the sequins of her royal blue dress, and it sparkles and shimmers each time she moves. I feel as though I'm in some kind of slow-motion dream. Or nightmare.

The doors open and the couple steps out. A man with a hood over his face steps in and grabs my arm. I'm pushed along ahead of him down a dark hallway. It all has such a sense of unreality about it. I keep waiting to open my eyes and see my bedroom ceiling above me.

The hood muffles sounds but I think I hear a crowd of people in the distance. I do. I'm pushed onto a stage of sorts. Tables are filled with people smoking and drinking below me. They all wear masks. Some more covering than others. Some merely strips across the eyes. The hood only allows me to see directly in front of me. I'm turned and my worst fears are realized.

A padded trestle is bolted to the floor in the middle of the stage. I start with fear and turn my head as my arms are lifted and attached to a hook. The hook rises and I'm on tiptoe. Three people are with me on stage. All in the same position I am.

One is a man. Thin. Sinewy. His head is encased in leather. Nervous eyes meet mine. I follow the chain that encircles his waist. It ends in a ring that looks snug around the base of his dangling penis. I don't want to think about how he'll feel if he should harden.

The next is a woman. Naked except for the hood and a harness that separates and holds open her buttocks. When she's placed on the trestle her small brown hole will be like a bull's-eye to whomever is behind her. By the look in her eyes I think she knows it.

I shudder and then look again. She's large. Extremely buxom. The man is thin but tight. And then I know. Godfrey and Helga. This is Grant's doing.

I already know who the other woman is. One look at her beautiful hands clenching and unclenching high above her tells me I'm right. The thin silver flower ring catches the light. As always, Grant has been thorough. A thin leather belt encircles her waist. A cruel chain runs through the ends of the two dildos embedded deeply within her. The same as she'd done to me. Louise's eyes are wide and frantic. I imagine she is screaming uselessly into her gag.

I'm pivoted around and lose sight of them. The hook rises another notch and I groan under the pull in my arms. Someone is behind me. All eyes in front of me are on me. A touch of the bows and my dress falls silently to the floor. Appreciative murmurs run through the audience. I'm stretched to my limit. And naked except for heels, stockings, and garter belt. The black stockings and garter belt must do nothing but enhance my white skin. Especially the very white skin of my ass.

People stare at us and apparently discuss our pros and cons. I can only hear the people nearest to us. A table of four men. They're drinking and ogling at the same time. Two look like they'll burst their pants before long. Two look like this is something they do all the time.

"She looks scared."

"Nay. They all love this. You don't hear any screaming, do ya?"

"Well, no, but..."

"Relax. I'm telling ya. They're all here because they dig the pain. You should see what some of these guys are capable of taking. It's amazing. I'm telling ya you're gonna love this. A lot of times the guy with the whip will fuck 'em after. Must be a turn-on to feel the hot skin against your raging hard-on."

I sway slightly. I can't believe this is real. I don't want to believe it. Music sounds. Lights in the audience dim. The sparkle of royal blue sequins catches my eye. The couple raise their glasses to me when they see me looking at them. My belly clenches.

Helga is released and two burly hooded men take her arms and lead her to the trestle. Her feet are forced into two low stocks, wide apart. I can see a thin sheen of sweat breaking out on her body. She's laid over the padded end and attached at full stretch. Her ass is high in the air. I can see the tension in her legs as she strains against the inevitable.

They keep her waiting. Then the curtains part and a man in a long black robe and hood steps out. A nasty-looking whip dangles from his hand. A murmur spreads along the audience. He trails its ends along the length of Helga's back. You can almost see when the certainty of her fears hits her. Her body tightens and then loosens as she awaits the man's pleasure.

Helga has done this with others before. She knows what to expect. The sight of the whip terrifies me as I've never been before. It will cut. It will be torture. I have to tighten hard to control my water.

Louise isn't so lucky. I hear the cries of outrage and laughter from the audience and try to turn. Louise has lost control of her bladder. The men and women are laughing, shouting, drumming their feet on the floor. Louise's hands are frantic in their bindings. I can see a tiny speck of blood oozing out of the leather that holds her tight to the hook. She's rubbing herself raw.

A spotlight finds her and shows her more clearly in her shame. Her bare feet slip in the fluid, and I watch her body jerk in pain when her arms take her weight. A man steps into the light from behind her and lashes her body with five quick jerks of the tawse in his hand. I do hear her muted scream this time. Or is it mine?

Welts rise along her belly, breasts, and thighs. He's left her ass alone. The other man will attend to that.

My insides are like jelly. I'm shaking from the center of my being. Grant had promised me no permanent physical or mental trauma. I repeat the words over and over to myself. No permanent physical trauma. No scars. No cuts. Nothing to lend support to any claims I might try to make.

My eyes are drawn to the whip in the man's hand. How can it not cut? How can it not scar? I watch as if in a daze as he raises his hand. It pauses, descends. The crack judders through me. Helga tightens like a bowstring and then releases, tightens and releases in response to the pain radiating through her body. He lets her feel all of it before the whip descends again. Five hard strikes across her buttocks. She's writhing in agony. Small drops of blood ooze from where the tip has burrowed in. The man steps back and runs the length of the whip along the crevice of her buttocks. I see every muscle in her body tense and turn away when he takes aim at her puckered hole.

I hear every kiss of the whip. I hear every muted scream of agony. I swear I'm going to be ill.

Time seems to stop. I see nothing even though my eyes are open and looking at the audience. I hear nothing but the sound of leather on flesh. None of this can be real. Nothing like this really happens. Places like this don't exist.

Yes, they do.

Louise is struggling frantically between the two men who walk her toward the man. She pulls and kicks and does nothing but annoy the man and arouse the audience. They're shouting encouragement, but whether it's to her or the man with the whip I cannot tell. By the tightening of the man's lips I think she's bought herself more pain.

One man releases her arm and kneels with a knee up. The other tugs her back hard, and she lies draped over the first man's knee at the small of her back. Her hands are pulled to the floor, stretching her cruelly into an arch. The whip is exchanged for a cat-o'-nine-tails. He's merciless as he uses it over her breasts and belly. I see the man flinch slightly whenever a tip hits his thigh. I see her agony whenever one strikes her mound.

She's lifted, turned, and attached to the trestle. She's shaking uncontrollably. I watch her try to lift her throbbing breasts from contact with the bench. The blow of the whip throws her down tight to the leather padding. I close my eyes and shake.

Godfrey catches my eyes once before they take him. I honestly can't say if it's fear or excitement I see. Probably both.

Godfrey's feet are put in the stocks. They're pulled back so his belly isn't tight to the padded trestle. His penis hangs in full view. It's already hardening just with the anticipation.

The first catches him full under his buttocks. He tightens. His hands clench. His penis thickens. The next is full across the width of his ass. His penis throbs visibly and darkens. I see the man measure his aim and turn away. Four more hard licks of the whip and then my arms are being lowered.

I walk between them calmly because I know this can't be real. This is all a dream. A nightmare. This is my guilt and hate taking over my subconscious at night. I'm going to wake up soon and it'll all be over.

Strange how real the people look. Strange how I feel no embarrassment walking along a stage, naked for all to see. But then you don't feel emotions in dreams, do you? I stop when I see the small pool of thick white semen. My dream is so detailed.

They let me stare at it another moment and then a touch on my arm startles me. I look into the man's eyes. They're calculating. Hard. He holds a tawse in his hand. Not a whip. No permanent trauma. The words snap me out of my daze.

I turn and lock onto two crinkling ice blue eyes at the nearest table. A glass is lifted in a silent toast. A camera sits on the table. A photograph album rests beside it.

My feet are surrounded by wood. I'm bent. The leather is damp and warm. I can smell Louise's fear. I can smell Godfrey's excitement. My belly clenches when I feel the pressure on my wrists keeping me still. It's strange that I feel no fear.

I turn and lay my head down. The blue eyes I love are staring at me. He won't be able to see my expression. Or will my eyes be enough?

The lips I know so well spread into a small smile. It seems to hold regret, not nastiness. Not anger. I swallow around the gag and force myself to relax and keep my eyes open.

I think about this summer. I think about the breezes I'll feel. The new scents I'll smell. I think about being with Grant. I don't think I'll experiment on my own anymore.

The Masquerade Erotic Newsletter

◆◆◆◆◆◆◆◆◆◆◆◆◆◆◆◆◆◆◆◆◆◆

FICTION, ESSAYS, REVIEWS, PHOTOGRAPHY, INTERVIEWS, EXPOSÉS, AND MUCH MORE!

"One of my favorite sex zines featuring some of the best articles on erotica, fetishes, sex clubs and the politics of porn." —*Factsheet Five*

"I recommend a subscription to *The Masquerade Erotic Newsletter*.... They feature short articles on "the scene"...an occasional fiction piece, and reviews of other erotic literature. Recent issues have featured intelligent prose by the likes of Trish Thomas, David Aaron Clark, Pat Califia, Laura Antoniou, Lily Burana, John Preston, and others.... it's good stuff." —*Black Sheets*

"A classy, bi-monthly magazine..." —*Betty Paginated*

"It's always a treat to see a copy of *The Masquerade Erotic Newsletter*, for it brings a sophisticated and unexpected point of view to bear on the world of erotica, and does this with intelligence, tolerance, and compassion." —Martin Shepard, co-publisher, The Permanent Press

"Publishes great articles, interviews and pix which in many cases are truly erotic and which deal non-judgementally with the full array of human sexuality, a far cry from much of the material which passes itself off under that title.... *Masquerade Erotic Newsletter* is fucking great." —*Eddie, the Magazine*

"We always enjoy receiving your *Masquerade Newsletter* and seeing the variety of subjects covered...." —*body art*

"*Masquerade Erotic Newsletter* is probably the best newsletter I have ever seen." —*Secret International*

"The latest issue is absolutely lovely. Marvelous images...." —*The Boudoir Noir*

"I must say that the *Newsletter* is fabulous...."
—Tuppy Owens,
Publisher, Author, Sex Therapist

"Fascinating articles on all aspects of sex..." —*Desire*

◆◆◆◆◆◆◆◆◆◆◆◆◆◆◆◆◆◆◆◆◆◆

The Masquerade Erotic Newsletter

"Here's a very provocative, very professional [newsletter]...made up of intelligent erotic writing... Stimulating, yet not sleazy photos add to the picture and also help make this zine a high quality publication." —Gray Areas

From **Masquerade Books**, the World's Leading Publisher of Erotica, comes *The Masquerade Erotic Newsletter*—the best source for provocative, cutting-edge fiction, sizzling pictorials, scintillating and illuminating exposes of the sex industry, and probing reviews of the latest books and videos.

Featured writers and articles have included:

Lars Eighner • *Why I Write Gay Erotica*
Pat Califia • *Among Us, Against Us*
Felice Picano • *An Interview with Samuel R. Delany*
Samuel R. Delany • *The Mad Man* (excerpt)
Maxim Jakubowski • *Essex House: The Rise and Fall of Speculative Erotica*
Red Jordan Arobateau • *Reflections of a Lesbian Trick*
Aaron Travis • *Lust*
Nancy Ava Miller, M. Ed. • *Beyond Personal*
Tuppy Owens • *Female Erotica in Great Britain*
Trish Thomas • *From Dyke to Dude*
Barbara Nitke • *Resurrection*
and many more....

The newsletter has also featured stunning photo essays by such masters of fetish photography as **Robert Chouraqui**, **Eric Kroll**, **Richard Kern**, and **Trevor Watson**.

A one-year subscription (6 issues) to the *Newsletter* costs $30.00. Use the accompanying coupon to subscribe now—for an uninterrupted string of the most provocative of pleasures (as well as a special gift, offered to subscribers only!).

Free GIFT

WHEN YOU SUBSCRIBE TO:
The Masquerade Erotic Newsletter

Receive two **Masquerade, Badboy or Rosebud** books of your choice.

Please send me these two books free!

1. _____

2. _____

☐ I've enclosed my payment of $30.00 for a one-year subscription (six issues) to: *THE MASQUERADE EROTIC NEWSLETTER.*

Name _____

Address _____

_____

City _____ State _____ Zip _____

Tel. (___) _____

Payment ☐ Check ☐ Money Order ☐ Visa ☐ MC

Card No. _____

Exp. Date _____

Please allow 4–6 weeks delivery. No C.O.D. orders. Please make all checks payable to Masquerade Books, 801 Second Avenue, N.Y., N.Y., 10017. Payable in U.S. currency only. Order by phone: 1-800-375-2356 or fax, 212 986-7355

Y74L

ROSEBUD BOOKS

THE ROSEBUD READER
Rosebud Books—the hottest-selling line of lesbian erotica available—here collects the very best of the best. Rosebud has contributed greatly to the burgeoning genre of lesbian erotica—to the point that authors like Lindsay Welsh, Aarona Griffin and Valentina Cilescu are among the hottest and most closely watched names in lesbian and gay publishing. Here are the finest moments from Rosebud's contemporary classics. $5.95/319-8

K. T. BUTLER

TOOLS OF THE TRADE
A sparkling mix of lesbian erotica and humor. A sizzling encounter with ice cream, cappucino and chocolate cake; an affair with a complete stranger; a pair of faulty handcuffs and love on a drafting table. Seventeen delightful tales.
$5.95/420-8

LOVECHILD

GAG
From New York's thriving poetry scene comes this explosive volume of work from one of the bravest, most cutting young writers you'll ever encounter. The poems in *Gag* take on American hypocrisy with uncommon energy, and announce Lovechild as a writer of unique and unforgettable rage. $5.95/369-4

ALISON TYLER

THE VIRGIN
Does he satisfy you? Is something missing? Maybe you don't need a man at all—maybe you need me. Veronica answers a personal ad in the "Women Seeking Women" category—and discovers a whole sensual world she never knew existed! And she never dreamed she'd be prized as a virgin all over again, by someone who would deflower her with a passion no man could ever show.... $5.95/379-1

THE BLUE ROSE
The tale of a modern sorority—fashioned after a Victorian girls' school. Ignited to the heights of passion by erotic tales of the Victorian age, a group of lusty young women are encouraged to act out their forbidden fantasies—all under the tutelage of Mistresses Emily and Justine, two avid practitioners of hard-core discipline! $5.95/335-X

ELIZABETH OLIVER

THE SM MURDER: Murder at Roman Hill
Intrepid lesbian P.I.s Leslie Patrick and Robin Penny take on a really hot case: the murder of the notorious Felicia Roman. The circumstances of the crime lead the pair on an excursion through the leatherdyke underground, where motives—and desires—run deep. But as Leslie and Robin soon find, every woman harbors her own closely guarded secret.... $5.95/353-8

PAGAN DREAMS
Cassidy and Samantha plan a vacation at a secluded bed-and-breakfast, hoping for a little personal time alone. Their hostess, however, has different plans. The lovers are plunged into a world of dungeons and pagan rites, as the merciless Anastasia steals Samantha for her own. B&B—B&D-style! $5.95/295-7

SUSAN ANDERS

CITY OF WOMEN
A collection of stories dedicated to women and the passions that draw them together. Designed strictly for the sensual pleasure of women, Anders' tales are set to ignite flames of passion from coast to coast. The residents of *City of Women* hold the key to even the most forbidden fantasies. $5.95/375-9

ROSEBUD BOOKS

PINK CHAMPAGNE
Tasty, torrid tales of butch/femme couplings—from a writer more than capable of describing the special fire ignited when opposites collide. Tough as nails or soft as silk, these women seek out their antitheses, intent on working out the details of their own personal theory of difference. $5.95/282-5

LAVENDER ROSE
Anonymous
A classic collection of lesbian literature: From the writings of Sappho, Queen of the island Lesbos, to the turn-of-the-century *Black Book of Lesbianism*; from *Tips to Maidens* to *Crimson Hairs*, a recent lesbian saga—here are the great but little-known lesbian writings and revelations. $4.95/208-6

EDITED BY LAURA ANTONIOU

LEATHERWOMEN II
A follow-up volume to the popular and controversial ***Leatherwomen***. Laura Antoniou turns an editor's discerning eye to the writing of women on the edge—resulting in a collection sure to ignite libidinal flames. Leave taboos behind—because these Leatherwomen know no limits.... $4.95/229-9

LEATHERWOMEN
These fantasies, from the pens of new or emerging authors, break every rule imposed on women's fantasies. The hottest stories from some of today's newest and most outrageous writers make this an unforgettable exploration of the female libido. $4.95/3095-4

LESLIE CAMERON

THE WHISPER OF FANS
"Just looking into her eyes, she felt that she knew a lot about this woman. She could see strength, boldness, a fresh sense of aliveness that rocked her to the core. In turn she felt open, revealed under the woman's gaze—all her secrets already told. No need of shame or artifice...." $5.95/259-0

AARONA GRIFFIN

PASSAGE AND OTHER STORIES
An S/M romance. Lovely Nina is frightened by her lesbian passions until she finds herself infatuated with a woman she spots at a local café. One night Nina follows her and finds herself enmeshed in an endless maze leading to a world where women test the edges of sexuality and power. $4.95/3057-1

VALENTINA CILESCU

THE ROSEBUD SUTRA
"Women are hardly ever known in their true light, though they may love others, or become indifferent towards them, may give them delight, or abandon them, or may extract from them all the wealth that they possess." So says *The Rosebud Sutra*—a volume promising women's inner secrets. One woman learns to use these secrets in a quest for pleasure with a succession of lady loves.... $4.95/242-6

THE HAVEN
J craves domination, and her perverse appetites lead her to the Haven: the isolated sanctuary Rus and Annie call home. Soon J forces her way into the couple's world, bringing unspeakable lust and cruelty into their lives. $4.95/165-9

MISTRESS MINE
Sophia Cranleigh sits in prison, accused of authoring the "obscene" *Mistress Mine*. For Sophia has led no ordinary life, but has slaved and suffered—deliciously—under the hand of the notorious Mistress Malin. How long had she languished under the dominance of this incredible beauty? $5.95/445-3

ROSEBUD BOOKS
LINDSAY WELSH

MILITARY SECRETS
Colonel Candice Sproule heads a highly-specialized boot camp. Assisted by three dominatrix sergeants, Col. Sproule takes on the talented submissives sent to her by secret military contacts. Then comes Jesse Robbins —whose pleasure in being served matches the Colonel's own. This new recruit sets off fireworks in the barracks—and beyond—and soon earns the respect of even her stern Commander.... $5.95/397-X

ROMANTIC ENCOUNTERS
Beautiful Julie, the most powerful editor of romance novels in the industry, spends her days igniting women's passions through books—and her nights fulfilling those needs with a variety of lovers. Julie's two worlds come together with the type of bodice-ripping Harlequin could never imagine! $5.95/359-7

THE BEST OF LINDSAY WELSH
A collection of this popular writer's best work. This author was one of Rosebud's early bestsellers, and remains highly popular. A sampler set to introduce some of the hottest lesbian erotica to a wider audience. $5.95/368-6

PROVINCETOWN SUMMER
This completely original collection is devoted exclusively to white-hot desire between women. From the casual encounters of women on the prowl to the enduring erotic bonds between old lovers, the women of *Provincetown Summer* will set your senses on fire! A national bestseller. $5.95/362-7

NECESSARY EVIL
What's a girl to do? When her Mistress proves too systematic, too by-the-book, one lovely submissive takes the ultimate chance—choosing and creating a Mistress who'll fulfill her heart's desire. Little did she know how difficult it would be—and, in the end, rewarding,.... $5.95/277-9

A VICTORIAN ROMANCE
Lust-letters from the road. A young Englishwoman realizes her dream—a trip abroad under the guidance of her eccentric maiden aunt. Soon the young but blossoming Elaine comes to discover her own sexual talents, as a hot-blooded Parisian named Madelaine takes her Sapphic education in hand. Another Welsh winner! $5.95/365-1

A CIRCLE OF FRIENDS
The author of the nationally best-selling *Provincetown Summer* returns with the story of a remarkable group of women. Slowly, the women pair off to explore all the possibilities of lesbian passion, until finally it seems that there is nothing—and no one—they have not dabbled in. A stunning tribute to truly special relationships. $4.95/250-7

PRIVATE LESSONS
A high voltage tale of life at The Whitfield Academy for Young Women— where cruel headmistress Devon Whitfield presides over the in-depth education of only the most talented and delicious of maidens. Elizabeth Dunn arrives at the Academy, where it becomes clear that she has much to learn—to the delight of Devon Whitfield and her randy staff of Mistresses! Another contemporary classic from Lindsay Welsh. $4.95/116-0

BAD HABITS
What does one do with a poorly trained slave? Break her of her bad habits, of course! The story of the ultimate finishing school, *Bad Habits* was an immediate favorite with women nationwide. "Talk about passing the wet test!... If you like hot, lesbian erotica, run—don't walk...and pick up a copy of *Bad Habits*."—*Lambda Book Report* $5.95/446-1

ROSEBUD BOOKS

ANNABELLE BARKER
MOROCCO
A luscious young woman stands to inherit a fortune—if she can only withstand the ministrations of her cruel guardian until her twentieth birthday. With two months left, Lila makes a bold bid for freedom, only to find that liberty has its own excruciating and delicious price.... $4.95/148-9

A.L. REINE
DISTANT LOVE & OTHER STORIES
A book of seductive tales. In the title story, Leah Michaels and her lover Ranelle have had four years of blissful, smoldering passion together. One night, when Ranelle is out of town, Leah records an audio "Valentine," a cassette filled with erotic reminiscences.... $4.95/3056-3

RHINOCEROS BOOKS

EDITED BY THOMAS S. ROCHE
NOIROTICA: An Anthology of Erotic Crime Stories
A collection of darkly sexy tales, taking place at the crossroads of the crime and erotic genres. Thomas Roche has gathered together some of today's finest writers of sexual fiction, all of whom explore the murky terrain where desire runs irrevocably afoul of the law. Carol Queen, Bill Brent, Simon Sheppard, Cecilia Tan, Amelia G., M. Christian and many others are represented by their most hard-bitten, hard-hitting tales. $6.95/390-2

DAVID MELTZER
UNDER
Under is the story of a sex professional, whose life at the bottom of the social heap is, nevertheless, filled with incident. Other than numerous surgeries designed to increase his physical allure, he is faced with an establishment intent on using any body for genetic experiments. These forces drive the cyber-gigolo underground—where even more bizarre cultures await.... $6.95/290-6

ORF
He is the ultimate musician-hero—the idol of thousands, the fevered dream of many more. And like many musicians before him, he is misunderstood, misused—and totally out of control. Every last drop of feeling is squeezed from a modern-day troubadour and his lady love. $6.95/110-1

EDITED BY AMARANTHA KNIGHT
FLESH FANTASTIC
Humans have long toyed with the idea of "playing God": creating life from nothingness, bringing Life to the inanimate. Now Amarantha Knight, author of the "Darker Passions" series of erotic horror novels, collects stories exploring not only the allure of Creation, but the lust that follows.... $6.95/352-X

GARY BOWEN
DIARY OF A VAMPIRE
"Gifted with a darkly sensual vision and a fresh voice, [Bowen] is a writer to watch out for." —Cecilia Tan

The chilling, arousing, and ultimately moving memoirs of an undead—but all too human—soul. Bowen's Rafael, a red-blooded male with an insatiable hunger for same, is the perfect antidote to the effete malcontents haunting bookstores today. *Diary of a Vampire* marks the emergence of a bold and brilliant vision, firmly rooted in past *and* present. $6.95/331-7

RHINOCEROS BOOKS

RENÉ MAIZEROY

FLESHLY ATTRACTIONS

Lucien Hardanges was the son of the wantonly beautiful actress, Marie-Rose Hardanges. When she decides to let a "friend" introduce her son to the pleasures of love, Marie-Rose could not have foretold the erotic excesses that would lead to her own ruin and that of her cherished son. $6.95/299-X

EDITED BY LAURA ANTONIOU

NO OTHER TRIBUTE

A collection of stories sure to challenge Political Correctness in a way few have before, with tales of women kept in bondage to their lovers by their deepest passions. Love pushes these women beyond acceptable limits, rendering them helpless to deny the men and women they adore. $6.95/294-9

SOME WOMEN

Over forty essays written by women actively involved in consensual dominance and submission. Professional mistresses, lifestyle leatherdykes, whipmakers, titleholders—women from every conceivable walk of life lay bare their true feelings about about issues as explosive as feminism, abuse, pleasures and public image. $6.95/300-7

BY HER SUBDUED

Stories of women who get what they want. The tales in this collection all involve women in control—of their lives, their loves, their men. So much in control, in fact, that they can remorselessly break rules to become the powerful goddesses of the men who sacrifice all to worship at their feet. Woman Power with a vengeance! $6.95/281-7

JEAN STINE

SEASON OF THE WITCH

"A future in which it is technically possible to transfer the total mind... of a rapist killer into the brain dead but physically living body of his female victim. Remarkable for intense psychological technique. There is eroticism but it is necessary to mark the differences between the sexes and the subtle altering of a man into a woman." —*The Science Fiction Critic* $6.95/268-X

JOHN WARREN

THE TORQUEMADA KILLER

Detective Eva Hernandez has finally gotten her first "big case": a string of vicious murders taking place within New York's SM community. Piece by piece, Eva assembles the evidence, revealing a picture of a world misunderstood and under attack—and gradually comes to understand her own place within it. A hot, edge-of-the-seat thriller from the author of *The Loving Dominant*—and an exciting insider's perspective on "the scene." $6.95/367-8

THE LOVING DOMINANT

Everything you need to know about an infamous sexual variation—and an unspoken type of love. Mentor—a longtime player in the dominance/submission scene—guides readers through this world and reveals the too-often hidden basis of the D/S relationship: care, trust and love. $6.95/218-3

GRANT ANTREWS

SUBMISSIONS

Once again, Antrews portrays the very special elements of the dominant/submissive relationship...with restraint—this time with the story of a lonely man, a winning lottery ticket, and a demanding dominatrix. One of erotica's most discerning writers. $6.95/207-8

RHINOCEROS BOOKS

MY DARLING DOMINATRIX
When a man and a woman fall in love it's supposed to be simple, uncomplicated, easy—unless that woman happens to be a dominatrix. Curiosity gives way to unblushing desire in this story of one man's awakening to the joys to be experienced as the willing slave of a powerful woman. A perennial favorite
$6.95/447-X

LAURA ANTONIOU WRITING AS "SARA ADAMSON"

THE TRAINER
The long-awaited conclusion of Adamson's stunning Marketplace Trilogy! The ultimate underground sexual realm includes not only willing slaves, but the exquisite trainers who take submissives firmly in hand. And it is now the time for these mentors to divulge their own secrets—the desires that led them to become the ultimate figures of authority. $6.95/249-3

THE SLAVE
The second volume in the "Marketplace" trilogy. *The Slave* covers the experience of one exceptionally talented submissive who longs to join the ranks of those who have proven themselves worthy of entry into the Marketplace. But the price, while delicious, is staggeringly high.... Adamson's plot thickens, as her trilogy moves to a conclusion in *The Trainer*. $6.95/173-X

THE MARKETPLACE
"Merchandise does not come easily to the Marketplace.... They haunt the clubs and the organizations.... Some are so ripe that they intimidate the poseurs, the weekend sadists and the furtive dilettantes who are so endemic to that world. And they never stop asking where we may be found...." $6.95/3096-2

THE CATALYST
After viewing a controversial, explicitly kinky film full of images of bondage and submission, several audience members find themselves deeply moved by the erotic suggestions they've seen on the screen. "Sara Adamson"'s sensational debut volume! $5.95/328-7

DAVID AARON CLARK

SISTER RADIANCE
A chronicle of obsession, rife with Clark's trademark vivisections of contemporary desires, sacred and profane. The vicissitudes of lust and romance are examined against a backdrop of urban decay and shallow fashionability in this testament to the allure—and inevitability—of the forbidden. $6.95/215-9

THE WET FOREVER
The story of Janus and Madchen, a small-time hood and a beautiful sex worker, *The Wet Forever* examines themes of loyalty, sacrifice, redemption and obsession amidst Manhattan's sex parlors and underground S/M clubs. Its combination of sex and suspense led Terence Sellers to proclaim it "evocative and poetic." $6.95/117-9

ALICE JOANOU

BLACK TONGUE
"Joanou has created a series of sumptuous, brooding, dark visions of sexual obsession and is undoubtedly a name to look out for in the future."
—*Redeemer*

Another seductive book of dreams from the author of the acclaimed *Tourniquet*. Exploring lust at its most florid and unsparing, *Black Tongue* is a trove of baroque fantasies—each redolent of the forbidden. Joanou creates some of erotica's most mesmerizing and unforgettable characters. $6.95/258-2

RHINOCEROS BOOKS

TOURNIQUET
A heady collection of stories and effusions from the pen of one our most dazzling young writers. Strange tales abound, from the story of the mysterious and cruel Cybele, to an encounter with the sadistic entertainment of a bizarre after-hours cafe. A sumptuous feast for all the senses. $6.95/3060-1

CANNIBAL FLOWER
"She is waiting in her darkened bedroom, as she has waited throughout history, to seduce the men who are foolish enough to be blinded by her irresistible charms....She is the goddess of sexuality, and *Cannibal Flower* is her haunting siren song."—Michael Perkins $4.95/72-6

MICHAEL PERKINS

EVIL COMPANIONS
Set in New York City during the tumultuous waning years of the Sixties, *Evil Companions* has been hailed as "a frightening classic." A young couple explores the nether reaches of the erotic unconscious in a shocking confrontation with the extremes of passion. With a new introduction by science fiction legend Samuel R. Delany. $6.95/3067-9

AN ANTHOLOGY OF CLASSIC ANONYMOUS EROTIC WRITING
Michael Perkins, acclaimed authority on erotic literature, has collected the very best passages from the world's erotic writing—especially for Rhino*ceros* readers. "Anonymous" is one of the most infamous bylines in publishing history—and these steamy excerpts show why! $6.95/140-3

THE SECRET RECORD: Modern Erotic Literature
Michael Perkins surveys the field with authority and unique insight. Updated and revised to include the latest trends, tastes, and developments in this misunderstood and maligned genre. $6.95/3039-3

HELEN HENLEY

ENTER WITH TRUMPETS
Helen Henley was told that woman just don't write about sex—much less the taboos she was so interested in exploring. So Henley did it alone, flying in the face of "tradition" by producing *Enter With Trumpets*, a touching tale of arousal and devotion in one couple's kinky relationship. $6.95/197-7

PHILIP JOSE FARMER

FLESH
Space Commander Stagg explored the galaxies for 800 years. Upon his return, the hero Stagg is made the centerpiece of an incredible public ritual—one that will repeatedly take him to the heights of ecstasy, and inexorably drag him toward the depths of hell. $6.95/303-1

A FEAST UNKNOWN
"Sprawling, brawling, shocking, suspenseful, hilarious..."
—Theodore Sturgeon
Farmer's supreme anti-hero returns. "I was conceived and born in 1888." Slowly, Lord Grandrith—armed with the belief that he is the son of Jack the Ripper—tells the story of his remarkable and unbridled life. His story begins with his discovery of the secret of immortality.... $6.95/276-0

THE IMAGE OF THE BEAST
Herald Childe has seen Hell, glimpsed its horror in an act of sexual mutilation. Childe must now find and destroy an inhuman predator through the streets of a polluted and decadent Los Angeles of the future. One clue after another leads Childe to an inescapable realization about the nature of sex and evil.... $6.95/166-7

RHINOCEROS BOOKS

LEOPOLD VON SACHER-MASOCH
VENUS IN FURS
This classic 19th century novel is the first uncompromising exploration of the dominant/submissive relationship in literature. The alliance of Severin and Wanda epitomizes Sacher-Masoch's dark obsession with a cruel, controlling goddess and the urges that drive the man held in her thrall. Includes the letters exchanged between Sacher-Masoch and Emilie Mataja—an aspiring writer he sought as the avatar of his forbidden desires. $6.95/3089-X

SAMUEL R. DELANY
THE MAD MAN
"The latest novel from Hugo- and Nebula-winning science fiction writer and critic Delany...reads like a pornographic reflection of Peter Ackroyd's *Chatterton* or A. S. Byatt's *Possession*.... The pornographic element... becomes more than simple shock or titillation, though, as Delany develops an insightful dichotomy between [his protagonist]'s two worlds: the one of cerebral philosophy and dry academia, the other of heedless, 'impersonal' obsessive sexual extremism. When these worlds finally collide...the novel achieves a surprisingly satisfying resolution...." —*Publishers Weekly*
Science fiction legend Samuel R. Delany's most provocative novel. For his thesis, graduate student John Marr researches the life and work of the brilliant Timothy Hasler: a philosopher whose career was cut tragically short over a decade earlier. On another front, Marr finds himself increasingly drawn toward more shocking, depraved sexual entanglements with the homeless men of his neighborhood, until it begins to seem that Hasler's death might hold some key to his own life as a gay man in the age of AIDS. $8.99/408-9/mass market

EQUINOX
The *Scorpion* has sailed the seas in a quest for every possible pleasure. Her crew is a collection of the young, the twisted, the insatiable. A drifter comes into their midst, and is taken on a fantastic journey to the darkest, most dangerous sexual extremes—until he is finally a victim to their boundless appetites. $6.95/157-8

DANIEL VIAN
ILLUSIONS
Two tales of danger and desire in Berlin on the eve of WWII. From private homes to lurid cafés, passion is exposed and explored in stark contrast to the brutal violence of the time. A singularly arousing volume. $6.95/3074-1

PERSUASIONS
"The stockings are drawn tight by the suspender belt, tight enough to be stretched to the limit just above the middle part of her thighs..." A double novel, including the classics ***Adagio*** and ***Gabriela and the General***, this volume traces desire around the globe. International lust! $6.95/183-7

ANDREI CODRESCU
THE REPENTANCE OF LORRAINE
"One of our most prodigiously talented and magical writers."
—*NYT Book Review*
By the acclaimed author of *The Hole in the Flag* and *The Blood Countess*. An aspiring writer, a professor's wife, a secretary, gold anklets, Maoists, Roman harlots—and more—swirl through this spicy tale of a harried quest for a mythic artifact. Written when the author was a young man, this lusty yarn was inspired by the heady days of the Sixties. Includes a new Introduction by the author, painting a portrait of ***Lorraine***'s creation. $6.95/329-5

RHINOCEROS BOOKS

SOPHIE GALLEYMORE BIRD
MANEATER

Through a bizarre act of creation, a man attains the "perfect" lover—by all appearances a beautiful, sensuous woman but in reality something far darker. Once brought to life she will accept no mate, seeking instead the prey that will sate her hunger for vengeance. A biting take on the war of the sexes, this debut goes for the jugular of the "perfect woman" myth. $6.95/103-9

TUPPY OWENS
SENSATIONS

A piece of porn history. Tuppy Owens tells the unexpurgated story of the making of *Sensations*—the first big-budget sex flick. Originally commissioned to appear in book form after the release of the film in 1975, *Sensations* is finally released under Masquerade's stylish Rhino*ceros* imprint. $6.95/3081-4

LIESEL KULIG
LOVE IN WARTIME

An uncompromising look at the politics, perils and pleasures of sexual power. Madeleine knew that the handsome SS officer was a dangerous man. But she was just a cabaret singer in Nazi-occupied Paris, trying to survive in a perilous time. When Josef fell in love with her, he discovered that a beautiful and amoral woman can sometimes be wildly dangerous. $6.95/3044-X

Email Us!
MasqBks @ aol.com

FOR A FREE COPY OF THE COMPLETE MASQUERADE CATALOG,
MAIL THIS COUPON TO:
MASQUERADE BOOKS/DEPT Y74K
801 SECOND AVENUE, NEW YORK, NY 10017
OR FAX TO 212 986-7355
All transactions are strictly confidential and we never sell, give or trade any customer's name.

NAME _____

ADDRESS _____

CITY _____ STATE _____ ZIP _____

MASQUERADE BOOKS

TABITHA'S TEASE *Robin Wilde*
The Valentine Academy: an ultra-exclusive, all-girl institution, soon to receive its first male charge. When poor Robin arrives, he finds himself subject to the tortuous teasing of Tabitha—the Academy's most notoriously domineering co-ed. What Robin doesn't realize—but soon learns—is that Tabitha is pledge-mistress of a secret sorority dedicated to enslaving young men. Soon he finds himself a captive of Tabitha & Company's weird desires! $5.95/387-2

HELLFIRE *Charles G. Wood*
A vicious murderer is running amok in New York's sexual underground—and Nick O'Shay, a virile detective with the NYPD, plunges deep into the case. He soon becomes embroiled in an elusive world of fleshly extremes, hunting a madman seeking to purge America with fire and blood sacrifices.
"[Wood] betrays a photographer's eye for tableau and telling detail in his evocation of the larger-than-life figures of the late-'70s to mid-'80s sexual demimonde."　　—David Aaron Clark, author of *The Wet Forever*
$5.95/358-9

PIRATE'S SLAVE *Erica Bronte*
Lovely young Erica is stranded in a country where lust knows no bounds. Desperate to escape, she finds herself trading her firm, luscious body to any and all men willing and able to help her. Her adventure has its ups and downs, ins and outs—all to the undeniable pleasure of lusty Erica! $5.95/376-7

THE MISTRESS OF CASTLE ROHMENSTADT
Olivia M. Ravensworth
Lovely Katherine inherits a secluded European castle from a mysterious relative. Upon arrival, she discovers, much to her delight, that the castle is a haven of sensual pleasure. Katherine learns to shed her inhibitions and enjoy her new home's many delights. $5.95/372-4

TENDER BUNS *P. N. Dedeaux*
Meet Marc Merlin, the wizard of discipline! In a fashionable Canadian suburb, Merlin indulges his yen for punishment with an assortment of the town's most desirable and willing women. Things come to a rousing climax at a party planned to cater to just those whims Marc is most able to satisfy.... $5.95/396-1

COMPLIANCE *N. Whallen*
Fourteen stories exploring the pleasures of release. Characters from many walks of life learn to trust in the skills of others, only to experience the thrilling liberation of submission. Here are the real joys to be found in some of the most forbidden sexual practices around.... $5.95/356-2

LA DOMME: A DOMINATRIX ANTHOLOGY *Edited by Claire Baeder*
A steamy smorgasbord of female domination! Erotic literature has long been filled with heartstopping portraits of domineering women, and now the most memorable come together in one beautifully brutal volume. $5.95/366-X

THE GEEK *Tiny Alice*
"An adventure novel told by a sex-bent male mini-pygmy. This is an accomplishment of which anybody may be proud."—Philip José Farmer
The Geek is told from the point of view of, well, a chicken who reports on the various perversities he witnesses as part of a traveling carnival. When a gang of renegade lesbians kidnaps Chicken and his geek, all hell breaks loose. A strange tale, filled with outrageous erotic oddities. $5.95/341-4

SEX ON THE NET *Charisse van der Lyn*
Electrifying erotica from one of the Internet's hottest and most widely read authors. Encounters of all kinds—straight, lesbian, dominant/submissive and all sorts of extreme passions—are explored in thrilling detail. Discover what's turning on hackers from coast to coast! $5.95/399-6

MASQUERADE BOOKS

BEAUTY OF THE BEAST *Carole Remy*
A shocking tell-all, written from the point-of-view of a prize-winning reporter. And what reporting she does! All the secrets of an uninhibited life are revealed, and each lusty tableau is painted in glowing colors. Join in on her scandalous adventures—and reap the rewards of her extensive background in Erotic Affairs! $5.95/332-5

NAUGHTY MESSAGE *Stanley Carten*
Wesley Arthur, a withdrawn computer engineer, discovers a lascivious message on his answering machine. Aroused beyond his wildest dreams by the unmentionable acts described, Wesley becomes obsessed with tracking down the woman behind the seductive voice. His search takes him through strip clubs and no-tell motels—and finally to his randy reward.... $5.95/333-3

The Marquis de Sade's JULIETTE *David Aaron Clark*
The Marquis de Sade's infamous Juliette returns—and at the hand of David Aaron Clark, she emerges as the most powerful, perverse and destructive nightstalker modern New York will ever know. Under this domina's tutelage, two women come to know torture's bizarre attractions, as they grapple with the price of Juliette's promise of immortality.
Praise for Dave Clark:
"David Aaron Clark has delved into one of the most sensationalistically taboo aspects of eros, sadomasochism, and produced a novel of unmistakable literary imagination and artistic value." —Carlo McCormick, *Paper*
$5.95/240-X

THE PARLOR *N.T. Morley*
Lovely Kathryn gives in to the ultimate temptation. The mysterious John and Sarah ask her to be their slave—an idea that turns Kathryn on so much that she can't refuse! But who are these two mysterious strangers? Little by little, Kathryn comes to know the inner secrets of her stunning keepers. $5.95/291-4

NADIA *Anonymous*
"Nadia married General the Count Gregorio Stenoff—a gentleman of noble pedigree it is true, but one of the most reckless dissipated rascals in Russia..." Follow the delicious but neglected Nadia as she works to wring every drop of pleasure out of life—despite an unhappy marriage. A classic title providing a peek into the secret sexual lives of another time and place. $5.95/267-1

THE STORY OF A VICTORIAN MAID *Nigel McParr*
What were the Victorians really like? Chances are, no one believes they were as stuffy as their Queen, but who would have imagined such unbridled libertines! One maid is followed from exploit to smutty exploit, and all secrets are revealed! $5.95/241-8

CARRIE'S STORY *Molly Weatherfield*
"I had been Jonathan's slave for about a year when he told me he wanted to sell me at an auction. I wasn't in any condition to respond when he told me this..." Desire and depravity run rampant in this story of uncompromising mastery and irrevocable submission. $5.95/444-5

CHARLY'S GAME *Bren Flemming*
A rich woman's gullible daughter has run off with one of the toughest leather dykes in town—and sexy P.I. Charly's hired to lure the girl back. One by one, wise and wicked women ensnare one another in their lusty nets! $4.95/221-3

ANDREA AT THE CENTER *J.P. Kansas*
Lithe and lovely young Andrea is, without warning, whisked away to a distant retreat. There she is introduced to the ways of the Center, and soon becomes quite friendly with its other inhabitants—all of whom are learning to abandon restraint in their pursuit of the deepest sexual satisfaction. $5.95/324-4

MASQUERADE BOOKS

ASK ISADORA *Isadora Alman*
An essential volume, collecting six years' worth of Isadora Alman's syndicated columns on sex and relationships. Alman's been called a "hip Dr. Ruth," and a "sexy Dear Abby," based upon the wit and pertinence of her advice. Today's world is more perplexing than ever—and Isadora Alman is just the expert to help untangle the most personal of knots. $4.95/61-0

THE SLAVES OF SHOANNA *Mercedes Kelly*
Shoanna, the cruel and magnificent, takes four maidens under her wing—and teaches them the ins and outs of pleasure and discipline. Trained in every imaginable perversion, from simple fleshly joys to advanced techniques, these students go to the head of the class! $4.95/164-0

LOVE & SURRENDER *Marlene Darcy*
"Madeline saw Harry looking at her legs and she blushed as she remembered what he wanted to do.... She casually pulled the skirt of her dress back to uncover her knees and the lower part of her thighs.... She tugged at her skirt again, pulled it back far enough so almost all of her thighs were exposed...." $4.95/3082-2

THE COMPLETE *PLAYGIRL* FANTASIES *Editors of* Playgirl
The best women's fantasies are collected here, fresh from the pages of *Playgirl*. These knockouts from the infamous "Reader's Fantasy Forum" prove, once again, that truth can indeed be hotter, wilder, and *better* than fiction. $4.95/3075-X

STASI SLUT *Anthony Bobarzynski*
Need we say more? Adina lives in East Germany, far from the sexually liberated, uninhibited debauchery of the West. She meets a group of ruthless and corrupt STASI agents who use her as a pawn in their political chess game as well as for their own perverse gratification—until she uses her talents and attractions in a final bid for total freedom! $4.95/3050-4

BLUE TANGO *Hilary Manning*
Ripe and tempting Julie is haunted by the sounds of extraordinary passion beyond her bedroom wall. Alone, she fantasizes about taking part in the amorous dramas of her hosts, Claire and Edward. When she finds a way to watch the nightly debauch, her curiosity turns to full-blown lust—and soon Julie's eager to join in! $4.95/3037-7

LOUISE BELHAVEL

FRAGRANT ABUSES
The saga of Clara and Iris continues as the now-experienced girls enjoy themselves with a new circle of worldly friends whose imaginations match their own. Perversity follows the lusty ladies around the globe! $4.95/88-2

DEPRAVED ANGELS
The final installment in the incredible adventures of Clara and Iris. Together with their friends, lovers, and worldly acquaintances, Clara and Iris explore the frontiers of depravity at home and abroad. $4.95/92-0

TITIAN BERESFORD

THE WICKED HAND
With a special Introduction by *Leg Show*'s Dian Hanson. A collection of fanciful fetishistic tales featuring the absolute subjugation of men by lovely, domineering women. From Japan and Germany to the American heartland—these stories uncover the other side of the "weaker sex." $5.95/343-0

CINDERELLA
Beresford triumphs again with this intoxicating tale, filled with castle dungeons and tightly corseted ladies-in-waiting, naughty viscounts and impossibly cruel masturbatrixes—nearly every conceivable method of erotic torture is explored and described in lush, vivid detail. $4.95/305-8

MASQUERADE BOOKS

JUDITH BOSTON
Young Edward would have been lucky to get the stodgy old companion he thought his parents had hired for him. Instead, an exquisite woman arrives at his door, and Edward finds his compulsively lewd behavior never goes unpunished by the unflinchingly severe Judith Boston! $4.95/273-6

NINA FOXTON
An aristocrat finds herself bored by run-of-the-mill amusements for "ladies of good breeding." Instead of taking tea with proper gentlemen, naughty Nina invents a contraption to "milk" them of their most private essences. No man ever says "No" to Nina! $5.95/443-7

A TITIAN BERESFORD READER
Wild dominatrixes, perverse masochists, and mesmerizing detail are the hallmarks of the Beresford tale—and encountered here in abundance. The very best scenarios from all of Beresford's bestsellers make this a must-have for the Compleat Fetishist. $4.95/114-4

CHINA BLUE
KUNG FU NUNS
"When I could stand the pleasure no longer, she lifted me out of the chair and sat me down on top of the table. She then lifted her skirt. The sight of her perfect legs clad in white stockings and a petite garter belt further mesmerized me. I lean particularly towards white garter belts." China Blue returns! $4.95/3031-8

HARRIET DAIMLER
DARLING • INNOCENCE
In *Darling*, a virgin is raped by a mugger. Driven by her urge for revenge, she searches New York in a furious sexual hunt that leads to rape and murder. In *Innocence*, a young invalid determines to experience sex through her voluptuous nurse. Two critically acclaimed novels. $4.95/3047-4

LYN DAVENPORT
DOVER ISLAND
Off the coast of Oregon, Dr. David Kelly has planted the seeds of his dream—a Corporal Punishment Resort. Soon, many people from varied walks of life descend upon this isolated retreat, intent on fulfilling their every desire. Included in this elite gathering is Marcy Harris, who will prove the perfect partner for the lonely but lustful Doctor.... $5.95/384-8

TESSA'S HOLIDAYS
Tessa Duncan dreads the thought of another long winter in her small, drab Midwestern town—particularly after a summer filled with the intrigue and erotic surprise provided by her voracious lover, Grant. Soon however, Tessa learns that she needn't fear being bored—not with lusty Grant on the job! He soon makes sure that each of Tessa's holidays is filled with the type of sensual adventure most young women only dream about. What will her insatiable man dream up next? Only he knows—and he keeps his secrets until the lovely Tessa is ready to explode with desire! $5.95/377-5

THE GUARDIAN
Felicia grew up under the tutelage of the lash—and she learned her lessons well. Sir Rodney Wentworth has long searched for a woman capable of fulfilling his cruel desires, and after learning of Felicia's talents, sends for her. Upon arrival in his home, Felicia discovers that the "position" offered her is delightfully different than anything she could have expected! $5.95/371-6

MASQUERADE BOOKS

AKBAR DEL PIOMBO

SKIRTS
Randy Mr. Edward Champdick enters high society—and a whole lot more—in his quest for ultimate satisfaction. For it seems that once Mr. Champdick rises to the occasion, nothing can bring him down. $4.95/115-2

DUKE COSIMO
A kinky romp played out against the boudoirs, bathrooms and ballrooms of the European nobility, who seem to do nothing all day except each other. The lifestyles of the rich and licentious are revealed in all their glory. $4.95/3052-0

A CRUMBLING FAÇADE
The return of that incorrigible rogue, Henry Pike, who continues his pursuit of sex, fair or otherwise, in the most elegant homes of the most debauched aristocrats. No one can resist the irrepressible Pike! $4.95/3043-1

PAULA
This canny seductress tests the mettle of every man who comes under her spell—and every man does! $4.95/3036-9

ROBERT DESMOND

PROFESSIONAL CHARMER
A gigolo lives a parasitical life of luxury by providing his sexual services to the rich and bored. Traveling in the most exclusive circles, this gun-for-hire will gratify the lewdest and most vulgar sexual cravings! This dedicated pro leaves no one unsatisfied. $4.95/3003-2

THE SWEETEST FRUIT
Connie is determined to seduce and destroy Father Chadcroft. She corrupts the unsuspecting priest into forsaking all that he holds sacred, destroys his parish, and slyly manipulates him with her smoldering looks and hypnotic aura. $4.95/95-5

MICHAEL DRAX

SILK AND STEEL
"He let his robe fall to the floor. She could offer no resistance as the shadowy figure knelt before her, gazing down upon her. Why would she resist? This was what she wanted all along...." $4.95/3032-6

OBSESSIONS
Victoria is determined to become a model by sexually ensnaring the powerful people who control the fashion industry: Paige, who finds herself compelled to watch Victoria's conquests; and Pietro and Alex, who take turns and then join in for a sizzling threesome. $4.95/3012-1

LIZBETH DUSSEAU

TRINKETS
"Her bottom danced on the air, pert and fully round. It would take punishment well, he thought." A luscious woman submits to an artist's every whim—becoming the sexual trinket he had always desired. $5.95/246-9

THE APPLICANT
"Adventuresome young woman who enjoys being submissive sought by married couple in early forties. Expect no limits." Hilary answers an ad, hoping to find someone who can meet her needs. Beautiful Liza turns out to be a flawless mistress; with her husband Oliver, she trains Hilary to be submissive. $4.95/306-6

SPANISH HOLIDAY
She didn't know what to make of Sam Jacobs. He was undoubtedly the most remarkable man she'd ever met.... Lauren didn't mean to fall in love with the enigmatic Sam, but a once-in-a-lifetime European vacation gives her all the evidence she needs that this hot man might be the one for her.... $4.95/185-3

MASQUERADE BOOKS

CAROLINE'S CONTRACT
After a life of repression, Caroline goes out on a limb. On the advice of a friend, she meets with the alluring Max Burton—a man more than willing to indulge her fantasies of domination and discipline. Caroline soon learns to love his ministrations—and agrees to a very *special* arrangement.... $4.95/122-5

MEMBER OF THE CLUB
"Deep down inside, I had the most submissive thoughts: I imagined myself under the grip of men I hardly knew. If there were a club to join, it could take my deepest dreams and make them real. My only question was how far I'd really go?" A woman finally goes all the way in a quest to satisfy her hungers, joining a club where she *really* pays her dues—with any one of the many men who desire her! $4.95/3079-2

SARA H. FRENCH

MASTER OF TIMBERLAND
"Welcome to Timberland Resort," he began. "We are delighted that you have come to serve us. And...be assured that we will require service of you in the strictest sense. Our discipline is the most demanding in the world...." A tale of sexual slavery at the ultimate paradise resort. $5.95/327-9

RETURN TO TIMBERLAND
It's time for a trip back to Timberland, the world's most frenzied sexual resort! Prepare for a vacation filled with delicious decadence, as each and every visitor is serviced by unimaginably talented submissives. These nubile maidens are determined to make this the raunchiest camp-out ever! $5.95/257-4

SARAH JACKSON

SANCTUARY
Tales from the Middle Ages. *Sanctuary* explores both the unspeakable debauchery of court life and the unimaginable privations of monastic solitude, leading the voracious and the virtuous on a collision course that brings history to throbbing life. $5.95/318-X

HELOISE
A panoply of sensual tales harkening back to the golden age of Victorian erotica. Desire is examined in all its intricacy, as fantasies are explored and urges explode. Innocence meets experience time and again. $4.95/3073-3

JOCELYN JOYCE

PRIVATE LIVES
The lecherous habits of the illustrious make for a sizzling tale of French erotic life. A widow has a craving for a young busboy; he's sleeping with a rich businessman's wife; her husband is minding his sex business elsewhere! Mind boggling sexual entanglements! $4.95/309-0

CANDY LIPS
The world of publishing serves as the backdrop for one woman's pursuit of sexual satisfaction. From a fiery femme fatale to a voracious Valentino, she takes her pleasure where she can find it. Luckily for her, it's most often found between the legs of the most licentious lovers! $4.95/182-9

KIM'S PASSION
The life of a beautiful English seductress. Kim leaves India for London, where she quickly takes upon herself the task of bedding every woman in sight! $4.95/162-4

CAROUSEL
A young American woman leaves her husband when she discovers he is having an affair with their maid. She then becomes the sexual plaything of various Parisian voluptuaries. Wild sex, low morals! $4.95/3051-2

MASQUERADE BOOKS

SABINE
There is no one who can refuse her once she casts her spell; no lover can do anything less than give up his whole life for her. Great men and empires fall at her feet; but she is haughty, distracted, impervious. It is the eve of WW II, and Sabine must find a new lover equal to her talents. $4.95/3046-6

THE WILD HEART
A luxury hotel is the setting for this artful web of sex, desire, and love. A newlywed sees sex as a duty, while her hungry husband tries to awaken her to its tender joys. A Parisian entertains wealthy guests for the love of money. Each episode provides a new variation in this lusty Grand Hotel! $4.95/3007-5

JADE EAST
Laura, passive and passionate, follows her husband Emilio to Hong Kong. He gives her to Wu Li, a connoisseur of sexual perversions, who passes her on to Madeleine, a flamboyant lesbian. Madeleine's friends make Laura the centerpiece in Hong Kong's infamous underground orgies. Slowly, Laura descends into the depths of depravity, where she becomes just another steamy slave—for sale! $4.95/60-2

RAWHIDE LUST
Diana Beaumont, the young wife of a U.S. Marshal, is kidnapped as an act of vengeance against her husband. Jack Beaumont sets out on a long journey to get his wife back, but finally catches up with her trail only to learn that she's been sold into white slavery in Mexico. $4.95/55-6

THE JAZZ AGE
The time: the Roaring Twenties. A young attorney becomes suspicious of his mistress while his wife has an fling with a lesbian lover. *The Jazz Age* is a romp of erotic realism from the heyday of the speakeasy—when all pleasures were taken in private. $4.95/48-3

AMARANTHA KNIGHT

THE DARKER PASSIONS: *THE FALL OF THE HOUSE OF USHER*
The Master and Mistress of the house of Usher indulge in every form of decadence, and are intent on initiating their guests into the many pleasures to be found in utter submission. But something is not quite right in the House of Usher, and the foundation of its dynasty begins to crack.... $5.95/313-9

THE DARKER PASSIONS: *FRANKENSTEIN*
What if you could create a living, breathing human? What shocking acts could it be taught to perform, to desire, to love? Find out what pleasures await those who play God.... $5.95/248-5

THE DARKER PASSIONS: *DR. JEKYLL AND MR. HYDE*
It is an old story, one of incredible, frightening transformations achieved through mysterious experiments. Now, Amarantha Knight explores the steamy possibilities of a tale where no one is quite who—or what—they seem. Victorian bedrooms explode with hidden demons. $4.95/227-2

THE DARKER PASSIONS: *DRACULA*
The infamous erotic retelling of the Vampire legend.
"Well-written and imaginative, Amarantha Knight gives fresh impetus to this myth, taking us through the sexual and sadistic scenes with details that keep us reading.... This author shows superb control. A classic in itself has been added to the shelves."   —*Divinity* $5.95/326-0

MASQUERADE BOOKS

ALIZARIN LAKE

THE EROTIC ADVENTURES OF HARRY TEMPLE
Harry Temple's memoirs chronicle his amorous adventures from his initiation at the hands of insatiable sirens, through his stay at a house of hot repute, to his encounters with a chastity-belted nympho! Here's one hot stud who's always in demand. $4.95/127-6

MORE EROTIC ADVENTURES OF HARRY TEMPLE
Harry Temple's lustful adventures continue. This time he begins his amorous pursuits by deflowering the ample and eager Aurora. Harry soon discovers that his little protégée is more than able to match him at every lascivious game and very willing to display her own talents. An education in sensuality that only Harry Temple can provide! $4.95/67-X

CLARA
The mysterious death of a beautiful, aristocratic woman leads her old boyfriend on a harrowing journey of discovery. His search uncovers a woman on a quest for deeper and more unusual sensations, each more shocking than the one before. $4.95/80-7

DIARY OF AN ANGEL
A long-forgotten diary tells the story of angelic Victoria, lured into a secret life of unimaginable depravity. "I am like a fly caught in a spider's web, a helpless and voiceless victim of their every whim." $4.95/71-8

EROTOMANIA
The bible of female sexual perversion! It's all here, everything you ever wanted to know about kinky women past and present. From simple nymphomania to the most outrageous fetishism, all secrets are revealed in this look into the forbidden rooms of feminine desire. $4.95/128-4

AN ALIZARIN LAKE READER
A selection of wicked musings from the pen of Masquerade's perennially popular author. It's all here: *Business as Usual, The Erotic Adventures of Harry Temple, Festival of Venus,* the mysterious *Instruments of the Passion,* the devilish *Miss High Heels*—and more. $4.95/106-3

MISS HIGH HEELS
It was a delightful punishment few men dared to dream of. Who could have predicted how far it would go? Forced by his sisters to dress and behave like a proper lady, Dennis finds he enjoys life as Denise much more! $4.95/3066-0

THE INSTRUMENTS OF THE PASSION
All that remains is the diary of a young initiate, detailing the twisted rituals of a mysterious cult institution known only as "Rossiter." Behind sinister walls, a beautiful young woman performs an unending drama of pain and humiliation. Will she ever have her fill of utter degradation? $4.95/3010-5

FESTIVAL OF VENUS
Brigeen Mooney fled her home in the west of Ireland to avoid being forced into a nunnery. But the refuge she found in the city turned out to be dedicated to a very different religion. The women she met there belonged to the Old Religion, devoted to the ways of sex and sacrifices. $4.95/37-8

PAUL LITTLE

THE DISCIPLINE OF ODETTE
Odette's family was harsh, but not even public humiliation could keep her from Jacques. She was sure marriage would rescue her from her family's "corrections." To her horror, she discovers that Jacques, too, has been raised on discipline. A shocking erotic coupling! $5.95/334-1

MASQUERADE BOOKS

THE PRISONER
Judge Black has built a secret room below a penitentiary, where he sentences the prisoners to hours of exhibition and torment while his friends watch. Judge Black's House of Corrections is equipped with one purpose in mind: to administer his own brand of rough justice! $5.95/330-9

TUTORED IN LUST
This tale of the initiation and instruction of a carnal college co-ed and her fellow students unlocks the sex secrets of the classroom. Books take a back seat to secret societies and their bizarre ceremonies in this story of students with an unquenchable thirst for knowledge! $4.95/78-5

DANGEROUS LESSONS
Incredibly arousing morsels of Paul Little classics: *Tears of the Inquisition, Lust of the Cossacks, Poor Darlings, Captive Maidens, Slave Island*, even the scandalous *The Metamorphosis of Lisette Joyaux*. $4.95/32-7

THE LUSTFUL TURK
The majestic ruler of Algiers and a modest English virgin face off—to their mutual delight. Emily Bartow is initially horrified by the unrelenting sexual tortures to be endured under the powerful Turk's hand. But soon she comes to crave her debasement—no matter what the cost! $4.95/163-2

TEARS OF THE INQUISITION
The incomparable Paul Little delivers a staggering account of pleasure and punishment. *"There was a tickling inside her as her nervous system reminded her she was ready for sex. But before her was...the Inquisitor!"* $4.95/146-2

DOUBLE NOVEL
Two of Paul Little's bestselling novels in one spellbinding volume! *The Metamorphosis of Lisette Joyaux* tells the story of an innocent young woman initiated into a new world of lesbian lusts. *The Story of Monique* reveals the sexual rituals that beckon the ripe and willing Monique. $4.95/86-6

CHINESE JUSTICE AND OTHER STORIES
The story of the excruciating pleasures and delicious punishments inflicted on foreigners under the leaders of the Boxer Rebellion. Each foreign woman is brought before the authorities and grilled. Scandalous tortures are inflicted upon the helpless females by their relentless, merciless captors. $4.95/153-5

SLAVES OF CAMEROON
This sordid tale is about the women who were used by German officers for salacious profit. These women were forced to become whores for the German army in this African colony. The most perverse forms of erotic gratification are depicted in this unsavory tale of women exploited in every way possible. $4.95/3026-1

ALL THE WAY
Two excruciating novels from Paul Little in one hot volume! *Going All the Way* features an unhappy man who tries to purge himself of the memory of his lover with a series of quirky and uninhibited women. *Pushover* tells the story of a serial spanker and his celebrated exploits in California. $4.95/3023-7

CAPTIVE MAIDENS
Three beautiful young women find themselves powerless against the wealthy, debauched landowners of 1824 England. They are banished to a sexual slave colony, and corrupted by every imaginable perversion. $5.95/440-2

SLAVE ISLAND
A leisure cruise is waylaid, finding itself in the domain of Lord Henry Philbrock, a sadistic genius. The ship's passengers are kidnapped and spirited to his island prison, where the women are trained to accommodate the most bizarre sexual cravings of the rich, the famous, the pampered and the perverted. $5.95/441-0

MASQUERADE BOOKS

MARY LOVE

MASTERING MARY SUE
Mary Sue is a rich nymphomaniac whose husband is determined to pervert her, declare her mentally incompetent, and gain control of her fortune. He brings her to a castle where, to Mary Sue's delight, she is unleashed for a veritable sex-fest! $5.95/351-1

THE BEST OF MARY LOVE
Mary Love leaves no coupling untried and no extreme unexplored in these scandalous selections from *Mastering Mary Sue, Ecstasy on Fire, Vice Park Place, Wanda,* and *Naughtier at Night.* $4.95/3099-7

ECSTASY ON FIRE
The inexperienced young Steven is initiated into the intense, throbbing pleasures of manhood by the worldly Melissa Staunton, a well-qualified teacher of the sensual arts. Soon he's in a position—or two—to give lessons of his own! Innocence and experience in an erotic explosion! $4.95/3080-6

NAUGHTIER AT NIGHT
"He wanted to seize her. Her buttocks under the tight suede material were absolutely succulent—carved and molded. What on earth had he done to deserve a morsel of a girl like this?" $4.95/3030-X

RACHEL PEREZ

ODD WOMEN
These women are lots of things: sexy, smart, innocent, tough—some even say odd. But who cares, when their combined ass-ettes are so sweet! There's not a moral in sight as an assortment of Sapphic sirens proves once and for all that comely ladies come best in pairs. $4.95/123-3

AFFINITIES
"Kelsy had a liking for cool upper-class blondes, the long-legged girls from Lake Forest and Winnetka who came into the city to cruise the lesbian bars on Halsted, looking for breathless ecstasies...." A scorching tale of lesbian libidos unleashed, from an uncommonly vivid writer. $4.95/113-6

CHARLOTTE ROSE

A DANGEROUS DAY
A new volume from the best-selling author who brought you the sensational *Women at Work* and *The Doctor Is In*. And if you thought the high-powered entanglements of her previous books were risky, wait until Rose takes you on a journey through the thrills of one dangerous day! $5.95/293-0

WOMEN AT WORK
Hot, uninhibited stories devoted to the working woman! From a lonesome cowgirl to a supercharged public relations exec, these women know how to let off steam after a tough day on the job. Includes "A Cowgirl's Passion," ranked #1 on Dr. Ruth's list of favorite erotic stories for women! $4.95/3088-1

THE DOCTOR IS IN
"Finally, a book of erotic writing by a woman who isn't afraid to get down—and with deliciously lavish details that open out floodgates of lust and desire. Read it alone ... or with somebody you really like!"
—Candida Royalle

A delectable trio of fantasies inspired by one of life's most intimate relationships. Charlotte Rose once again writes about women's forbidden desires, this time from the patient's point of view. $4.95/195-0

MASQUERADE BOOKS

SYDNEY ST. JAMES

RIVE GAUCHE
Decadence and debauchery among the doomed artists in the Latin Quarter, Paris circa 1920. Expatriate bohemians couple with abandon—before eventually abandoning their ambitions amidst the intoxicating temptations waiting to be indulged in every bedroom. $5.95/317-1

THE HIGHWAYWOMAN
A young filmmaker making a documentary about the life of the notorious English highwaywoman, Bess Ambrose, becomes obsessed with her mysterious subject. It seems that Bess touched more than hearts—and plundered the treasures of every man and maiden she met on the way. $4.95/174-8

GARDEN OF DELIGHT
A vivid account of sexual awakening that follows an innocent but insatiably curious young woman's journey from the furtive, forbidden joys of dormitory life to the unabashed carnality of the wild world. Pretty Pauline blossoms with each new experiment in the sensual arts. $4.95/3058-X

ALEXANDER TROCCHI

THONGS
"...In Spain, life is cheap, from that glittering tragedy in the bullring to the quick thrust of the stiletto in a narrow street in a Barcelona slum. No, this death would not have called for further comment had it not been for one striking fact. The naked woman had met her end in a way he had never seen before—a way that had enormous sexual significance. My God, she had been..." $4.95/217-5

HELEN AND DESIRE
Helen Seferis' flight from the oppressive village of her birth became a sexual tour of a harsh world. From brothels in Sydney to harems in Algiers, Helen chronicles her adventures fully in her diary. Each encounter is examined in the scorching and uncensored diary of the sensual Helen! $4.95/3093-8

THE CARNAL DAYS OF HELEN SEFERIS
P.I. Anthony Harvest is assigned to save Helen Seferis, a beautiful Australian who has been abducted. Following clues in her explicit diary of adventures, he pursues the lovely, doomed Helen, the ultimate sexual prize. $4.95/3086-5

WHITE THIGHS
A fantasy of obsession from a modern erotic master. This is the story of Saul and his sexual fixation on the beautiful, tormented Anna. Their scorching passion leads to murder and madness every time. $4.95/3009-1

SCHOOL FOR SIN
When Peggy leaves her country home behind for the bright lights of Dublin, her sensuous nature leads to her seduction by a stranger. He recruits her into a training school where no one knows what awaits them at graduation, but each student is sure to be well schooled in sex! $4.95/89-0

MY LIFE AND LOVES (THE 'LOST' VOLUME)
What happens when you try to fake a sequel to the most scandalous autobiography of the 20th century? If the "forgers" are two of the most important figures in modern erotica, you get a masterpiece, and THIS IS IT! One of the most thrilling forgeries in literature. $4.95/52-1

MARCUS VAN HELLER

TERROR
Another shocking exploration of lust by the author of the ever-popular *Adam & Eve*. Set in Paris during the Algerian War, *Terror* explores the place of sexual passion in a world drunk on violence. $5.95/247-7

MASQUERADE BOOKS

KIDNAP
Private Investigator Harding is called in to investigate a mysterious kidnapping case involving the rich and powerful. Along the way he has the pleasure of "interrogating" an exotic dancer named Jeanne and a beautiful English reporter, as he finds himself enmeshed in the crime underworld. $4.95/90-4

LUSCIDIA WALLACE

KATY'S AWAKENING
Katy thinks she's been rescued after a terrible car wreck. Little does she suspect that she's been ensnared by a ring of swingers whose tastes run to domination and unimaginably depraved sex parties. With no means of escape, Katy becomes the newest initiate into this sick private club—much to her pleasure! $4.95/308-2

FOR SALE BY OWNER
Susie was overwhelmed by the lavishness of the yacht, the glamour of the guests. But she didn't know the plans they had for her: Sexual torture, training and sale into slavery! How many maids had been lured onto this floating prison? And how many gave as much pleasure as the newly wicked Susie? $4.95/3064-4

THE ICE MAIDEN
Edward Canton has ruthlessly seized everything he wants in life, with one exception: Rebecca Esterbrook. Frustrated by his inability to seduce her with money, he kidnaps her and whisks her away to his remote island compound, where she emerges as a writhing, red-hot love slave! $4.95/3001-6

DON WINSLOW

THE MANY PLEASURES OF IRONWOOD
Seven lovely young women are employed by The Ironwood Sportsmen's club for the entertainment of gentlemen. A small and exclusive club with seven carefully selected sexual connoisseurs, Ironwood is dedicated to the relentless pursuit of sensual pleasure.

CLAIRE'S GIRLS
You knew when she walked by that she was something special. She was one of Claire's girls, a woman carefully dressed and groomed to fill a role, to capture a look, to fit an image crafted by the sophisticated proprietess of an exclusive escort agency. High-class whores blow the roof off! $5.95/440-2

GLORIA'S INDISCRETION
"He looked up at her. Gloria stood passively, her hands loosely at her sides, her eyes still closed, a dreamy expression on her face ... She sensed his hungry eyes on her, could almost feel his burning gaze on her body...." $4.95/3094-6

THE MASQUERADE READERS

THE COMPLETE EROTIC READER
The very best in erotic writing together in a wicked collection sure to stimulate even the most jaded and "sophisticated" palates. $4.95/3063-6

INTIMATE PLEASURES
Forbidden liaisons, bizarre public displays of carnality and insatiable cravings abound in these excerpts from six bestsellers. $4.95/38-6

THE VELVET TONGUE
An orgy of oral gratification! *The Velvet Tongue* celebrates the most mouthwatering, lip-smacking, tongue-twisting action. A feast of fellatio and *soixanteneuf* awaits readers of excellent taste at this steamy suck-fest. $4.95/3029-6

A MASQUERADE READER
Strict lessons are learned at the hand of *The English Governess*. Scandalous confessions are found in *The Diary of an Angel*, and the story of a woman whose desires drove her to the ultimate sacrifice in *Thongs* completes the collection. $4.95/84-X

MASQUERADE BOOKS
THE CLASSIC COLLECTION

PROTESTS, PLEASURES AND RAPTURES
Invited for an allegedly quiet weekend at a country Vicarage, a young woman is stunned to find herself surrounded by shocking acts of sexual sadism. Soon her curiosity is piqued, and she begins to explore her own capacities for cruelty—leading to an all-out search for an appropriately punishable partner. Latent depravity explodes! $5.95/400-3

THE YELLOW ROOM
Two legendary erotic stories. The "yellow room" holds the secrets of lust, lechery, and the lash. There, bare-bottomed, spread-eagled, and open to the world, demure Alice Darvell soon learns to love her lickings. Even more exciting is the second torrid tale of hot heiress Rosa Coote and her adventures in punishment and pleasure. Feverishly erotic! $5.95/378-3

SCHOOL DAYS IN PARIS
The rapturous chronicles of a well-spent youth! Few Universities provide the profound and pleasurable lessons one learns in after-hours study—particularly if one is young and available, and lucky enough to have Paris as a playground. A stimulating look at the pursuits of young adulthood. $5.95/325-2

MAN WITH A MAID
The adventures of Jack and Alice have delighted readers for eight decades! A classic of its genre, *Man with a Maid* tells an outrageous tale of desire, revenge, and submission. Over 200,000 copies in print! $4.95/307-4

MAN WITH A MAID II
Jack's back! With the assistance of the perverse Alice, he embarks again on a trip through every erotic extreme. Jack leaves no one unsatisfied—least of all, himself, and Alice is always certain to outdo herself in her capacity to corrupt and control. An incendiary sequel! $4.95/3071-7

MAN WITH A MAID: The Conclusion
The final chapter in the epic saga of lust that has thrilled readers for decades. The adulterous woman who is corrected with enthusiasm and the maid who receives grueling guidance are just two who benefit from these lessons! Don't miss this conclusion to erotica's most famous tale. $4.95/3013-X

CONFESSIONS OF A CONCUBINE III: PLEASURE'S PRISONER
Filled with pulse-pounding excitement—including a daring escape from the harem and an encounter with an unspeakable sadist—*Pleasure's Prisoner* adds an unforgettable chapter to this thrilling confessional. $5.95/357-0

CONFESSIONS OF A CONCUBINE II: HAREM SLAVE
The concubinage continues, as the true pleasures and privileges of the harem are revealed. For the first time, readers are invited behind the veils that hide uninhibited, unimaginable pleasures from the world.... $4.95/226-4

CONFESSIONS OF A CONCUBINE
What *really* happens behind the plush walls of the harem? An inexperienced woman, captured and sentenced to service the royal pleasure, tells all in an outrageously unrestrained memoir. No affairs of state could match the passions of a young woman learning to relish a life of ceaseless sexual servitude. $4.95/154-3

INITIATION RITES
Every naughty detail of a young woman's breaking in! Under the thorough tutelage of the perverse Miss Clara Birchem, Julia learns her wicked lessons well. During the course of her amorous studies, the resourceful young lady is joined by an assortment of lewd characters who contribute to her carnal education in unspeakable ways.... $4.95/120-9

MASQUERADE BOOKS

TABLEAUX VIVANTS
Fifteen breathtaking tales of erotic passion. Upstanding ladies and gents soon adopt more comfortable positions, as wicked thoughts explode into sinfully scrumptious acts. $4.95/121-7

LADY F.
An uncensored tale of Victorian passions. Master Kidrodstock suffers deliciously at the hands of the stunningly cruel and sensuous Lady Flayskin—the only woman capable of taming his wayward impulses. $4.95/102-0

SACRED PASSIONS
Young Augustus comes into the heavenly sanctuary seeking protection from the enemies of his debt-ridden father. Within these walls he learns lessons he could never have imagined and soon concludes that the joys of the body far surpass those of the spirit. $4.95/21-1

CLASSIC EROTIC BIOGRAPHIES

JENNIFER III
The further adventures of erotica's most daring heroine. Jennifer, the quintessential beautiful blonde, has a photographer's eye for detail—particularly details of the masculine variety! A raging nymphomaniac! $5.95/292-2

JENNIFER AGAIN
One of contemporary erotica's hottest characters returns, in a sequel sure to blow you away. Once again, the insatiable Jennifer seizes the day—and extracts from it every last drop of sensual pleasure! $4.95/220-5

JENNIFER
From the bedroom of an internationally famous—and notoriously insatiable—dancer to an uninhibited ashram, *Jennifer* traces the exploits of one thoroughly modern woman. $4.95/107-1

ROSEMARY LANE *J.D. Hall*
The ups, downs, ins and outs of Rosemary Lane. Raised as the ward of Lord and Lady D'Arcy, after coming of age she discovers that her guardians' generosity is boundless—as they contribute to her carnal education! $4.95/3078-4

THE ROMANCES OF BLANCHE LA MARE
When Blanche loses her husband, it becomes clear she'll need a job. She sets her sights on the stage—and soon encounters a cast of lecherous characters intent on making her path to sucksess as hot and hard as possible! $4.95/101-2

THE FURTHER ADVENTURES OF MADELEINE
"What mortal pen can describe these driven orgasmic transports?" writes Madeleine as she explores Paris' sexual underground. She discovers that the finest clothes may cover the most twisted personalities of all—and sexual desires that match even those of the wicked Madeleine! $4.95/04-1

KATE PERCIVAL
Kate, the "Belle of Delaware," divulges the secrets of her scandalous life, from her earliest sexual experiments to the deviations she learns to love. Nothing is secret, and no holes barred in this titillating tell-all. $4.95/3072-5

THE AMERICAN COLLECTION

LUST *Palmiro Vicarion*
A wealthy and powerful man of leisure recounts his rise up the corporate ladder and his corresponding descent into debauchery. A tale of a classic scoundrel with an uncurbed appetite for sexual power! $4.95/82-3

WAYWARD *Peter Jason*
A mysterious countess hires a tour bus for an unusual vacation. Traveling through Europe's most notorious cities, she picks up friends, lovers, and acquaintances from every walk of life in pursuit of pleasure. $4.95/3004-0

MASQUERADE BOOKS

LOVE'S ILLUSION
Elizabeth Renard yearned for the body of Dan Harrington. Then she discovers Harrington's secret weakness: a need to be humiliated and punished. She makes him her slave, and together they commence a journey into depravity that leaves nothing to the imagination—*nothing!* $4.95/100-4

DANCE HALL GIRLS
The dance hall in Modesto was a ruthless trap for women of all ages. They learned to dance under the tutelage of sexual professionals. So grateful were they for the attention, they opened their hearts and legs! $4.95/44-0

THE RELUCTANT CAPTIVE
Kidnapped by ruthless outlaws who kill her husband and burn their prosperous ranch, Sarah's journey takes her from the bordellos of the Wild West to the bedrooms of Boston, where she's bought by a stranger from her past. The ultimate erotic road novel! $4.95/3022-9

A RICHARD KASAK BOOK

EDITED BY MICHAEL BRONSKI

FLASHPOINT: The Best Gay Male Sexual Writing
A collection of the most compelling, provocative testaments to gay eros. Longtime cultural critic Michael Bronski (*Culture Clash: The Making of Gay and Lesbian Sensibility*) presents over twenty of the genre's best writers, exploring areas such as Enlightenment, Violence, True Life Adventures and more. Sure to be one of the most talked about and influential volumes ever dedicated to the exploration of gay sex and sexuality. $12.95/424-0

CECILIA TAN, EDITOR

SM VISIONS: The Best of Circlet Press
"Fabulous books! There's nothing else like them."
—Susie Bright, *Best American Erotica* and *Herotica 3*.
A volume of the very best speculative erotica available today. Circlet Press, the first publishing house to devote itself exclusively to the erotic science fiction and fantasy genre, is now represented by the best of its very best: *SM Visions*—sure to be one of the most thrilling and eye-opening rides through the erotic imagination ever published. $10.95/339-2

FELICE PICANO

DRYLAND'S END
Set five thousand years in the future, *Dryland's End* takes place in a fabulous techno-empire ruled by intelligent, powerful women. While the Matriarchy has ruled for over two thousand years, and altered human language, thought and society, it is now unraveling. Military rivalries, religious fanaticism and economic competition threaten to destroy the empire from within—just as a rebellion also threatens human existence throughout the galaxy. $12.95/279-5

EDITED BY RANDY TUROFF

LESBIAN WORDS: State of the Art
One of the widest assortments of lesbian nonfiction writing in one revealing volume. Dorothy Allison, Jewelle Gomez, Judy Grahn, Eileen Myles, Robin Podolsky and many others are represented by some of their best work, looking at not only the current fashionability the media has brought to the lesbian "image," but important considerations of the lesbian past via historical inquiry and personal recollections. A fascinating, provocative volume. $10.95/340-6

A RICHARD KASAK BOOK

MICHAEL ROWE

WRITING BELOW THE BELT: Conversations with Erotic Authors

Journalist Michael Rowe interviewed the best erotic writers—both those well-known for their work in the field and those just starting out—and presents the collected wisdom in *Writing Below the Belt*. Rowe speaks frankly with cult favorites such as Pat Califia, crossover success stories like John Preston, and up-and-comers Michael Lowenthal and Will Leber. $19.95/363-5

EURYDICE

f/32

"Its wonderful to see a woman...celebrating her body and her sexuality by creating a fabulous and funny tale." —Kathy Acker

With the story of Ela (whose name is a pseudonym for orgasm), Eurydice won the National Fiction competition sponsored by Fiction Collective Two and Illinois State University. A funny, disturbing quest for unity, *f/32* prompted Frederic Tuten to proclaim "almost any page ... redeems us from the anemic writing and banalities we have endured in the past decade..." $10.95/350-3

LARRY TOWNSEND

ASK LARRY

Starting just before the onslaught of AIDS, Townsend wrote the "Leather Notebook" column for *Drummer* magazine. Now, readers can avail themselves of Townsend's collected wisdom as well as the author's contemporary commentary—a careful consideration of the way life has changed in the AIDS era. $12.95/289-2

RUSS KICK

OUTPOSTS:
A Catalog of Rare and Disturbing Alternative Information

A huge, authoritative guide to some of the most offbeat and bizarre publications available today! Rather than simply summarize the plethora of controversial opinions crowding the American scene, Kick has tracked down and compiled reviews of work penned by political extremists, conspiracy theorists, hallucinogenic pathfinders, sexual explorers, religious iconoclasts and social malcontents. Each review is followed by ordering information for the many readers sure to want these publications for themselves. $18.95/0202-8

WILLIAM CARNEY

THE REAL THING

Carney gives us a good look at the mores and lifestyle of the first generation of gay leathermen. A chilling mystery/romance novel as well. —Pat Califia

With a new introduction by Michael Bronski. Out of print for years, *The Real Thing* has long served as a touchstone in any consideration of gay "edge fiction." First published in 1968, this uncompromising story of New York leathermen received instant acclaim. Out of print for years, *The Real Thing* returns, ready to thrill a new generation. $10.95/280-9

MICHAEL LASSELL

THE HARD WAY

Lassell is a master of the necessary word. In an age of tepid and whining verse, his bawdy and bittersweet songs are like a plunge in cold champagne. —Paul Monette

The first collection of renowned gay writer Michael Lassell's poetry, fiction and essays. As much a chronicle of post-Stonewall gay life as a compendium of a remarkable writer's work. $12.95/231-0

A RICHARD KASAK BOOK

AMARANTHA KNIGHT, EDITOR
LOVE BITES
A volume of tales dedicated to legend's sexiest demon—the Vampire. Includes such names as Ron Dee, Nancy A. Collins, Nancy Kilpatrick, Lois Tilton and David Aaron Clark. Not only the finest collection of erotic horror available—but a virtual who's who of promising new talent. $12.95/234-5

LOOKING FOR MR. PRESTON
Edited by Laura Antoniou, *Looking for Mr. Preston* includes work by Lars Eighner, Pat Califia, Michael Bronski, Joan Nestle, and others who contributed interviews, essays and personal reminiscences of John Preston—a man whose career spanned the industry. Preston was the author of over twenty books, and edited many more. Ten percent of the proceeds from sale of the book will go to the AIDS Project of Southern Maine. $23.95/288-4

MICHAEL LOWENTHAL, EDITOR
THE BEST OF THE BADBOYS
A collection of the best of Masquerade Books' phenomenally popular Badboy line of gay erotic writing. The very best of the leading Badboys is collected here, in this testament to the artistry that has catapulted these "outlaw" authors to bestselling status. John Preston, Aaron Travis, Larry Townsend, John Rowberry, Clay Caldwell and Lars Eighner are here represented by their most provocative writing. Michael Lowenthal both edited this remarkable collection and provides the Introduction. $12.95/233-7

GUILLERMO BOSCH
RAIN
An adult fairy tale, *Rain* takes place in a time when the mysteries of Eros are played out against a background of uncommon deprivation. The tale begins on the 1,537th day of drought—when one man comes to know the true depths of thirst. In a quest to sate his hunger for some knowledge of the wide world, he is taken through a series of extraordinary, unearthly encounters that promise to change not only his life, but the course of civilization around him. $12.95/232-9

LUCY TAYLOR
UNNATURAL ACTS
"A topnotch collection..." —Science Fiction Chronicle
A remarkable debut volume from a provocative writer. *Unnatural Acts* plunges deep into the dark side of the psyche, far past all pleasantries and prohibitions, and brings to life a disturbing vision of erotic horror. Unrelenting angels and hungry gods play with souls and bodies in Taylor's murky cosmos: where heaven and hell are merely differences of perspective; where redemption and damnation lie behind the same shocking acts. $12.95/181-0

SAMUEL R. DELANY
THE MOTION OF LIGHT IN WATER
"A very moving, intensely fascinating literary biography from an extraordinary writer. Thoroughly admirable candor and luminous stylistic precision; the artist as a young man and a memorable picture of an age."
—William Gibson
Award-winning author Samuel R. Delany's riveting autobiography covers the early years of one of science fiction's most important voices. Delany paints a vivid and compelling picture of New York's East Village in the early '60s—a time of unprecedented social transformation. *The Motion of Light in Water* traces the roots of one of America's most innovative writers. $12.95/133-0

ORDERING IS EASY!

MC/VISA orders can be placed by calling our toll-free number
PHONE 800-375-2356 / FAX 212 986-7355
or mail this coupon to:
MASQUERADE BOOKS
DEPT. Y74A, 801 2ND AVE., NY, NY 10017

BUY ANY FOUR BOOKS AND CHOOSE ONE ADDITIONAL BOOK, OF EQUAL OR LESSER VALUE, AS YOUR FREE GIFT.

QTY.	TITLE	NO.	PRICE
			FREE
			FREE

Y74A — SUBTOTAL / POSTAGE and HANDLING

We Never Sell, Give or Trade Any Customer's Name. — **TOTAL**

In the U.S., please add $1.50 for the first book and 75¢ for each additional book; in Canada, add $2.00 for the first book and $1.25 for each additional book. Foreign countries: add $4.00 for the first book and $2.00 for each additional book. No C.O.D. orders. Please make all checks payable to Masquerade Books. Payable in U.S. currency only. New York state residents add $8^{1/4}$% sales tax. Please allow 4-6 weeks delivery.

NAME _____

ADDRESS _____

CITY _____ STATE _____ ZIP _____

TEL ( ) _____

PAYMENT: ☐ CHECK ☐ MONEY ORDER ☐ VISA ☐ MC

CARD NO. _____ EXP. DATE _____